Coquina Key

This book is a work of fiction. Names, characters, places, and incidents are the product of the author's imagination or used fictitiously. Any resemblance to actual events, locales, or persons, living or dead, is coincidental.

1st edition, 2004 ISBN:
0-976-0050-1-8

© 2004 Backwater Press and the author, Micah O'Brien.
Web: www.backwaterpress.net
Email: Micahobrien@backwaterpress.net

All rights reserved. No part of this book may be reproduced or utilized in any form or by any means, electronic or mechanical, including photocopying and recording or by any information storage and retrieval system, without permission in writing from the author and/or publisher.

Printed and bound in the United States of America

Cover art by Carol Sakellarios
Cover design by Martin Lass – Galactic Publications Book Service

To: Betty Malonie —

# Coquina Key

*Micah O'Brien*

Backwater Press
Fully Rely On God

To Diann Phelps Bowman

# One

There was no one near the old grove house the night Ben Ivan died. Tava later said the orange groves and Silver Lake itself stood completely still as if they were in shock and wondering what to do next. The water in the lake lay flat, not moving, and noiseless like a quiet backwater, something looking like a background of a watercolor print. Ben Ivan's main hand, Tommy, found him as the night was quitting and as the morning was just beginning to show.

Ivey Hayes knew when it happened. He was six hundred miles away in Virginia and in the middle of the same mystical night. He sat up in bed as if someone had called him, looked at Addie still asleep beside him, reached for his robe, then walked quietly down the back stairs to the kitchen. He moved carefully so as not to awaken the children or make a sound that would cause anyone to wonder why he was out of bed so early on a Sunday morning.

He sat for an hour in the dim yellow glow from the kitchen nightlight, knowing something was wrong, something had happened. The red dot between the changing numbers on the stove clock blinked as if it was a blinking warning itself. It took Tommy's call to tell him for sure. He knew it when he picked up the phone on its first ring. He knew that his father, Ben Ivan Hayes, had died.

That was three days ago now, two days since he left. Getting someone to take his single class then the canceling of appointments used up most of the first day. Then getting Addie and the children to the airport and the flight down to Orlando. Since getting back home, talking to those who needed consoling, then making the arrangements for a proper and fitting funeral, and those other things an eldest son seemed responsible for—it all took time.

Now he walked along the edge of the lake as he cooled down from his run, looking at the grassed yard running down from the house and down to the edge of the water. No one was around except for the pooreyed dog that lived there at the grove house—Ben Ivan's dog, and it not even knowing. It tore along the wide packed-sand path in front of him where the lake was down. He ran with those two old strays that sometimes come by when the shallows of the lake are warm and still and the air is cool, all three running and looking like they are almost young again. It seemed as though there was something they wanted, or needed. Maybe it was just to open up and to let anything hiding inside of them escape. Like people, he thought as he watched them. Those wanting something, needing something, needing somebody like a Ben Ivan Hayes. Maybe they're right, maybe the right idea is to keep on going, to start something over again, start it even a second time.

He reached out to one of the orange trees and pulled off his morning's juice and breakfast. Then he took off his running shoes, tied the laces together to hang the shoes over his shoulder, and waded out into the lukewarm water of the lake. He stepped back into the shallow water and held the orange to his nose to smell the ripeness. Ivey squeezed it and felt the spindly squirt of juice as he began peeling it with his thumbnail and fingers just as he had done all those years before. It was as he had done when he was even in high school, back before he left those years ago, back before; somehow, most of a lifetime was sneaking by. With only some of the rust colored peel off, he bit into the orange, letting anything that dripped fall onto his sweat-drenched shirt or into the water.

Minds wander on the lake. Its post card beauty and only the sound of a new day coming across the water made sure of that.

He looked at the dock running out from the shore—the pier for getting out to the boat. Then, at the boathouse at the end of the dock—both things that he, his dad, and Tommy built all those years before. Built, the best he remembered, that only summer he was home. Apparently, no one used it anymore. His father sold the boat, somebody told him. Now the dock and the boathouse sat abandoned and looking like parts of a desolate and closed-down park once used for amusement.

He jumped at an unexpected sound of his name and turned to see Tommy watching him.

"I said, 'Good morning, Ivey.' You must have been a thousand miles away."

"You startled me, Tommy."

Tommy stepped toward him and handed him a folded-over newspaper. The sun was up just enough and lighting the house and Silver Lake so that he could read it. "Brought the obituary. Thought you might want to see it."

Tom Ripington knew Ivey had already seen it. At one time, it seemed as if he knew him as well as he knew himself. Knew him maybe too well—Ivey leaving and only making quick trips home with Addie anymore, the one no one ever knew or had ever known for that matter. Then, the two later-in-life children, children most people did not even know by name. Now, despite all that, and whether Ivey wanted to admit it to himself or not, he was home again.

Ivey bent over and shook the front of his shorts and a seed sticking to it, then washed the juice from his hands and wiped them on the back of his shorts. He took the paper Tommy gave him and looked at yet another notice about his father.

> Ben Ivan Hayes died Sunday after a short illness. President of Summer Tree Inc. Local businessman, investor, and civic leader. Former State Senator from District IV (See Article Pg A-1) Member of Mt. Dora Baptist Church. Survived by his wife Martha Ripington Hayes, a daughter, Mary Celeste King of Winter Park, two sons, Ripington of Orlando and Ivey of Lynchburg, Va., and two grandchildren, Virginia Rand Hayes and Mark Hayes. Services will be at Mt. Dora Baptist Church on Wednesday at 12 noon. Interment will be at family cemetery. The family requests memorial donations to the American Cancer Society in lieu of flowers.

The Hayes dog ambled up and looked straight up at Ivey. Ivey reached out and rubbed the top of his head, down his nose, then patted him on his wide, lake-dampened back. Ivey remembered the dog from when he was there before. So much was coming back. Ben Ivan and Tommy's dogs all looked the same: short hair, brown or tan colored, outdoor dogs. He would stay around the house or jump into the back of Tommy's pickup and ride into town to stay until the next morning. Ivey remembered when he and Tommy both had dogs and both from the same litter. The two dogs would run around the lake, barking and chasing each other. And that old cat that belonged to Addie and the kids back in Lynchburg—sleeping all day, contrary as all hell when awake, and then only getting up to eat. After that, it would search out a place to hide again. Then his last dog—the one his dad gave to one of the pickers who said he would give him a good home, and after he knew Ivey was not coming home any more. *How could anyone give someone's dog away?*

The two stood without speaking, each awakening with the bluing sky and smelling the orange blossom fragrance in the morning dew. "Got to put a little PVC bushing on that irrigation line coming up from the water there," Tommy said, "it leaking the way it's doing and all. Forgot it in the truck. Left it on the da-burn seat, but I'll be back in a minute." He turned and walked up the pathway with the dog trailing along behind him.

On the side sat an old wooden chair with both arms and legs splitting from time.

He pulled it closer to the water and sat down on its front edge. He stuck his feet back into the water and looked at the sun's breaking and its settling in over the corn-row lines of orange trees across the lake.

He ran extra early that morning, as he did when he was younger and all those years before. He left by going north and away from Ben Ivan Hayes and Summer Tree Corporation, the years before Addie and the children. It seemed so natural to be running again, then cooling down beside the lake, the groves with oranges hanging on the trees for him to pull off as he ran by, just as he did back then—his salute to nature and all that was good about out-of-doors. All that was back before responsibility, places to be, cellular telephones, fax machines, megabytes, percentage breakdowns, and probability ratios took their place in his life. He ran with only enough light to dimly outline the path and before the sun rose high enough to bake the groves and the shallow water of the lake. Nevertheless, the sun would brighten even more, and he would eventually have to face the people already there: grievers still stopping by the house in town—the house on *Coventry Road,* she called it. All that and more was to come. His mother would need the shoulder of her oldest—to deal with the well-wishers they all knew and many at the funeral he didn't know at all.

"It'll only take a minute," Tommy called. He had waded out to his knees and was pulling up on a white plastic pipe running out from the shore and into the water. The dog swam beside him with his nose stuck high in the air.

Ivey watched, then stood up and pulled his over-sized *University of Virginia* t-shirt away from his warm and still sticky-wet body while fanning any air there over his at-one-time marathoner's body. He turned his sweating arm up, looked at the underside, then down at the matted wet hair on the top of his arm. He looked at his lack of tan—at the natural but bland whiteness covering his arm. He smiled knowing it was all anyone could get by standing in front of a 400 Statistics class trying to breath interest into columns of computer-compiled numbers of no interest to those in the class whatsoever. *Or* his sitting around some linencovered table at a management seminar, expounding man's changing but still proprietary role in an electronic world.

He put a leg up on the arm of the chair and stretched out his Achilles' tendon. He kept his now-fifty-year-old body still in shape with twice-a-week basketball with his mid-aged cronies and pick-up game with college Phys-Ed majors—runs that were once more regimented, but still done almost daily… when it wasn't raining or there was no snow or ice on the ground. That and Sunday afternoon "A" team tennis at the club—that club where Hampton-Chase faculty were expected to be seen at Saturday evening receptions and at Sunday lunch with their family.

He pushed his damp sandy-brown hair back, hair once streaked by the sun but now starting to tinge with gray. He kept it too long and full, perhaps, but it was one of the few things he could still do for his hidden Sixties rebellion against academia and its solemn images. Besides, his thoughts continued, Hampton-Chase College is becoming a thing of the past anyway. He went to the private and at the time all-male school himself so many years ago that he did not want to remember. He went for his masters and Doctorate at the University of Virginia, and then returned to teach for another twenty-plus years while sitting for most as the Dean of the School of Business Administration. Those titles, those over-blown jobs. Now it was a class a week he somehow maintained, the computer nerds trying to take over the business world, and the outside programs he found himself involved in to keep up with and to monitor on solving the inadequacies of the world. He published in both business and academic circles and ran the fledgling Hampton-Chase School of Advanced Studies in Communications—a task taking him from computer programming to speaking to trade groups, seminars, and other eastern business schools on what he called Effective Management in a Capitalistic Society.

He put the other leg up and stretched the muscle of his calf.

They cannot ask a person to leave. But you can tell—politically, academically. Then, I guess they can do it, he thought—if they know how to tell someone that they do not fit well with the new twelve-year plan. Downsizing. Huh. I probably came up with that phrase; now they are quietly turning it against me. Tighten-up, cut-down, and all that running rampant in faculty meetings and referenced as subject on e-mail and inter-office memos, "The Future Is Now At Hampton-Chase", or whatever their credo of the moment happens to be.

Then there was Frederick Bey back at Washington and Lee calling. Fred always seemed to have some kind of a hidden tap on what the rest of the world was doing as well as Ivey's love of literature and his growing disdain of anything that was not. He could always sense that first and undying love before the need for business school and the training of minds-of-commerce for the future. It showed with the offer he sent. Then the returning of the obligatory acceptance of W & L's invitation to speak at the Bard Series on pre-Shakespearian letters in order to sell worth and liberal arts knowledge, as well as business mind, to those few who somehow still don't know of him and needed to be sold.

But, it *is* a college position, he thought, and *is* in literature, even if it does mean picking up and relocating. I still might have to. The private sector—no, I can't do that. I wouldn't back then, and I don't want to now. But with nobody else now that he is gone?

Not like other things, anyway. And this lake. No one ever drains it dry—the rain comes and restores it. It doesn't have to change. You leave; you come back. It's as if you never left.

Many things somehow go—somehow don't ever last. For no reason, they just leave. No warning, just leave. Or they just break down, and they cannot be fixed again. You have to adjust... maybe not in the same direction, but you have to go on.

He looked toward the dog, toward the house, and toward Tommy on down the lake.

All this... it was still Ben Ivan Hayes and fit the picture he kept in his mind and what that was left of his father. He would go to the groves, to town, to the packing plants, but the house in the groves still saw him sitting on the screened back porch, and alone at night. It felt him on short weekends, alone or sometimes with his buddies. Or it would see him walking around the lake with Tommy every day when they met there after work. Or early in the mornings, both of them planning and talking and doing. Then, those times he was gone—more and more times toward the end.

He offered the house to Ivey when he first got out of school, when Ivey was young and not yet married to Adelaide Sellers of the Richmond Sellerses. It would always be Ivey's, he told him. All he had to do was to come home and take it. His dad always said he could have it at no cost whatsoever. He would work at Summer Tree, of course, and do what he was born to do. Addie, now the children. No, it is still his dad's world. It was Ben Ivan's house in the grove. Ivey was gone and despite what Ben Ivan thought, he somehow found a life and world of his own.

He peered out again at the lake, which looked as a huge silveredged mirror set down in a geometrically rowed orange grove, with bald-knobbed cypress knees serving as edge markers. Behind these wooden outcroppings were gray and twist-legged cypress trees rimming the lake like somebody's hand-drawn outline. They formed a blurry edge, like something drawn with a thick lead pencil then smudged over with a damp finger, showing where the water ended and where the groves of Ben Ivan Hayes and Summer Tree Corporation began. He looked at what was once nothing but vast sand and virgin Florida scrub lands where growers bought, sold, planted, and picked from there to the vegetable fields and truck farms to the south, stopped only by the Gulf to the west and the Atlantic Ocean to the east. It was all Hayes land now—Summer Tree land. He knew what was coming. All that was called Summer Tree would be his.

Maybe something to be controlled by a man who really did not want it at all.


Tommy's walking up startled Ivey, but then Tom Ripington was supposed to be at the lake—to be where Ben Ivan may have been. He remembered Tommy always being… slow to learn, but always remembering whatever he did. "Developmentally impaired," is what they said about him. Ben Ivan just called him "slow." Tom Ripington—kid brother of Martha Hayes. He had lived here since he was old enough to walk, Ivey knew, and he appreciated that. Both of them now had more years behind them than they had left to go. Tommy looks so sure of himself, Ivey thought. Him looking like this part of the world is his and he knows the reason for everything. Then, he probably does.

"What I figure is that if I change out from an inch and a half to an inch and three quarters, I can get enough of a head of water that I can irrigate a good five hundred feet further than I am now."

He watched as Tommy looked into the lake first, then into the grove—counting something and figuring something in his head. He never had the education of the rest of them. Only finished high school when they saw to it that he got to that special school at night for his GED—the school that Summer Tree saw to financially support. He stood shorter than Ivey or his younger brother Rip. Tommy was slight of build with thick black hair on his head; a burr cut that had not ever changed. He was always wearing one of those brown Summer Tree shirts with the red letters writing out Summer Tree and his name in scroll.

Anorexia is something else they would whisper. He went from student to man like walking out of one room and into another.

"I didn't expect to see anyone out and around this early," Ivey smiled as if showing he was glad Tommy was there. "Tava up in the house. Some things never change, do they? If I know my mother though, I bet she's behind Tava's leaving the big house in town and getting out here first thing. That's what it is, isn't it?"

Tommy turned to him and smiled as he always did when spoken to, but he did not answer.

"I mean, Tommy, this is before anybody ought to do anything. Much less be hauled out to do repairs or to do cleaning... especially at this hour in the morning."

They both looked as if wondering what to say next and waiting on the other to speak. They stood as if they were both hiding something that could possibly leak out to the other. They each knew that Ben Ivan was still there and on both their minds. They knew that, and they knew the reason they were both there and waiting. They knew that Summer Tree would have to go on and someone would have to be the one to make it go. But neither one wanted to say anything. Especially at that hour of the morning.

Ivey looked at Tommy then back at a spot in the grass where he found he could park his thoughts. They both knew; they all knew it would happen. Tommy knew. Martha knew. They all knew something else would have to be done. Time itself was the only unknown.

When Ben Ivan died, Tommy called the only daughter that early morning, but Mary Celeste didn't wake up for the call. Her husband, Sutton King did. So Tommy waited until she got to the phone so he could tell her personally. It was his responsibility—one of the last duties Ben Ivan gave him to do in a talk they shared one of the times Tommy was with him before it finally happened. After Ben Ivan's daughter Mary Celeste, Tommy called the younger son Rip. He wasn't there to answer the call, but then Rip was not around most nights to answer anyone's call.

Mainly, he called Ivey, and that was the hardest call of them all. That is why he called him last, trying to build up what to say after telling the others. He knew how Mary Celeste would take it. He didn't much care what Rip would say. But Ivey Hayes?

Oh, Ivey had to come back to stay. Everyone knew that. There was no one else in the overall scheme of things. With the groves and the packinghouses and whatever else Ben Ivan did to keep everybody working, Ivey would have to come back.

Tommy called each of them as Ben Ivan had said and as he had carefully written on his penciled-out list. He told Tommy not to wait on Martha to call, but to follow his list with the names and telephone numbers whenever anything happened. Call his children as soon as he could, he said. Martha would already know. Then, and after they were all called, call the attorney, Johnson Crews; he would know what had to be done. And the accountant, Sol Weinstein. They were all on the list penciled on a yellow legal sheet of paper, folded over in quarters, and kept by Tommy to open only when Ben Ivan was gone. He knew them all even without the list, and he had all their telephone numbers in his own folder by the telephone anyway. But he still kept the list Ben Ivan had given him.

He called each one that morning and called them after he made the call to the first name on the list. He knew to call that first name before any of the rest, the number that no one else knew. He knew the number in the Keys.

## Two

Beava hurried into the law offices, past the gold-leaf lettering on the wooden panel beside the front door: *"Tanner, Leigh, and Crews, Attorneys at Law, Established 1949,"* then past the smiling lady at the front desk.

She shared a wordless shrug as she fast-stepped past the receptionist and down the hallway to the back of the converted old-Orlando house. She climbed the *Employees Only* wooden stairs in back that the family members of the antique two-story had once used. Beava sauntered down the short hallway to Johnson Crews's office, did not knock or pause at the door, but barged in to stand at his desk in front of him. Johnson immediately made an excuse to whoever was on the other end of the telephone conversation and hung up the receiver.

"So, tell me," he said, adjusting a strap on his thin leather suspenders, straightening his tie as if making himself suddenly presentable, and giving her his total attention. "And don't skip any details."

She flipped open a leather folder to notes penciled on a limecolored legal pad and laid it flat in front of her. "It's what I can't tell you that still has me buffaloed. But all in all, it's just like we thought."

Beava stood tall in front of him with her blond close-cropped hair blown, gelled, and sprayed stiff into what could have been a man's styling. Three years out of law school and the daughter of the now retired senior partner, she was the youngest in the Tanner, Leigh, and Crews practice, the one Johnson Crews chose—with Judge Leigh's prodding— to take under his wing and be his protégé.

"Like you said, Essie and I both went down, checked in Key West on what seems like every site plan that was ever recorded. Every code or code exception in Monroe County. We found nothing but what we already know. That land is prime if there ever is any—a whole damn island sitting out in the water all by itself. A 'Key' to them, an 'island' to you and me, but a whole damn island."

She looked at Johnson for a response but did not get one. "We first went to the store on the mainland—the place where you park to get taken out to the key. For starters, you would not believe that place. It looks like someplace maybe fifty years ago: old, south Florida, stuffed fish on the walls, a few groceries, bait, pictures of men holding fish— real Hemingway stuff. A man named Bearclaw of all things runs it. Yeah, Bearclaw—Billy Bearclaw. He's an Indian if you haven't guessed—Indian in both name and appearance. I didn't ask, but probably one of those bingo-playing tribes. Anyway, one eye is crossed... almost spooky looking. A nice enough fellow though, but eerie-looking. We gave him ten dollars and he took us out to Coquina Key. He took us in an old wooden boat of some kind—looked like something stored on a movie lot somewhere waiting for the rebirth of a Humphrey Bogart movie."

Beava looked behind her and then sat down. She wore dark stockings or pantyhose under the short skirt of a near black suit she was fond of wearing. She rubbed over a knee as Johnson walked to the front of his desk, kept one foot planted and slid onto his glass-topped desk.

"Essie and I had a long talk with this Bearclaw character on the way out, but he didn't tell us anything we didn't already know. Your girl-buddy Esmeralda did most of the talking. The boatel out there gets most all of its customers by boat, he says. They go in, tie up, stay on their boat, or rent one of the rooms in one of the little motel units. Some go to Bearclaw's like we did, and he takes them out. Then they call, and he goes back and gets them. That or one of the ladies, one of the Trace ladies will take them in."

"So tell me what else you found."

"We of course heard about Ben Ivan. I guess we all knew it was getting time, but it still doesn't make it any easier, does it?"

"You were there then before you heard he died," Johnson said.

"Yeah. Helen told me about it when we called in from Key West that night. Last Tuesday it was... It seems like we've been gone forever."

"I think we were right in telling you to stay there and find what you went after, don't you? I don't think your missing his funeral hurt any-thing."

"You are probably right. Tommy Ripington is the only one I really know and I'm sure he didn't miss me. He thinks I was gone on business somewhere, anyway. The poor guy—not too bright, but a nice guy all the same. I bet he's going to have a rough time with the big man gone. Anyway, he doesn't need to know it was Coquina Key business."

Johnson reached to his collar as if to loosen his tie, felt it already pulled loose, touched the button on his opened collar, then pulled down on the collar to make sure it was straight. He picked up his now cold cup of coffee and spun around in his chair to face the window, thumbing the edge of his white coffee-stained mug as he did. For the moment, he seemed satisfied with her answer about Esmeralda Santo, Essie—the one the offshore money sent up to make sure everything was on the up and up—the one who wasn't a secret to anyone after she was sent from São Paulo to Ft. Lauderdale three months before. He was satisfied with Beava too, for that matter. But Beava he knew. Essie, the dark-skinned and red smiling Brazilian he personally knew well, but professionally, she was still a mystery.

She paused for a moment as if thinking of something else to say or something she might have forgotten. "Miss Emily was all talking away when we first got there but seemed to hush when the daughter walked up." She checked off her notes as she spoke, as if completing another item from her list. He watched her with a questioning stare while digesting every word being said. Johnson was the senior partner now that Beava's father, the judge, had retired. He was the glad hand, Ben Ivan would call him—the thinker, the public relations all rolled into one. For the last twelve years, he had only one client and its associated companies: Summer Tree Corporation, the parent company that owned Consolidated Realty and the other offshoots. He would joke about why he didn't work directly for Ben Ivan Hayes, but then he reminded himself that in truth that was exactly what he did.

Johnson Crews hid his age—pushing sixty—with his year-round tan, styled and waved silvery hair, and clothes from a Buckhead tailor he made a trip to Atlanta to see twice a year. In his younger days, he was Little All-American at Stetson, and then got his law degree from the University of Florida. Judge Leigh hired both him and Will Tanner, set them up in Orlando, then let them run. "Grab-it" and "Growl," he would call the two to his golfing and poker-playing cronies at Dubsdread Country Club. With Johnson's gift of gab and Will's brainpower, they and the firm prospered. It took Johnson all the way to a first-name basis and to being kept on a retainer by Ben Ivan Hayes, the biggest game around. But it was the game that was now gone.

Beava continued, "It's like it shows on the plot plan, only bigger, and a lot prettier. It's what the whole key, the whole dang island, what our whole plan is about. It's overgrown but looks to be kept that way—overgrown with nothing but scrub, palmetto, palm trees, and those odd-looking trees with the funny looking roots sticking out of the ground."

"Banyans."

"Right. And other trees, smaller and growing right out into the water."

"Mangroves."

"Yeah, mangroves. It wouldn't take much to get rid of them and open up the beach. And when I say beaches, I'm saying miles of it."

"So to get there from land, you travel from the Bearclaw place?"

"Right. Bearclaw's is just a little place, but with signs near the highway: diving, snorkeling, beer, bait, fishing, and rentals—all those Keys things that look like they are on every sign. It sits back on the water and off the road a little way. There is just a little what looks like a shell road leading from the highway to a good-sized parking lot. There are a couple boats tied up that look as if they might belong there. There is a sign out front of Bearclaw's and toward the road for the boatel itself. It is a brightly colored fish—funny looking. Under it is written—let me find it here... 'Rooms by the night or by the week, docking for boats and diving, fresh bait. Check inside Bearclaw's for more information.' But, that's about it. Oh, there's one of those red-and-white diving signs attached to it, but those signs are everywhere. Listen, that one Coquina Key sign with an arrow painted across the bottom is the only way you can tell anything but trees are out there."

"That surprises me," Johnson said. "You would think they would have something big or flashy on the road."

"They work by word of mouth to the boating crowd from what we heard—that's what brings in the business. If the few boats we saw were their business, it all must be part of the mystique. And laid back! You wouldn't believe those people, Johnson."

They sat for a moment, quiet and hidden in thought. Then Beava pulled a cigarette from a pack in the purse beside her, lit it, and continued. "In checking the courthouse in Key West, we didn't find any record of soil borings or any geotechnical surveys at all." Smoke blew from her nose after she had taken the first drag and then she seemed to let what tension was in her voice escape and her body to relax. She crossed her leg and then pulled down hard on her skirt, out of a seldom-practiced modesty. "From what we can tell, it's the same as the day the waters parted and they discovered land. The boatel—I still can't believe that's what they call it. I mean, is that as hokey as it comes or what? But it seems to work. It's all dutiful and licensed, pays taxes every quarter, on time, and has never had a lien filed against it. Not a one. And that's saying a lot—or so we gathered from the courthouse clerk that helped us— a lot for what they call a seasonal motel."

She reached over to the brown plastic coffee container that always sat on the edge of Johnson's desk, swished it around to see if there was anything in it, then set it back down. She looked at Johnson, snapping her head as if she just then remembered what she was going to ask.

"You did get to the funeral, didn't you?"

"Sure. Sol Weinstein and I went together... listen, there were more people there than you could ever imagine. It's an old, and I mean old church. I never even knew it was there, much less been in it. It looked like some old outer-island church off South Carolina or somewhere. Something you would expect to see with a black choir swinging and swaying. The windows were open and people were standing outside and listening. People were outside every window. It's a wonder the old wooden floor didn't give way with all the people on the inside. I'm glad we went, though. That was good for both Sol and me. His Yiddish eyes could not believe that place either. But I've known Ben Ivan and Martha Hayes for a long time."

"I still wish I had been in town and could have gone," Beava said.

Johnson said, "We're digressing, and you don't need to be seen around any more than you have to. Okay. You need to continue to see Tommy Ripington and let's keep it at that, okay? That's going all right, isn't it?"

"It's no problem, no problem at all. It's all in the palm of my hand."

"I know that Tommy's going to be seeing Ivey and hard telling who else," Johnson said. "You need to keep your ears open with that one. You agree, don't you? I mean, you don't mind that, do you?"

"No," she said. "I told you I'll let you know if I get anything from him worth telling. But so far, there's not anything there we don't already know." She smiled as she looked over his desk for a coffee cup. "The things I do... But I can say this, he knows an awful lot about what's going on with the Hayes clan here and what's going on in the Keys. He seems to keep his finger on the pulse of everybody and every thing. And that's not all bad. In fact, he seems to be asking me as many questions as I've been asking him. He is a nice fellow though, as pleasant and caring as anybody I have ever met. He's just not as bright as the others. But I'll keep you advised."

Johnson smiled for the first time since she walked in. "That's a trait you've already learned, huh?" Having a male where you can pump him for information."

"There's no learning to it," she answered. "The basics come when a girl is born. You get a little card to learn. The mastering comes with time, but I'd mastered all I'll ever need to know by junior high school."

Johnson turned in his chair and looked out the window behind him. "Keep on finding out what you can, but keep out of the way as much as possible, too. Martha Hayes or that voodoo housekeeper of hers will see through you like washed crystal goblets." He turned and looked right at Beava. "It's not every day a man loses his biggest client. And, if truth be known, for all the crap he put me through, it's going to take a lot to replace him around this office. Oh, we'll get more clients, but as far as movers and shakers like him? Naw, I don't think so. And one with cojones as big as Ben Ivan Hayes? It'll never happen."

"Golden cojones, the judge used to say," Beava added.

"Never again in this lifetime. No, he's the last one for a long, long time."

He gave his head a quick shake as if blotting out his last thought to clear the way for something that was to come. He turned around to the window, looked out again, and said, "That's enough about that. Excuse the rabbit trail where I seemed to get us sidetracked. Finish telling me about Coquina Key."

"Answer one more thing for me then, and I will. Did you talk to Ivey Hayes?"

"Sure I talked to him," he answered to her reflection in the window glass. "I saw him at the funeral, then later at the house. I didn't get to say much, just to offer my condolences. You don't worry yourself about Ivey. I can take care of him. If I can't, I'll sic you on him. Knowing Ivey Hayes—you'd like that, anyway."

"I look forward to meeting the all-illusive and now top-honcho Ivey Hayes. The man that everybody who knows him seems to describe differently."

"Never sell the man short, Beava. That's what I'm saying. You knew Ben Ivan before he died. You know Martha Hayes and you of course know Mary Celeste. The best way to describe Ivey is that whatever is crude about the daughter Mary Celeste is the complete opposite with Ivey. Ivey is as smooth as a greased baby's butt." He grinned. "Excuse my orange-picker metaphor."

"It beats the first time I heard Ben Ivan say something is slicker than owl shit."

Johnson got solemn and then spoke again. "Go on with your story, but remember now that Ivey Hayes himself, though he doesn't show it, got everything he will ever need and got it honestly from his old man, whether he wants to admit to it or not."

Beava said, "So you think that Mary Celeste is no problem as well as little brother Rip. What's Rip's story anyway?"

"You can probably get more from Tommy, but basically Rip is an overeducated playboy, graduated from the best the world has to offer, but has never worked a day, other than office help from time to time when Ben Ivan screamed loud enough. What do they say… cut from a different mold?"

Beava smiled her understanding then looked back at her notes. "So about the people… we talked directly to Miss Emily. Can you believe that's what everybody calls her? When I first heard it, I thought it was just some southern nicety. That changed when I met her. Listen, she's right out of Tennessee Williams—a cotton dress and barefoot drama that one is. Rough-talking, tanned, and sun-cracked face, but with a ring on her right hand big enough, as the judge would say, to choke a horse."

"I can very well imagine where she got that," Johnson said.

Beava looked at him and smiled. "Ben Ivan, right?"

"Probably."

"Essie came up with a story that we were looking for a place to put some people up for a week or so, like we were tourist agents or something. She has learned well—all her years working in Peru and dealing with American yo-yos, she says. After she said that, we got the royal treatment and were shown all around. It's like some ad for a Caribbean getaway of some sort, maybe something sitting on the water in Cuba that civilization has seen fit to go on by for awhile. Yeah, it's easy to see why people go there. I mean view. And quiet. And dock. Now, when I say dock, I mean a walkway right into the Gulf of Mexico. We checked in Key West, and the dock was constructed twelve years ago and got every Corp. of Engineers approval imaginable. The owner is listed as Coquina Key Boatel and submitted for approval under a name you would readily recognize."

"Ben Ivan Hayes."

"None other. And like everything else, the permit was approved, unblemished and crystal clean."

"And the land itself. What else about the land?"

Beava again checked her notes. "Basically, what's there is five little buildings, each with two rental units in them. A Tiki Hut is next to the pier but it looks like it's never used. Then, toward the end of the long pier, there's a sailboat. It's not very big. The *Doubloon* it's called. There are two, no three of their own boats—I mean all painted alike and *Carefree* names on them. I mean *Carefree Eight, Carefree Nine, Carefree Ten.* Isn't that adorable? "

"Adorable," he smirked. "The pier. Tell me about the pier again.

"It's what the land management people call a T-shaped pier, with boats tied up. Some are monstrously big, some small. Some are power-boats, some sailboats."

"Nothing special about them? They're just docked there?"

"Just docked? It's the *Carefree* boats they charter. Both Miss Emily and Genna have captain's licenses, but Genna is the one with the reputation. You know, a pretty captain woman who always leads to fish. Bearclaw talked about her as if she were some fishing goddess or something. Besides that, there's a bait shop—ship's store, much smaller than Bearclaw's. It sits right at the start of the dock. No name is on the store but letters are painted crudely on the side giving hours, rates on boat usage, and prices on bait fish. There's a steady flow of water dripping out of a plastic PVC pipe and into the Gulf—from ice melting, I figured. Oh yeah, and pink ornamental flamingos—there are a couple of them around."

"You must have arrived back late. I called Essie's after eleven and she wasn't home. You mustn't have gotten in just before the sun came up this morning if you were that late in dropping her off in Lauderdale."

"She was with me, don't you be worrying about that. We've got bigger things to be thinking about than your boy-girl needs and what you're thinking about you and your latest."

"I know, I was just asking. Excuse my schoolboy curiosity." His gaze at her changed as he dove back into the problem at hand. "So there's no reason in the world we can come up with—I mean legally—that will cause them to sell. Is that what you're getting to? ...I was afraid that's what you two would find. Something, anything you could find in the woodpile would help." He was disappointed as he reached for his coffee, his mind busy digesting.

"Everything is on the up and up, believe me. It's the original Mom and Pop but without the Pop. Just the Grandmamma and a single parent mother who nobody warned me about and didn't give a damn about talking to us. She's maybe the biggest mystery, maybe the biggest problem of it all. I think she sensed something, the way she looked at us. She looks to be one of those God-save-the-world, the snail-darters, and the manatee types. A pretty person, but hard—unmoving, uncompromising. Won't change her values, no matter what. You know what I mean? What I'm saying?"

"Yeah, I've heard."

"A pretty lady like I said—Indian-looking, tanned. She has blue eyes though, eyes that are light and sparkly. Eyes that have a way of piercing right through you. Eerie-looking. You know what I mean? She's one of those left-over-from-the-sixties idealists, I figure. She loves that land. You can pick that up the first time you talk to her. She dates some PhD very sporadically, we found out. Strictly platonic they say. Some marine brain. Alex Roan—with some fisheries department of the state. All we know there is that they've dated a long time, but we didn't see a need to follow that up."

She looked at her notes, then said, "And... oh, here—here's the appraiser's report."

He spun his chair back around in apparent vexation. "I can't believe they own the whole damn island and don't do a thing but rent out a few rooms, dock a few boats overnight, and sell cut bait and fishhooks to Yankee fishermen. You said something about there being a little girl. How about the father? Did you find out about that? Even in the Keys they don't find babies growing under conch shells."

She stood up and moved to the edge of the desk. She opened the top lid on the coffee thermos, swished around maybe a half-cup in the bottom, and then set it back down. She walked around, opened the side of the credenza behind the desk, and pulled out a semi-clean cup with the name of a Savings and Loan gold-etched on it and poured what was left from the bottom of the thermos.

"They're separated. Divorce papers are recorded, but there's no address for him." She turned up two or three sheets in her legal pad. "Riggs is his name. He has no visitation rights and looks to have all but disappeared. He apparently never calls, is always late with child support, when he sees fit to send it at all. But I think that comes with little-boy packages when they're born.

"Now, Miss Emily—she's pulling in a Social Security check every month. It is not much, but it's steady income. And the daughter—the tree hugger, the born-again hippie lady—besides the erratic child support checks, she makes what she does from charters, from a part-time job in some environmental office in Marathon, and from a class and workshop she teaches at the University of Miami."

"And the motel—the *boatel*. Is it making them any money?"

"Not appreciably," Beava answered, turning another sheet. "It's rented about half the time. As I understand, it's the same crowd staying there year after year. You know... fishermen or old salts of the sea on extended vacations... anyone who will pay to stay close to their precious boats. But even with half-occupancy, it breaks about even. The place was paid for years and years ago. All they have now is upkeep, the cost of utilities, and what a few new sheets and towels can cost them."

Johnson kept staring out the window as she spoke. Finally, Beava sat down in the other one of the chairs facing the desk. A monotone voice came over the telephone intercom reminding him of an eleven o'clock meeting downtown, but he didn't respond.

"It sounds like you two did a good job, even if we don't have the answers we need. You do your dad proudly." They both sat in silence again until Johnson continued. "So the easiest way is to just offer to buy. Anybody will sell if the price is right, and I think we can offer that number."

He picked up the appraiser's report, and then put it down. "That can be six million if it has to be. Maybe even more if we redo some development numbers. I have already set the groundwork for that. But once everything is sorted out and Ivey Hayes is in control. Once he finds out what the Keys property is worth "as is," he will sell. There's a screwball addendum to the title about the wives and children of Ben Ivan Hayes and Wiley Trace needing to approve the sale, but that's just paperwork. Nothing to worry about.

"Other than that, Solly will get into his accountant world and explain the Hayes cash flow being what it is. With the taxes owed, that's all he can do. We will make an offer to buy through the corporation we talked about you setting up, and he'll jump all over it. Of course, we'll start a hell of a lot lower and ease up as we need to, but we'll get there. You just watch this ol' country-boy deal. Those two island ladies will have to break once we get into serious money and get Ivey serious about it, too. You can be rest-assured of that."

"That worries me—I mean those big numbers you're throwing around."

"I told you, Miss Doubter. Your south-of-the-border compadres have agreed to the deal, and they know about what this thing could be. Besides, putting some glitz into that part of the world is needed. I mean new motel units, good for the one-nighters, the "weekenders." We'll fill the rest of the place up with timeshare units—low units, new units, maybe a single high-rise, maybe just a bunch of low rise. Who knows? Think about it now—think about the view—a condo with water view on all four sides. Apartments with water front and back. Can you picture all that? We could buy out your Indian friend, run a taxi service from there to the island with pontoon boats, and have a calypso singer on every trip. It would be the best thing south Florida has ever seen. We'd get full and stay full. God knows, Disney has taught us how to do that."

Johnson stood up, straightened his chair, and then sat back down. He picked up a pencil from his top drawer, made a note with it, and then started tapping the eraser lightly on the desk. "Think about it like your man Carlos says. We're not only providing a vacation spot, we're giving jobs to an area where jobs are needed. Those people have tried diving and fishing for a living. They see what that pays, which is nil. We'll have ten applications for every job and be the biggest employer between Miami and Key West."

"But what if it doesn't work?"

He stood back up, moved around to the back of his chair, and leaned on it as he continued. "That's the beauty of it. It's offshore landacquisition and developmental money, and they have a lot of it to put someplace."

Johnson moved around to the front of his desk and to directly in front of Beava. "You can't allow yourself to forget, these aren't just dreamers and businessmen we're working with—Essie and her buddies from home. No, they're people who know what they're doing. Nevertheless, suppose for conversation, it doesn't work? Just suppose. What if things don't sell after we buy the land? What do we have then? We may tear up some beaches for a few miles, but the ocean has a way of repairing anything we could ever do. A little dredging if need be, a little fixing up, that's okay. Then, the land will be sold and for a big number. And I've got no doubt whatsoever that it can be sold so that we can move it more one beautiful profit."

"You are well into millions now. Big millions. Is that what I'm hearing?"

"They need to do things with their cash, Beava. They get the land, then borrow on it and borrow in cash. At least that's what I'm going to advise them to do. To them, it's mainly cash flow. You know, trading dollars for dollars. But after the land is built on, things run for a year or so and show a profit, you know what time it is then. It's gravy time, well-off lady. Boat coming in time. That's what it is. Walking down the street like Charlie Potatoes time. That horn you'll hear is your boat pulling into port loaded down with dollars. And, with the deal they've agreed to cut going in, and the both-equity-and-participation deal I'm going to get the firm in the black again for being the maestro of this whole thing, we're both going to get well. Now, how bad is all that? Huh, tell me now. How bad is that? It'll be everybody's retirement time then—you, Solly, Mary Celeste and Sutton, me, even Essie, we can all hang it up. You can be a full partner and have so much money you'll only have to practice if you want to. You can pick up and go to South America, the Caribbean, or wherever you want to go. We'll get what we want out of the deal, and then we're home free, all of us. We won't even have to worry about Coquina Key or anything else again."

She straightened up, reached down and smoothed out the front of her skirt, then did the same to her blouse. "Expand again," she said, "as to what you think can happen if they're adamant and won't agree to sell."

"Technically, of course," he said as he started pacing across the front of the office, "but just technically, the Traces owe Summer Tree money—some hundred fifty thousand, the best Solly can tell. One of those Ben Ivan sugar deals. If the corporation needs the money, they can call in the loan. Old lover-boy Ben Ivan never intended for it to be repaid, and they haven't paid a red cent on it since it was made. But if the loan is called in, and they can't pay, then we can foreclose for payment on the loan. All we'd have to do is to convince Ivey to call it in and let some third party buy it. But Ivey? You don't worry about him. Ivey Hayes will ultimately be an asset."

He looked thoughtfully at Beava as if searching for something that would convince her—convince him, that all he had said, all he had done, was right. "Think about it now. If those Trace people sell—no, *when* those Trace people sell—Hayes can get paid and forgive the amount of the loan. The Traces will be happy—you know they think about it from time to time. Ivey can pay most of his horrendous tax bills—he'll be happy. And our people can take down the land in their name. There's still some work to do, but the ship's coming in. I can see the smokestacks out there in the distance. We just have to think positive. That's something Ben Ivan taught this old barrister. And this deal is ours."

Beava said, "You do know that at one time Ivey Hayes knew Genna Trace. It's been years and years ago now. I told you that, didn't I? It was back when they were high school kids or something. Maybe college kids."

"Yeah. You told me, but I don't see it as relevant. I mean, all those years ago."

"You're probably right," Beava said. "But do one thing for me."

"What's that?"

"Make them the cash offer first. I mean, before you start thinking about foreclosing or calling in loans or getting Ivey in a position where he has to deal monetarily with the Traces. Make it in whatever name you need to hide under, but make them the offer first. An offer to buy. Let's work that angle until we know it won't work. Okay? Then, I mean as a last resort, you can force the calling in of the loan and anything else you have to do. I mean, my feminine intuition says to keep Ivey Hayes and Genna Trace apart as much as possible."

"We could, I suppose, if you're all that sensitive about it."

"I am. And I can tell she is too. They're good people. And if Ivey is all you say he is, we don't want him taking sides with them." Beava stood up and walked to the window. "That may be the main thing that my trip has reconfirmed. Genna Trace may turn out to be a problem."

"I admit that she could be a hard sell... the one who could screw the whole deal. I don't think so, but... We don't know everything we need to know about her. Maybe you need to ask Tommy Ripington some more. I mean, what is it going to take to sell her?"

"She's a nice lady, Johnson. I hope I look that good someday. But she's just as Tommy Ripington described. You're not going to pull anything over on her. She's too shrewd for that. But will she sell? Hey, she's the one you have to convince, not Miss Emily. I've got no doubt the mama would sell without any problem at all."

The receptionist from downstairs interrupted by bringing in a fresh thermos pitcher of coffee and setting it on the table, picking up the empty as she left. Neither Johnson nor Beava spoke while she was in the room.

"It all makes sense if we can do one thing, and we can't forget the other important part of the puzzle."

"What's that?"

"Ole church-going Ivey Hayes," Beava answered. "Everything is based on him selling and getting the others to approve the sale of the land."

His eyes locked again on Beava. "You just stand back and watch this old boy do his thing. You just watch Ivey, and watch him do the things we need him to do."

# Three

Ivey was out early again the next morning. Tommy's dog, and one from somewhere else, ran before him, with only enough light to expose a remembered foot trail he had taken so many times before. He showered at the Gotha house, dressed in shorts and another tee-shirt he had left in his old bedroom for such unplanned occasions, then walked down to the edge of the lake's still-warm morning water. After he had returned from cleaning up and a quick bite of toast, the sun was "early-bright" as Tava called it. Gleaming crystals were produced on the surface of the lake and shot out gold-tinted rays, as if the water was reflecting back the orange groves on the far side and showing them to whoever was watching.

He fixed his stare past the glare of the new sun and onto the unmoving silence in the center of the lake. Along Silver Lake's edge, a bird glided over the lapping soundings of ripples waltzing their way onto the shore, called, then dropped down to something in the shallow waters below. Ivey felt the warmth of the coffee, and an old UofVa. cup in his hand. He squinted at the sun, and watched as another bird flew off, as if—like him—it wanted to be alone and to search for what was in yet another part of its world. His mind stayed in what he had seen so many times before. However, in those earlier years, it was too slow to have held his attention at all. Now the lake and its surrounding groves were somehow new to him, something he had unknowingly watched all those many times before but never really seen. Or maybe now just seeing it a different way—something like singing an old-old song but with words and tune being heard for the very first time.

He snapped back into his reality and looked down at his watch. Addie was still asleep back at the house on Coventry Road and not to be bothered. She would stay as much as possible in the upstairs room they used on those rare occasions when they went there for a visit. Or now, when it was Ivey's responsibility. And the children themselves, young and Virginia-born, maybe overprotected to a fault and indifferent to the Hayes name and the sand-floored groves. Ginny Hayes, the sixteen-year old blond-haired photographic negative of Addie. Then Mark, twelve years old, mesmerized with television sports, computers, and professional athletics. Neither of them was demurring at the possibility of leaving their beautiful Jeffersonian home nor the pomp and the correctness of Hampton-Chase, its stepping stone Deerfield Academy, and Ginny's down-the-road Anne Markham School. But theirs was to do as their parents directed. Doctor Ivey Hayes, as the college would call him on days of show and ceremony. And Addie Hayes, the middle-aged but youthful-looking emblem of Virginia aristocracy, as it once was and, around their home, still survived. An aristocracy that, it was thought by Addie and her oxford-button-down intimates—Ivey, too, if he were ever to admit it—represented all that was right about heritage, being right, and learning.

The sound of truck doors slamming caused him to turn and look toward the back of the grove house even though he knew it was Tommy. Tom Ripington, wearing a light tan windbreaker—the one, like the shirts, with Summer Tree stitched over the left pocket—walked toward him. Tava stepped down from the other side of the cab, quickly looked, saw the unlocked and partly open back door of the house and realized Ivey was already there.

"Good morning, Tommy. What brings you out here so early again?" Ivey spoke quietly, feeling as if there must be a rule somewhere dictating a certain degree of quiet in the presence of the early-awakened water.

"Told you I come out a couple times every week. Even before… You know, check on things and stuff. Tava tells me if I forget."

"I changed inside and got a cup of instant coffee. There's an old coffee maker beside the sink, but I didn't know where to look for the real coffee. I'm going to sit here and finish it, though. Running through orange groves and sugar sand isn't the same as morning runs on hills and hard pavement." He leaned forward while rubbing his leg and squeezing a sore muscle he hoped might just be pulled.

"Tava has fresh made now." Tommy looked toward the house then back at Ivey. "I'll bring you a refill if you want. Ben Ivan always got a refill when he stayed out here. Drinking coffee, I mean. Coffee without any lace in it."

"No," he said. He gave his near-empty cup to Tommy, then watched as he turned the last of the old coffee out onto the sand. "But you go do what you need to do. I just want some quiet time." He watched as

Tommy walked away, angling up the wild-grassed and pine-needled back yard toward the house. Damn, he looks good, he thought. He hasn't aged at all.

He looked past him to the screened back porch and the sun-faded cedar siding—wood cut from lake-soaked trees that Ben Ivan as a young man had hauled down to a mill in Bartow where they were split into the rough-faced boards he used to side the house. It was one living room and one kitchen wide, two bedrooms in back, plain and unadorned for something belonging to a Ben Ivan Hayes, much less a Martha Ripington Hayes. Probably the only things she liked about the house were the azaleas, those bushes planted by Ben Ivan and Martha themselves before the children were even born and now left for Tommy to take care of.

The house had been kept for Ben Ivan as a quiet seclusion, where Martha would know where he was. Not that anything could be "allowed" to Ben Ivan Hayes, but if he had to have something—a "plaything"—maybe the old house would be his. Tommy would unlock it, sweep it out, and pick up anything left lying about. He would put it back in its rustic, backwater state, and ready to welcome the likes of Ben Ivan Hayes and his good-ole-boy cronies—the king of orange and his landhungry court. It was his place for supposedly playing cards, drinking expensive liquor, and generally doing whatever he wanted. Then, those who knew, those few who were that close to him—Tommy, even Ivey if he would ever admit it—all knew better.

I can't remember when Tommy wasn't here, he thought. He's always here. Always happy with something good to say. And tan. I guess there's something to be said about pickup trucks and orange groves... They beat air conditioning and asphalt parking lots.

Ivey looked at the boathouse—the sides painted white but the old wooden dock aged to a natural gray. He walked over to the dock and stepped up on it to walk the few feet to the door of the boathouse. He opened the door, but there was nothing inside but an old rod and reel hung on nails on the wall.

Ivey looked at the platform that extended two or three feet inward from the walls on either side—an inside dock cut out just enough and in the right shape for a boat to be lowered into the water. He remembered Tommy, Mary Celeste, and himself—he twelve or so—swimming underwater from the outside and coming up inside the boathouse. It was a secret hiding place for the three that could only be reached through their magical underwater entrance while swimming in old jeans, cutoffs, or sometimes, when no one was around to tell, nothing at all. The davits were still there, looking as if they had been greased and ready to be used. Probably something else Tommy takes care of, he thought. He pulled off part of a twig lying on the dock and dropped it into the water. It didn't move but set and rested on top like a praying mantis standing on a silver tray. Or like an outsider looking into where he might have been sometime before.

He walked out of the boathouse and closed the door on the childhood memories of all that time before they moved onto Coventry Road and the oversized and opulent monstrosity of his mother's new house. He stood in the simplicity of the lake and boathouse and groves. He stood for a moment, making it hard to think about the Coventry Road columns, turrets, finials, and gingerbread, the exposition and claim of Martha Ripington to Central Florida solidity, affluence, and old-Florida poise. Tommy had his two rooms over the garage behind the big house on Coventry Road—the *House of Martha,* Ben Ivan called it when she couldn't hear. Ben Ivan never liked it, even when it was first built, back when things were hard but somehow simple—back before Disney, before the expressways, and before people started pouring in those thirty years ago, as though it was Florida's own gold rush—or their rush for gold, and many thought it had never changed.

That's when Tava came… the time when Ben Ivan hired the Haitian girl with a Haitian father and a Spanish mother, away from the migratory pickers one year—one year before she was good and near legally grown. She took to the big house as well as to the house in the grove. And she took to Tommy. She taught Tommy about why and how people do what they do. Things no special school for the slow-to-learn could ever teach, or probably even knew about. And what was on the inside. She educated him about that as well. No one would admit it, but that and love and touch and caring… it all came from Tava de Herrera. According to Martha Hayes and after those times she would catch them together, talking, sometimes even touching, perhaps, she taught him too well.

At one time, Tommy even admitted to a schoolboy crush on her, as Ben Ivan was to call it. Back when he and Tava were both young and exploring and not knowing who or what the other one was all about. Back when Tommy was just becoming old enough to know about such things and before he knew the difference between the two was black and white, as Ben Ivan would say, and had to stay that way. Most especially with her being what Ben Ivan openly called "colored." It was on one of

Tommy's first drinking nights, one of those early nights when he was still trying out and seeing what he should see. It was one when the weather turned cold and he and the Haitians working the groves had to cover all the young tree plantings and plants in Gotha. It was a night when they stayed up all night lighting and keeping smudge pots going— fires in the groves to warm the trees and the fruit against the freeze. He—or at least it was what everyone thought—tried to show off to the world his thoughts about the Haitian girl. He took a concoction that one of the Haitians gave him and, with a needle another one handed him, tattooed T.H. on his left shoulder. According to Martha when she heard about it, it was both immature and unthinking, slow as he was or not. He never said anything about it after that but wore a tee shirt all the time to keep it covered up, even while swimming and soaking wet in the lake.

Tava had a rental house in town at first. Down in "the quarters," Ben Ivan called them. That was before he and Martha's children left and before she finally agreed to move into two rooms and a bath set aside for her in the big house on Coventry Road. It was rumored that she was married once and to a man who, through the years, people would see, but no one could ever say they really knew. The story was that they were married back home before she left for the States and to work for Ben Ivan Hayes. But the Haitian man would never let go of her. Ben Ivan never admitted it, but like an angry father, he kept him away from town as much as morally and legally possible and away from Tava when he came around. He was a big man as Haitians go, with long dreadlocks hanging around his island-black face. He stayed on the road with the crops, went back to Haiti from time to time, then one day he went back for no reason that people would say, and he never returned.

Tommy brushed off the bottom of his shoes on the first step, walked onto the screened-in back porch, and into the house. He walked into the kitchen, startling Tava and causing the cabinet door under the sink to slam shut as if being slapped hard with a closing knee.

"It be good to see Ivey back," Tava said as she straightened up, smoothed down her lap after fingering something under the waistband of her apron. "Good to see Ivey even if he's out there alone and probably talking to his own self. He still do that?" Tommy nodded as he walked over to the sink and past another newspaper with the previous day's obituary opened and lying on the counter. He opened the cabinet door behind where Tava was standing and saw the mayonnaise jar under the sink that hid five pieces of dried and bleached white chicken bone. He had seen Tava shaking the jar and the pieces around many times before, then opening it and tossing the fragments out onto the hard kitchen floor. She would look secretively at the bones and the way they landed and study them as though she was reading a writ of the Holy Spirit.

Tommy looked at the paper, then at the jar of bones.

"Is he all right?"

Tava nodded her head. "Ben Ivan Hayes is all right. Now Ivey Hayes I'm more worried about," she almost whispered, as if someone besides Tommy could hear. "And Miss Martha Hayes. She I'm most fretful about, too." Her Haitian accent seemed to get stronger whenever she worried—like falling back to some place only she would know.

Tava de Herrera's hair was slicked back as always and in a bun, her face thin but smooth as if just washed and motioned, her color the reddish brown of unbaked cinnamon. She was much younger looking than her age, an age just older than Tommy's. She wore stone-washed denim jeans with a black cotton top, something she insisted on doing, only giving in and wearing a dress for one of Martha Hayes's parties. Her sole admission to working was a strip of floral material tied around her waist for an apron, something she wore every day as her own signature uniform while working at one of the houses. Thin-laced sandals showed brightly painted toenails looking like ruby-red buttons and inappropriate for anyone other than Tava. She was in constant motion as she worked, now watching what Tommy was doing in the house and Ivey down by the water. She often spoke with her island words, Tommy would call them—words still inside that as much as she tried, and as much as she practiced, would never leave her. That was especially true when her mind was too busy thinking in her words, and thinking about something where only her mind was aware.

"It's the fuse that's blown," Tommy said. "That's what it is . . . it may be just blown. The fuse I mean. Probably blown to hell and back, as Ben Ivan would say." He walked over and closed the door from the kitchen so he could get to the white-painted fuse box on the wall behind it. He took down a year-old calendar hanging over the fuse box, then tugged open the little metal door that hid the fuses.

Tava said, "Something else like you be worn out if you don't get the fan turning like I told you. If the attic fan no work, it's got to be a fuse. Ain't ever seen it no work before. Can't be no other reason." Tommy looked at the fuses and ran his finger down each side and over the top of the round, glass-topped, quarter-shaped fuses as he did.

"You touch the wrong thing in there and I know something else," Tava said.

"What you know?"

"I know we can bury two people in the same week, that's what I know. Ms. Martha's baby brother can get his little *cul blanc* shocked as well as anybody."

He twisted out the round fuse on the kitchen circuit then held it up so he could see if the thin metal strip on the inside was burned in two. He dropped it in his shirt pocket as if to save it, or to throw it away later.

"That's it. Yes, ma'am, that's it all right. I think there are a couple of extras around here somewhere. Ben Ivan told me to put some in a drawer in case Tava ever needs them. I remember him saying that."

He pushed shut the little door on the electrical panel and walked across the room to the sink. He pulled open a drawer on the painted white kitchen cabinet beside it. He fingered then pushed unsorted things around as he looked—string, dabs of cotton, books of matches, a few pencils of various lengths, and a 30-amp fuse. He walked back to the fuse box, put in the one, closed the little hinged door, and put the calendar back over the box to hide it.

"It mean that Ivey Hayes is going have to jump into the catbird seat," Tava said. "That's what else I know. Growing and picking and shipping I mean. Somebody has to make sure all that gets done. I heard Ben Ivan talking about that to mister Johnson Crews, mister skinnypant-legs attorney, not too long back. Ivey Hayes is going have to quit whatever keeps him up there and get his own *school-teaching*s *cul blanc* on down here. That's what I know. Carrying on, I call it. That's what he has to do." Tava looked at Tommy through squinted eyes, a glare she uses when she was serious about what she was about to say or had just spoken. "I checked, and all the signs tell me that, too. They say he has got no choice about it. No choice at all."

She looked in the direction of the lake, breathed out as if she had already said what she had to say, but still went on. "Did you know about him, I mean Ivey Hayes? Did you know about him coming out to here early this morning? Did he say to you he is coming? You saw him after he got in. Why didn't you get up and come out with him? Him out there half-dressed and looking like he ought to be on some New York beach or somewhere. Him all white-legged like some water standing ghost."

Tommy walked across the room and pried open the grove house windows Tava had not yet opened. He stood there at attention as if he were a sentry, set there and ordered not to move again until told it was all right to do so.

"He just wanted to run, Tava. I mean, his shorts on under his pants and running shoes on. He did it yesterday, too. Ivey Hayes does things like that."

"He thinks he's a kid again, is what he thinks," Tava said. "That man wishes he's still back here, that's what I think."

Tommy looked out at Ivey's warm-up pants crumpled over on the top step. He hesitated, as if seeing something in particular, then walked closer to them and to something lying loose and peering out from the pocket. It looked like a gold coin, a piece of old jewelry sliding out from the pocket. He looked down toward Ivey, staring as if in a trance until he remembered. Then it all came back to him—a gold ornament, round like a half dollar, with tiny turquoise stones smoothly set in a circle on the outer gold edge, like hours on the face of a clock. Yeah, he remembered. There were two of them, just alike. Miss Emily had one. Wiley Trace gave it to her. And she gave hers to Genna. Yeah, and Ben Ivan—he had one that he gave to Ivey.

It had been years since he had even thought about those coins.

They pulled into the gas station in Ocoee, Ben Ivan turning his weight toward the door and waiting until a young attendant with a torn T-shirt came out from the open garage and walked toward the car. Ben Ivan laid his thick and sun-splotched arm across the back of the seat as he watched, then shifted his eyes to Tommy.

"While this young man gets us some gas, you go in and get us a couple of co-colas. Get us a couple of those tall ones in bottles. Don't get those new tin-can things that make you think you're drinking from some miner's cup somewhere." He reached into his pocket and pulled out his change; four or five coins along with a large, round, gold-looking coin, shinny with blue stones somehow embedded in it. He gave Tommy fifty cents then put the change back into his pocket. Tommy looked up from watching the coin disappearing into Ben Ivan's khaki pants pocket then looked at him as if expecting him to say something else.

"What you looking at? That gold coin?" He reached back into his pocket, felt around with his fingers then brought it out again. "I got this the last time I was down," he said as he handed it to Tommy. "I don't know what in the sam-hill it's good for, but I got it anyway. Supposedly, it's an old Spanish doubloon set with those stones in it for luck. Carried by those old south Florida people—the conchs, the Seminoles up in the swamp. Coins that years ago they would strip off Spanish soldiers, then add those colored stones they would find and somehow attach. Signs of love, they would say—love, fertility, and all that good crap."

Tommy turned it over in his own hands, studying both sides of the coin and looking at the blue chips set around the edge. "Must be worth something," he said as he fingered and smoothed over it. "I mean, it gold and all."

"Naw, I don't think so. Wiley Trace and me, we each got one. A matching pair they are. One is supposed to be given to your first-born. It gives them good fortune with... you know. You know those tribal witch's-brew things. Then, or as the story goes, if a male with one of them finds a female with a matching one, those two are meant for each other and supposed to live happy and productive together for the rest of their natural born lives."

Tommy gave it back and watched it as Ben Ivan put it back in his pocket.

"Old Bearclaw is bad," said Ben Ivan. "Then Wiley Trace is the same, even Miss Emily—if they don't know a hundred legends about everything anyone would ever think to ask about. Anyway, I got this one after I saw Wiley Trace with his'n. Bearclaw says he found them both while he was out diving for lobsters. It's just a bunch of hocus-pocus, not as bad as Tava's bone throwing now, but hocus-pocus just the same. All those legends... when to fish, what to fish for, ladies, money, about everything including the full moon."

He spun around to look back across the other side and at the kid pumping gas into the car.

"And a full blue moon is going to be here before he gets through with the gas and before you get back with those co-colas if you don't go on and get 'em."

Tommy looked over at Ben Ivan frowning at the kid, opened the door quickly, and walked into the store.

Tava finished wiping off the kitchen counter where she splashed water from washing up the dishes—the first part of those stacked but seldom used at the grove house and stored in the back of one of the cabinets. She turned and set out paper napkins on the white oilcloth covering the kitchen table. The Haitian knew everything she needed to know about the Gotha house, about the big house on Coventry Road, about everything in general, according to those who knew her. It was the other things, the people things that puzzled her—Ivey Hayes, now that Ben Ivan was gone, those places people went, who they saw, and why they even went there at all.

"You know, I still don't know all I need to know about going to the Keys like he does," Tava said. "Like he did, I mean. I guess I never will."

"You talking about Ben Ivan or you talking about Ivey now?"

"About Mister Ben Ivan Hayes. Ivey doesn't go to the Keys, does he?"

"Not in many, many years," Tommy said. "He's going to go down now though. He told me that."

"No, I was talking about Mr. Ben Ivan Hayes. He never acted as if he wanted to say anything about it. The trips I'm talking about now. Or for me to know anything about it. You know what I mean?"

"You know as much as anybody," Tommy said.

Tava spoke again, almost in a whisper. "Mr. Trace from down there—he was a nice man. He never call much, but when I answered, I tell he was a nice man."

"Real nice man. You can always tell a real nice man. He was better than that missus person who called after Mr. Trace passed on. You know, like being too nice? You know what I say?"

"I know what you mean. I know her and her daughter, too. Nice people, those Traces. You maybe just heard her wrong. Her, her daughter, even her little granddaughter—she's eight in June—they're all really nice people. I'll see them again sometime soon, maybe."

Tommy's mouth rounded as if he was forming a word to say, then he decided against it before Tava said, "Then, Miss Adeline. You know, I didn't even see her at the funeral come to think about it. I saw her at the house and spoke to her—her all yellow-headed with her hair cut like a bowl, quiet and off in a corner like she always is, with those big round glasses on her face. I spoke to her as well as anybody speaks to her. I saw Ivey at the funeral, of course. I even hugged him. But I didn't see her. Of course, that's not saying much. You never see them together anymore. Last time they were down, I noticed that. He goes one way, she goes another... I never have understood that woman. Never understood her at all."

"I like Addie Hayes," Tommy said.

"But Ivey Hayes. He's in the catbird seat now. He's the one going to run things. It scares me some, but not as much as those others. You know Ivey Hayes has to do it. It's, how you say, a formality. Someone has to and it can't be Mr. Rippy Hayes. He and the way he does and the way he gets all drunken up and stays that way. All that fancy schooling—a real waste, I say." She almost grinned as she thought about something to do with Rip but didn't as she thought about the next one. "Or Mary Celeste. We would all be in trouble for sure, if she has anything to do with anything. That has to be the most hateful one person in the world to act so goody-goody trying to help this and help that. The devil is planted in that one's heart—planted deep and growing stronger by the day. I know that for a fact. I know it well. And it's not just talk either. It's fact, pure fact." Tava looked from side to side then lowered her voice almost to a whisper. "The woman has a fire raging in her mind, that's what I know. And she's trying to put it somewhere. She's going to be that way till she finds some place to put it, and I don't want to be around when she does. Naw, Ivey coming back is in back of Miss Martha's mind. I overheard her talking that way and it's not all that long ago, either. She hushed when she saw me, but I still heard her talking...."

Silence hung between the two before she spoke again. This time, she stopped what she was doing, walked, and stood in front of him. "But, tell me mister man who knows everything. All those people at the funeral. There were some there I hadn't seen before. Most of them had been to the house at some time or the other. You know, local people that you know their faces, even if you don't know their names. Some of them were just field hands with a clean shirt on. I could tell that. Some were *uppities*—you know, government people, the governor, and all them. But one lady—one lady sitting in back all by herself. Back in the very back pew, she was. All the women I saw there were with someone, but that one lady sat by herself. You could tell. She never looked up, just sat there. Looking down—crying she was. She would touch her eyes with a handkerchief and looked like she didn't care to see anybody else at all. A pretty lady. White hair—long white hair. I don't remember seeing her before. You don't see many white ladies with long white hair."

"There were a lot of people—lot of them I didn't even know."

"She was an older lady. Not old-old but a pretty old. Tan-faced she was with sunglasses pushed back on top of her head. After she was there awhile, she put them on. You must remember seeing her. I couldn't help but stare at her. She had a dark tan, dark like she was even from back home—from some island. But you could tell she was white. Just years of sunshine were on her. But she was a white lady."

"I don't know who you mean," he lied. "I don't think I saw her."

"You're not telling Tava right now, Tommy Ripington. I've caught you right out this time. You quit trying to hide yourself and what you know. You went up and hugged her even. You not only hugged her, you hugged her hard. And long. A long, long hug. You know her; don't you tell Tava different now."

"There were a lot of people there—a lot of people I knew. Some of them even hugged me like I was family or something."

"That was your Miss Emily lady, wasn't it? Her with all the gumption to show her face up here."

Tommy looked at her for a few full minutes without speaking with an expression on his face saying he wanted to say more, but he didn't. Besides, he would tell her when it was time. Ben Ivan taught him about doing that. Besides, his mind had fallen to other things.

Tava set out an oversized white mug for Tommy to fill slowly for Ivey. He wondered to himself what Ivey was thinking, what must be running through the man's mind. He picked up the cup and pushed open the screen door to the outside, being cautious not to spill the coffee. He walked through and caught the door with his knee as the taut spring pulled it shut.

As Tommy walked away from the house, Ivey rose up from sitting in the chair, turned, and set his stare toward him.

"You still drink your coffee black with sugar don't you?" Tommy said as he walked carefully with the two cups of coffee through the high-cut grass. "I brought coffee anyway. I know you. I brought one of those pink things Tava uses if it's okay. I told Tava to make sure you had some out here. I mean, I figured you don't use sugar anymore. I mean, you running and school and knowing about things like you do and all."

"That's fine," Ivey said. "And you still drink yours black, don't you?"

They both rested the warm cups in their hands and looked out and into the lake. "A lot of people were there yesterday, weren't they?" Ivey said. "At the funeral, I mean."

Tommy didn't answer.

Ivey spoke softly as he changed the subject, speaking in almost a whisper, as if again speaking also to the morning. "It was a little cool before the sun came up. I wore long pants over my running shorts when I came out and forgot and left the warm-ups on the back steps to the house. I figured no one would be out who would take them at this hour." He looked back at Tommy. "Is it just me or is the lake especially still this morning?"

Tommy looked around as though searching for an answer—as though it was written somewhere but then hidden. He only shrugged.

"Hey," Ivey suddenly said. "I met Beava Leigh yesterday. I didn't know you were seeing anyone. Her I mean. You picked a pretty one there."

"Yeah," he said. "We've been out a few times—nothing special... just out. She's not a girlfriend or anything like that."

"What do you think of her?" Ivey asked.

"Oh, she's nice. She's young, pretty. Ben Ivan knew her. He saw her with me one time."

"What did he say? Or shouldn't I ask?"

"He says I probably have old sweat socks older than she is.... Dab-burn sweat socks. I guess that means he didn't like her. He says she's too young for an old fart like me."

Ivey smiled as he pictured him saying that—the sort of thing only he would say. He looked at Tommy sipping his coffee and remembered the two of them, the two of them together, his dad and always-there Tommy. He taught Tommy things—work and life things he shared with him. There were things very few others ever knew; he taught him about the fruit on the trees, about telling the age of the fruit by the color of the leaves, of when it is ready to be picked by sniffing at its peel after you squeeze it. And land... Ben Ivan took him with him to see new groves— to check the soils, the drainage, how far the grove was from a packinghouse, and what it was worth. Ben Ivan could pick up a piece of paper cup or an old paper bag in a ditch beside a road somewhere and jot down figures with a piece of a pencil always in his pocket. Or figuring in his head, he would compute yield, interest, what he would have to pay with money, and what he would pay with only a promise until it would turn its first cash-producing crop. He taught Tommy well. Ben Ivan and Tava knew Tommy and knew who and what he was. To everyone else, Tommy was just that man always around the packinghouses, the man who wasn't too bright, but the man who seemed to know where everything was and why it was there.

"You just watch out for what Tommy thinks," Ivey said. "You're the one that matters."

Tommy didn't change his expression. "And Tava? Is she still a friend?"

"A friend. Yeah, that's what she is. Ben Ivan likes Tava. You never have to hide anything from Tava."

"But tell me something else, Tommy. Tell me something that might be my business. Tell me about the Keys. It's been brought up a few more times since I've been home this trip and each time it's said like there's something mysterious or something no one ought to be talking about. I mean, I remember going down to… you and I both went years and years ago… what was his name? Trace?"

"Yeah, Wiley Trace."

"Wiley. Wiley Trace. That was his name."

"I don't see anything mysterious about anything," Tommy answered. "Is that where you mean everybody talks about?" Ivey didn't answer, so Tommy continued. "I mean, Ben Ivan would go to the Keys, but he always did that. He did that for a long time—as far back as I can remember. Sometimes he took me along, sometimes he didn't. But there never was no mystery about it. Everyone knew it when he went."

"I remember going, but barely," Ivey said. "Years and years ago."

Tommy looked at Ivey with a slow and penetrating look—a look that Ben Ivan himself might have given him. "You need to go down there, Ivey. You go down as soon as you can, you hear."

"Well, yeah," Ivey answered. "I plan to."

"It's important, Ivey. I've told you now. Don't make me have to tell you again. You get on down there now. You hear!"

"Okay, Tommy. I didn't know it was suddenly so important. Until we decide what's going to be done with the company and all, I thought I would make a little tour *everywhere*. You know, to see what's what and what's where. I guess I could go down soon if it's somehow that important."

"It's that important, Ivey."

"I trust it's the Traces my dad went to see, and that's who you're talking about."

"You remember, don't you, Ivey? I mean going down, fishing, and staying with the Traces. I mean, you're bound to remember all that."

"I remember. The Traces... Coquina Key. I went with him two or three times the best I recall. Maybe I was busy doing something else. I think back now and don't remember why I didn't go more often. But then again, it might have been because he didn't want to take me."

"You remember though," Tommy asked. "You remember, don't you?"

"Sure I remember."

"You remember going with Ben Ivan some, then me and ole Billy Glen Ransom some. Then you going down alone and seeing Genna. I don't have to worry about you remembering that now, do I?"

"Genna! I haven't thought about her in years," Ivey lied. He looked at Tommy for his response, but didn't get one. "Have you seen her recently? I know she wasn't at the funeral."

"Every time I go. I mean her, and Katy, and Miss Emily."

"Miss Emily. Is that what Mrs. Trace is called?"

"Ben Ivan named her that... You really don't know, do you? It was back when he first started going down there. Back before Wiley passed on and all. I sure did hate to see that man go. You know, die like he did. I know where he went; I know that. But first him, then Ben Ivan."

"I assume Katy is Genna's daughter."

"That's her. Little Katy. Little as she can be but goes a mile a minute, that one does."

"And Genna?"

"She asks about you from time to time, Ivey. What you are doing and all that. She's a nice lady, Genna is."

Ivey stood up before he asked again. "So, tell me this. Did my dad ever buy any land down there? Any property?"

"Sure. Johnson Crews asked me that same thing. I thought everybody knew about that. Him helping out at Coquina Key, I mean." "Apparently they don't. Tell me about it."

"It was back many, many years ago now. You know that Wiley Trace was his best friend down there. And Wiley Trace... well Wiley had a fishing boat—a charter boat. He was the one who would take Ben Ivan out fishing. Sometimes I got to go along with them. It was a big boat—oh, twenty-eight foot long maybe. He had a smaller boat, too. Yeah, I remember when the four of us, me, you, Billy Glen Ransom, and Genna took it out one time. The smaller one, I mean. You remember, don't you?"

Ivey didn't answer so he went on. "The one they used when they didn't go out in deep water. The skiff, I mean. Bonefish sometimes. And reds… cobia. Ben Ivan liked all those. You can't eat bonefish though."

"Go on."

"But they would go out for bill fish on the big one; sometimes they even staying all night. He took me along to help a couple times. But I never cared about being out very far. When you get to where you can't see land, I start to worry a little."

"When you double the point," Ivey said.

"If that's what you call it. That sound's like some string puller's talk to me."

"You mean people on sailboats?" Ivey grinned.

"That's what Wiley Trace called them. He always fussed when sailboats would get in his way. Said the ocean wasn't big enough for him and them too. The *Doubloon* is there. It's a sailboat, of course. But Wiley, he never sailed it. Ben Ivan did… in the Gulf."

"I remember Wiley Trace, I think," Ivey continued. "Those times I went down there, I couldn't have been over sixteen or seventeen years old; I met him then."

"You can't tell me you forgot now, Ivey Hayes. I mean, you getting sweet on Genna and all. Ben Ivan and Wiley used to laugh about that."

"Laugh? What did they say? Or shouldn't I ask?"

"Said you were both in heat is what Ben Ivan said. I remember that."

Ivey looked away with a smirk on his face before Tommy went on. "Don't you tell me you don't remember her now? You don't do that, Ivey Hayes. It's been a long time but… " Ivey smiled, but guarded what he said as he answered. "It's strange how you can forget about things then all of a sudden, what you've forgotten all comes back to you. Yeah, sure I remember her. I remember she's a couple of years younger than I but a neat person…. a pretty lady. And yeah, I guess she was special to me at one time. I suppose you don't forget someone like that. That's been, let's see... that's been pushing thirty years."

The conversation died with Ivey staring into the edge of the water as it almost hit his shoes, and his eyes fixed into syncopation with the shore-lapping water.

"But about the land," Tommy said. "All I can remember is that Ben Ivan and Wiley Trace bought then owned it together. Coquina Key, I mean. There where the boatel is. Bought it from the Indian people. Wiley had some pull there somehow, him being a Seminole and all. He could buy it but other people couldn't. I guess that's how he and Ben Ivan worked their deal. The Key is pretty big, but Ben Ivan said you couldn't ever do anything with it cause of it sitting out there by itself and a boat being the only way you could get there. You remember that, don't you?"

"Vaguely—not very well."

"Yeah, well when Wiley and Ben Ivan bought it, I remember wondering what he was going to do with it. It being down where oranges won't grow. I mean, it wasn't what Ben Ivan took interest in. In fact, he never told anybody up here about it. I don't know why. Never said anything to Johnson Crews or Sol Weinstein or anybody. Or even put it on the books."

Ivey turned to Tommy and almost laughed. "You amaze me sometimes with your ability to remember things, Tommy. That's a trait I wish I had. Tell me what else you remember about it."

"Well.... I remember one spring—oh, this is way after you had gone off to school and all. I remember Wiley Trace's old boat, the one he had before the big one... it catching fire. It caught fire big time and then sank. Sitting right there at the old wooden dock."

"Did you see it afterwards? Did they pull it up or anything?"

"No. Ben Ivan just told me about it. Then I overheard him talking about it on the phone a few times. The best I remember is that Ben Ivan worked some kind of a deal where he ended up owning what must have been all the land and Wiley Trace ended up with a new boat. It was big and fast. Flying bridge and all. Then all kinds of equipment on it. The *Carefree X*. Then Wiley was on that one, the new one about a year later when he went out and didn't come back."

"Does anyone know for sure what happened to him? I think I heard it was heart problems."

"The Coast Guard found it adrift out in the Gulf Stream. Wiley Trace up against the bulkhead. That's all we know. It's been years ago now. I mean years and years ago."

"And my dad became more and more involved after that. Have I got all that right?"

"Yeah, that's true. But if you're thinking the way some people probably think, you're wrong. Ben Ivan was needed down there. Miss Emily, Genna, they were needing him."

"I'm not sure I want to know why," Ivey said.

"You just get yourself on down there, Ivey. I told Miss Emily at the funeral that I'd tell you that, and now I've done it. And I don't mean just a quick polite visit. Now, you get yourself on down there for awhile, you hear?"

# Four

The gray and fender-dented Camaro pulled into the crushed-shell parking lot next to *Bearclaw's Dive, Bait, and Convenience Store, (Open Can to Can't* written under it in smaller letters). The driver pulled past the building to one of the parking spaces between the bumper-scraped palms and among the fallen coconuts and hard yellow no-use fruit from the tropical almond trees. She pulled past the sign with the brightly colored fish and parked beside another sign, this one saying, *Check Inside for Information on Coquina Key Boatel* and *Charter Fishing,* and next to the one saying, *Parking for Coquina Key Only.*

The tag on the front of the Camaro was like the flag over the dive shop door: a solid red flag with a white line running diagonally across it. The driver swung her left leg out of the car, and then, with both arms wrapped around a paper grocery bag, stepped out. A canvas carry-bag hung from her shoulder with FECO in bold letters on the side and Florida Environmental Conservation Office in block letters under it. She didn't lock the car, just waved with a nod and a smile toward whoever was waving from inside the shop. She jaunted out onto the gulf intruding dock and walked to the very end of it as if being blown there by the afternoon breeze. She stepped into the *Carefree X* while maintaining her balance by shifting her weight from one leg to the other as the boat rolled gently from her stepping down into it. She stepped high in her flowered skirt, cotton top, and boat shoes across the boat's transom and set her packages on the passenger seat next to the wheel. She pulled out a silver knob at the controls three times and pushed it back in each time. The last time she adjusted it to just half way, turned the key, and pressed the starter button. She listened as the motor started, then roared that it was ready. She cut the wheel and headed out into the open Gulf water and toward the dark mound in the distance—to Coquina Key.

Genna accepted half-day fishing charters at the Key, but only if they fit her schedule and if she knew the people (she knew all the locals and most of the regulars). She spent her afternoons at the FECO on Little Pine Key. From fishing with her dad, and knowing Florida Bay on one side and the flats out to the reef on the other, she had caught bonefish, tarpon, and everything else the waters would allow. But overfishing, plastic six-pack holders, and monofilament line had caused her since to fish strictly on her own terms. Among the old-timers—among the conchs who would admit it—Genna Trace ranked with the best. Billy Bearclaw still swore that she smelled fish under the water—that she could even talk to them.

The whole Florida Bay ecosystem, and what people being on the water were doing to the gulf with all the pollution seeping out and onto the reef on the ocean side, changed her outlook on people using the gulf at all. Much less taking fish that were becoming fewer by the day. Her mornings were dedicated to her livelihood but her afternoons were married to keeping alive what was already there. Neil Roan, at Fisheries, started the FECO with both her and her enthusiasm behind him, and after getting a nonprofit grant to educate the public and the professional education channels. The talks to school kids, the letter writing, the prodding of the right people when they saw things not being done was Genna Trace at her dedicated best. That and the murderous screaming needed to let Tallahassee, Washington, and the world know that Florida Bay and its life-cultivating backwaters—the nursery for all that was alive in the waters of the Gulf of Mexico and throughout the Caribbean—was itself dying; that the Keys were not far behind it; that fishing, sea life, and the sea itself were passing away in front of them like some decayed and stagnant pool while, as Neil Roan put it, the world didn't seem to care. But besides the departing clean waters of Florida Bay, those who knew both Genna and Neil Roan, and cared about such things, wanted to think that she romantically kept the young botanist advised on everything else. They also knew that, with Genna, it was not the case.

As she cleared the end of the dock, she pushed the lever forward and felt the aft settle even deeper into the water as the boat opened up into the wide and blue-green gulf waters. Genna looked ahead as *Carefree X* split the waves in front of her and continued the short ten-minute ride out to the key. Salt spray blew around the sides of the curved plastic windshield, laying a fine mist and a rejuvenating sprinkle against her face and into her unbraided and free-flowing hair. She shook her head to make sure her long Indian-black hair was blowing and that she was experiencing the rush of ocean wind she felt so often on the morning rides going into civilization. Then, always in the afternoons, going home.

*Carefree X* was a low-draft, shallow skiff built for use on the flats. It was as short a boat as they had ever owned but one with a small and enclosed cuddy-cabin. With Katy going to school every day now, it was always being used to take her to the bus stop, or by Miss Emily, for reasons only she knew. The cabin was the place for Katy to ride as Genna or Miss Emily took her into the mainland in the morning, and for riding in after Billy Bearclaw met her at the school bus after school to take her on home. Then, return the boat to the Bearclaw docks for Genna to use later on.

Katy was standing alone on the end of the long dock at the key, waving her arms and jumping up and down as if doing a Welcome Home dance. She stood in her favorite too-large T-shirt, with her own dark and long hair blowing with the open water breezes. On the end of the dock closest to the mainland was a sign—a new sign saying Coquina Key Boatel – Moorings. Katy jumped as her mother threw her the line after cutting the engine of the boat and letting the boat float slowly to a stop and only lightly kissing the dock.

"Mama, did you see the sign?" Katy squealed. "Did you see the new sign?" Genna stopped immediately as she stepped up onto the dock and as the excited Miss Katy ran to her and wrapped her arms around her. She turned without moving her legs and looked at the new plywood sign; it was red and white like a diver's flag and big enough to be seen by those looking for dockage for the night. Besides the name, it said *Individual Units, Ship's Store, Diving and Snorkeling, Live Bait. Off Season Rates. Emily Trace, Manager.* A one-legged concrete flamingo attached permanently to one of the legs of the dock sat at an angle, as if reading the sign.

"What are you doing out here, young Miss Katy?" Genna asked, after quickly looking at the sign. "Where's your Grandmother?"

"Down on the end, Mama. She and Mango. We're both fishing. I've already caught a blow fish, a sting ray, and one damn catfish."

"Watch your language, little lady." She knelt down, looked closely at her daughter, hugged her, leaned back, and then pushed the hair back from Katy's beaming face. "I know that is what Miss Emily calls them, but we just call them catfish. Okay?"

She took her FECO bag from her shoulder and gave it to her daughter. She got a better grip on the brown paper bag from Winn-Dixie, then together, and holding hands, the two of them walked toward the other end of the dock. As they strolled down the dock, with Katy mocking her mother by trying to walk step by step along with her, they could hear only light syncopated splashes against the pilings of the dock, and the constant but barely noticed sounds of birds cackling and calling as they flew by—or their silence as they stood perched, as if cast in ceramics, then placed on the end of the dock and painted. And smells—the smells of live shrimp, poggies, and pen fish in the bait shop or laying drying on the dock before Miss Emily or Genna would push them off and into the water for the crabs.

They stepped off the dock and into the open area falling away from the boatel and their manager's unit, to a round concrete picnic table— one of five sitting in a grassed area behind the rooms. Genna carefully put the bags down on the table. Like the other tables at the back of the rental units, it was round and painted white with broken pieces of multicolored tile cast into the concrete top; it was something made and set in place when the little square painted block buildings were first built and long before Katy was even born—born right there in the front unit, unit number one. She left the bags on the table, turned around, and took Katy again by her outstretched hand. Genna stood tall, her hair dark and just beginning to streak lightly with gray—and this seen only by looking closely. With the exception of occasional quiet time with Neil Roan, the botanist and long time—and now only occasionally—"other" in her life, no one seemed to get that close to Genna Trace. Neil was there for her both during and after the divorce and remained her boss, confidant, and date for a drive into Key West or back up to Miami for dinner and a movie. Or to hear a speaker at the University of Miami about something the two of them could understand and somehow enjoy. Then, there were those times there was a Sunday afternoon trip to some picnic spot, or an outing of some kind with her and Katy in Alex Roan's boat or one of the *Carefree* boats in the afternoon sun. Nevertheless, Genna kept it at that. Her mother questioned why but only got the answer, "It is not time," or "Things will happen as they happen," or "Yes, I love having Neil around; yes, he loves the out-of doors; and yes, Miss Emily, he is probably a good catch for someone." Then, "No, I will not get involved with him and destroy our working relationship." That is as far as it ever went.

In the mornings, she wore khaki shorts for fishing and charters, then sometimes on to the FECO. Or jeans when the mornings were cool or if she was talking with school groups. But Genna could still wear colorful and flowery dresses when the spirit so moved her, or long sheer when she was to read aloud at her Wednesday night University of Miami poetry workshop. Alternatively, tailored and plain when her conservation work changed from environmental needs to political action.

She reached into her pocket and fiddled as though looking for something. "It looks like I forgot the key, Katy. I am getting more and more forgetful. Miss Emily has one though. We need to go and see her anyway. Do not let me forget the bags when we go in." They headed back to where Miss Emily was still sitting with her feet dangling from the other end of the dock. "You watch out for birds seeing the groceries setting there. Okay?"

"Or, raccoons, Mama? Or dogs like Mango?"

"Yes, raccoons or Mango too." Katy took Genna by the hand and pulled her along as they walked back onto the dock with Katy looking first ahead, then back at the groceries. Only a few boats were tied up, and only one with anyone on board. Genna spoke politely as she saw the solitary older man sitting in the late sun on a lawn chair and engrossed in a folded-over paperback. She looked toward the sun; it was not as bright but setting with thin and pink clouds arriving early for the later sunset.

"It is too quiet, Miss Emily," Genna said as they walked to within easy speaking distance. Miss Emily sat with her legs dangling and her shorts wet from water on the dock—water left from splashing from the bait bucket and from off the reel when she would wind it in. The hot afternoon sun caused sweat to appear through the back of the white sleeveless top she wore. A wide-brimmed cotton hat slowed the rays of the sun onto her head and face, her long-length white hair loosely tied into pigtails like some white-maned teenager. Her permanently tanned arms and legs, as well as her reason for being there, weren't hidden at all from the sun.

"Miss Katy caught a couple of throwbacks, but that's been about it," she called back. "It's quiet because it's too damn hot, that's what the problem is. Like your daddy use to say, when it gets hot, it gets quiet—too quiet. The only thing going on is out there somewhere—out there where it's deeper and cooler. It sure ain't around here." She looked back at Genna and caught her staring at her. "If there's something you want, sometimes it takes patience, but you have to go after it and don't let anything or anybody get in your way. But you know that, don't you?"

"Are you talking fishing or life in general?" Genna looked down the dock at the few boats tied up as she answered. "But fish are not what I am talking about. I mean customers. Have there been any calls?"

"Nary a one. I have that portable thing Ben Ivan bought right here beside me just in case. Telephone, ship to shore, whatever. It's still early though. We'll fill them up. Don't you be worrying none about that. That new sign's going to pull them in. It's stuck up there just like it's got a magic fishing hook in it. If a boat gets close, it'll jump out there, hook it good and tight, and reel it in."

Genna stood looking out to sea, glazing past her mother at the same view she watched every day for well over forty-five years now. Her thin skirt didn't stop the rays from the sun or the reflections from the water from passing through; like an ink eradicator, it took away any colorful shields of modesty and exposed young-looking, muscular legs that were more accustomed to shorts and to the open sun.

"Did you find what you went after? I mean, after the workshop today. I can't believe you still have your poetry thing like you do. I mean, as if your chartering and the conservation office didn't keep you busy enough by themselves."

"It ran a little long today. I ought not complain, though, when college students want to talk on and on. Even if it is just reciting something they wrote, or something I convinced them to read in order to get a grade. There is too much slamming down books and heading to wherever they might be going, but it did somehow delve into my time. But from what I can find out by telephone, the entire Key is in your name. I still think you will find that it cannot be sold without Ben Ivan's heirs or whatever having to sign some kind of rights away—even if they or we were dumb enough to try. We still need to check the Monroe County records in Key West sometime, but I think we're going to find exactly what we think and have thought all along. It all belongs to you."

"And you," Emily said.

"And Katy," Genna added. "We will never sell. It is just whatever Ben Ivan did to the title. And you still do not remember the details?"

"No."

"Well, we ought to know what that is, but if we do too much snooping around, we could open up a whole new can of worms, or poke at a manta-ray when it is asleep, as daddy used to say." She looked down at her mother as if to look her in the eye.

"I told you, that's the way it is. I mean, it being in our name, not about sleeping 'cudas or whatever your daddy told you."

"And I told you we're okay right here where we are. We can sell out when we want to, I will give you that. That is if we get the Hayes people to sign the right paper and we decide that selling is best for all concerned."

"I well know what you think of that. You've made that known, loud and clear."

"We can stay right out here without anyone bothering us. Taxes— we have always somehow taken care of taxes. Or at least so far. The last thing Ben Ivan told me is that the payback to Summer Tree for all he did and money he spent is all taken care of. I still do not understand all I know about that, but I feel that it is safe to assume it is true. You know, whatever he wrote out and is in that shoe box you hide under your bed."

"What's important is that we are still owners," Miss Emily said. "That's step one."

"We can keep it and let Katy's children, then their children, do the same thing. This is where we are supposed to be, despite your pumped up illusions about some over-built tourist Mecca with pumped-in sand and plastic palm fronds."

"Nothing wrong with air conditioning and somebody else 'doing for', Genna."

Emily stared at the line in the water as if it was her way of thinking of what Genna was saying. "I know what you're saying, lady. You're too much like your daddy—bless his soul. Both of you think the sun rises because of Coquina Key and sets for the same reason. Your daddy wouldn't have dreamed about doing anything with it, if there was a choice. I mean, getting what we could then us moving someplace dry and civilized where we could enjoy life for a change without it just enjoying us."

"I do not believe we are getting into this stale old conversation again," Genna said. "It is my fault, I guess, for bringing it up. If Daddy had not worked that deal with Ben Ivan—and I still think he did it just to get himself a new boat—we would still be standing right where we are standing. Maybe not on this dock, but we would still be right here on Coquina Key."

"Listen, if he hadn't worked that deal, as you call it, we wouldn't have been eating. Ben Ivan got the approvals; bought your dad the *Carefree I,* this dock, fixed things up around here, all that. All that out of the kindness of the man's heart."

"Well, I still do not know… Aw, forget it." Genna turned and started to head back to the "T" of the dock and to the land.

"You still don't know if it was help for your dad or help for me. Go on and say it again, lady. I know what's still in your soul-searching crawl. Ben Ivan Hayes was special to me. That's all I'm going to say about that, and you can take that any way you want it. You think what you want, Miss holier-than-thou. You just go right ahead. But I was there. I know. I know what went on."

"And I knew Ben Ivan, too. You forget that sometimes. I remember him and his big ole' belly laugh, him buying anything he wanted, the way he treated Daddy. That and the way he kept his eyes on you all the time, as if he was standing in a candy store. Anyone could have seen that—Ben Ivan and his big-timing, him the same as buying us."

"You won't ever forget will you, child? You won't forget what you think about him as long as you live, will you?"

Genna turned and looked again at the open sea, at the birds overhead, at the small waves gently and almost silently breaking against the piling. She remembered as she looked back all those years ago to her daddy, Wiley Trace's funeral. Then her mama coming home last week from another.

The engine died a few feet from the side of the pier. The blue and white *Carefree X* floated the last few feet into the old rubber-tired bumper as the boat gently touched its home again. Miss Emily stood up in the boat and braced her legs against the sides, as she had done more times than she could ever remember. With one hand, she tossed the manila rope to Genna and Katy standing on the dock. Katy caught the loosely flung rope and handed it to her mother.

"Hi, Miss Emily," Katy cried, her feet leaving the dock as she jumped up and down in her excitement. "Me and Mama fished again— fished off the end of the dock."

"You wait and tell her when she gets on the dock," Genna said. "In fact, you carry her bag for her." Genna pulled the seventeen-foot outboard tight to the bumpers then tied off the bowline to a brass cleat. She walked to catch the stern line thrown by her mother and tied it to yet another.

"Trip okay?" Genna asked. "I see you took Billy's car."

"I did," she answered as she lifted her suitcase from leaning against the console and strong-armed it onto the dock. "I figured you would need ours, and Billy Bearclaw owes us a little rental car use from time to time."

"I caught a red," Katy called. She looked at her mother as she put her fingers to her mouth. "Or was it a blue? I forget."

"It was a red," Genna answered.

"Yeah, I caught a red and I caught two damn catfish."

"Just catfish will suffice, Katy."

"Yeah. One red and two catfish."

"Sometimes you just have to call them the way you see them, don't you little Miss Katy?"

"You are turning my daughter into a drunken sailor," Genna said as Emily stepped onto the dock. Katy wrapped her arms around Miss Emily's legs as she did.

"I figured you knew where I went," she said.

"We knew." Genna stepped back a foot and looked at her mother. Genna wore one of the running tee shirts that she always wore as her at-home uniform and an old pair of saltwater-cured boat shoes with her khaki shorts. She looked down at her mother's long-legged black slacks—one of the few times, other than Mass, that she was seen in other than shorts. "You could have told someone before you left."

"You might have tried to talk me out of it if I did. Look at all the aggravation I saved you."

"Was it nice? Where there a lot of people there?" Genna smiled before Miss Emily answered. "I do not know why I say that. Nice is such an oxymoron to the rest of the sentence."

"Yes, my English-professor-speaking daughter. And no, before you ask. I didn't embarrass either you or me by talking to anyone. It was the correct thing to do. It was the proper thing to do. He was a close friend to your father."

"And my mother."

"Yes, and your mother," Emily answered. "I'm going to miss that old bear being around here."

She reached down and took hold of the suitcase, and with Katy helping, started walking up the dock.

"By the way—one person who I saw, but I of course didn't talk to, was…"

Genna interrupted. "Ivey Hayes. You are going to tell me about Ivey again."

"Just in conversation," Emily answered. "It's been years and years and years since I've seen him. He looked very nice—very 'in charge,' if you know what I mean. Back then, you two were what?—both in college the last time I saw him. I remember the first time he came down though—back when you were both barely in high school. Back then, you were barely into lipstick and combed hair. You would put on that one dress of yours at the time that you thought was so debonair and sexy, or too-short cut offs that I tried to keep you out of, and follow him around like some lost puppy dog. You would have thought you two were called to be with each other the way you both acted. He wasn't here long, but you two sure were thick when he was. Do you remember all that?"

"No. I do not remember," Genna lied.

"He would come down sometimes with those friends of his with him, even with young Tommy Ripington with him. It didn't skip a beat. I worried myself to death. But your daddy—your daddy said to let it go, it was just boy-girl stuff, puppy love he called it, not to worry none he would say, and you would be okay. Yeah, not to worry—me, your mother, he says it to—with both of you looking cross-eyed and gigglylike at each other. I didn't know who wanted to jump on who. Or is it whom? Anyway, he's done a good job of taking care of himself. He's just as tall and proud and good-looking. He's better looking than his father ever hoped to be."

"I am sure he is, Mother. Maybe we will get to see him again some day."

"It doesn't hurt to have someone around from time to time, Genna. Lord knows we wouldn't have gotten by without Ben Ivan being here from time to time like he was. After your father passed, it was like he was sent to us from above. A real blessing, that man was."

"I know what you are trying to say, Mother. The same thing you have hinted at more times than I have ever paid attention to. But if you saw him, you probably saw his wife and children. And that is all I care to say about that and hopefully need to say about that particular situation. You do know that he is active in her church."

Emily stopped as she and Katy put the suitcase down, and then let Genna pick it up before they walked on.

"He's a good Christian man, Genna. All I'm telling you is to be civil. I mean, don't put him up on some pedestal. Ben Ivan told me that about him. That's all I'm trying to say. I'm just telling you to be nice if he does call for any reason. You know what I mean, Genna?"

"I know what you mean, Mother. And I hope that you know what I mean. We will get by here. Even with Ben Ivan gone, somehow we will get by. Ivey Hayes is just a name from the past. He has his own world now. And with his father passing as he did, I would imagine it is going to be a very busy world. Probably a very busy world."

# Five

 Ivey and Addie were away for less than a week; then it took another week before their lives were back to anything resembling normal.
 Ivey's students seemed to like having him back. Someone had even bought a flowery condolence card, condolence which everyone had signed and which he found on his desk that first morning back in class. He heard enthusiastic comments about the young graduate student from the University of Virginia who had taken his classes for him while he was gone, but that was okay. Anyone as young-but-savvy as the graduate student they had sent had to have made an impression. But even with his youth and his too-long hair, his thin, round-framed glasses, and his big-legged pants, Ivey could keep up with him. Besides, security and tenure were things he was told to enjoy now—those things for older people, the ones who had done what they always wanted to do. They were the things that didn't mean too much when he first started teaching, but were now somehow becoming parts of his known and predictable life, whether he wanted them to or not.
 Despite his thoughts to the contrary, he enjoyed, in his own way, getting back to the sameness and the familiarity of things—back to the hallowed protection of academia. He enjoyed the lightness and seldom-caring freedom of so many of the kids; they reminded him sometimes of being back in Florida with Tommy—even Rip and Mary Celeste when they were that age. He had probably been that way, too. But with time and position, all that had long passed and gone by quicker than he would have ever thought—if he had ever taken the time to think about the past.
 Then there was the contrary massiveness of the old gray stone and red-brick buildings—those things that, along with classical and mystical writings, Elizabethan odes, and quest for chivalry, he grabbed onto during his college days. They were the things that he admitted and made a part of himself, as though they were the only roads away from Ben Ivan Hayes and all that was predetermined like an arranged marriage and laid out in front of him. He still remembered the running and hiding from not

only all that was expected of him then, but what was now being echoed from the trees, the rolling acres, the big business dictates, and the now Central Florida realm of Hayes Groves.

Maybe he was correct with the action at the time; maybe he could now live with what was so carved into stone for him to do. But as it was then, his classroom and his teaching would have to act again as a protective blanket he could crawl under to escape—a blanket he could use when something unsure or unsettling occurred, when he remembered something he wanted to hide, or when some person or some thing was taken away from him. But with it came the same—the continuing of what had been the month before and the year before that. Maybe the only answer was in all that he continually tried to forget.

Oh, it was nice getting home, but Florida was always nice to get back to, even though the good of taking Addie and the children there barely overcame the bad what with them treating it like something pretended, artificial, something maybe set up for a school play or carnival that would be taken down when they ventured back into the real world again. Neither she nor the children were ever close to Ben Ivan before he died. Or to Martha, for that matter. Addie seemed to treat Martha the same as everyone and everything else she saw and visited there: Martha and her new-found correctness, the state of Florida and its growing pains—so young and still trying to justify itself and its existence. At least that was what Virginia-born Adelaide Ward Hayes would have said both in look and attitude, as if she were answering while standing with wire hoops in a long, layered dress, and taking tours of Williamsburg when Ivey said anything about going home. Or once the children had seen and spent the time Addie thought appropriate in the lines of Epcot then the Magic Kingdom at Disney World.

Addie's life revolved first around the children, then around her little social groups—her "Daughters of the South Gatherings" someone in an off-campus William and Mary lampoon had once called them. She reluctantly agreed with that assessment, though she never mentioned it. Besides, as the wife of a faculty member and having a son at Deerfield School as well as a daughter at the Anne Mason School, there were many demands on both her time and her energy: the faculty teas, orientation booths, trips to be sponsored—all those things that took as much time as one could give them. It was only in the later years—years that saw the children getting older, both of them maturing and finding new interest in their own lives and new reasons to be away from Addie and their home—that she confessed a need to work, to "do something on a full-time basis back in the workplace", as she had read somewhere. It sounded like it had been written only to her. Ken Irwin and the Book Nook on Sumpter Square had given her that opportunity.

The bookstore was as well known to Ivey as it was to Addie. It had been there for Ken Irwin, his father, his father before him, and for all the years that their honorable business lived in their own little niche of the world. It was a specialty shop that made its reputation by stocking antiquarian books, finding out-of-print titles, and filling special orders. But its real income came from supplying textbooks to Hampton-Chase College, Deerfield School, Anne Mason School, and the other preparatory schools sprinkled throughout southeast Virginia. Ken and Addie had gone to school together, or so the story went and as told to Ivey. In earlier years, he even wondered if maybe there was more than he knew about. But time had never ferreted out anything like that. Besides, the wondering was now only academic. The closeness of the store, as well as the closeness of Ken to Addie, made the Book Nook and Ken Irwin the place and the person for Addie to turn to. There was never any doubt about that.

"Has Ken said anything about you being away?" Ivey asked Addie as she walked down the stairway off the foyer and into their woodpaneled basement. Addie spent time after the completion of dinner each day for an hour or so, sometimes even two, on the telephone with the myriad of ladies she knew who either called her or waited for a call from her as if the well being and the telling of each and every thing in their lives was like a religious edict that somehow had to be honored. Ivey was accustomed to losing her for that hour each evening while she "caught-up," as she would call it. He spoke of it one time in an essay he composed in his head but never put on paper—one written while he had been driving on the open expressway to Charlottesville—or Richmond or wherever he was driving that particular time—and composing things in his mind as he passed by the staid mile markers and informational signs on the highway. Women have a way of caring a little about a wide range of people, he had written in his head; men care just as deep, and maybe even deeper, but about one thing or just a few—and those things are often interrelated. But writing anything about the difference in the sexes was taboo these days. There would be someone somewhere who would read it and find him wrong and out of touch with the world of which he was so literally, and figuratively, a part.

"Ken understands," Addie said. "He has always understood these things." They gathered as they did every evening in their remodeled basement den—their place for family, television, reading, and the location of one of the old house's three fireplaces that they sometimes used. Ivey sat in his customary chair. The Times lay on the ottoman from when he brought it downstairs along with a low cholesterol frozen dinner he had heated in the microwave after being late and missing dinner with Addie and the kids—something he hated to do. The half-eaten dinner lay on a side table for later.

"I'm back now," Addie said. "Starting over again, so to speak. With what Ken's doing now, the changes, the adding on, he really needs someone. That space next door where the dress shops use to be—he has leased it and has cut a doorway through to the other side for even more space. Even Ken Irwin admits that he needs me now."

"It's always nice being needed, isn't it?" Ivey stood up, walked to the fireplace, prodded the top log into a better burning position on the fire, then put the brass mallard-headed poker back among the other long tools in the rack beside the fireplace opening. "It sounds like work is agreeing with you then."

"I have to admit that it is. I mean, working in my major of all things after all these years. Literature, I mean. We have the new space all stocked now, you know. Have you noticed as you fly by that we have even painted the brick on the outside?"

Ivey shook his head.

"Anyway, the added space gives us a better breakdown of genres into finer categories, and this makes it easier to show what we have in stock. Ken has even agreed to serve coffee now—a freebie for anyone who drops in. That should help business, I would think. That is, until someone spills something on a display of Grishams or sets a hot cup down on a coffee table book."

He sat back down and pushed aside an anthology of southern women writers he was reading. "I see you decided not to go up for the basketball game tonight. I suppose I should have stayed on at school and gone to the game myself. I ended up working so late—catching up on being gone, I mean. This is the first game with Mark I have missed since… well, I don't remember. But outlines, lesson plans, student mixes and breakdowns, individual learning curves, even my personal goals now. That new commission is about to ask for one thing too many."

"I decided not to go as well," Addie answered. "Mark and Ginny went. I let Ginny take my car if she promised not to go anywhere else and come straight home when it's over. Ginny doesn't care a thing about the game, of course, but went along, as mister-wonderful-of-the-week is supposed to be there. The school watches them though. Gin said, 'She's like going for like a little while, like, you know what I mean.' I'll be so glad when she gets over 'like' whatever this is she is 'like' going through."

"Did you get something worked out about getting your checks cashed? That whole money thing you were talking about?"

"I talked with Bill Jeffcoate at the bank… you know Sally Jeffcoate's Bill? He's opened up a regular account for me… said everyone needs one these days for credit purposes and what have you. He's getting me a VISA, too."

"Listen to miss independence there. You make sure you put me on the account. You know, just in case."

Addie didn't answer but just sat on the sofa and opened up the current edition of Southern Living she had been carrying.

Ivey looked past her and around the room. The book and the newspaper both sat on the ottoman, unopened. His eyes traveled along the wall looking at the pictures, the memorabilia, and the prints he had gathered. Scenes from only a week ago flowed into his mind as he looked…

The French doors leading to the porch at the grove house were open and filling the room with a yellow shade of light filtering through the screen and into the room where Martha and the family were meeting the very next day after the funeral. Even with the people inside— Martha, Mary Celeste and Ivey, as well as Rip, Tom, and even Tava fretting around with all the people there with only small sounds to be heard—the quiet from the lake and the groves filtered in as though it was noise itself. Martha's stare settled on the furniture with its dark wooden arms and legs, on pictures on the wall, on everything that had been stationary in the room since Ivey could remember at one or some time looking at all those things. Her look was slow and inquisitive enough that it appeared, to those watching and waiting for whatever was to be said, to be an invitation to join her in her visual tour.

The sofa had been upholstered at one time. Martha remembered Ben Ivan saying something about this back when it was done, but this was the first time she had noticed it. She remembered that Mr. Jernigan, the upholsterer, called for a color, but she told him anything that looked nice would do. That was, unless Ben Ivan cared, for some reason. She tried to think quickly what color it was before, but could not. Two overstuffed chairs were in front of the sofa, wooden armed and covered with the same nondescript but heavy knotted fabric as the sofa. A painting of two bird dogs hung on one wall, near it an unframed caricature of dogs dressed like men, playing cards and smoking cigars. Pictures of fish and old fishing trips hung on another.

On the third wall were more pictures—all framed, with some of them signed. Seeing her look, then seeing the pictures, Ivey stood up and walked over to them.

There was a picture of Ben Ivan and Governor Collins; Ivey remembered it again as he saw it. He looked at the picture of them shaking hands, both of them standing on what must have been the old Tallahassee Capital steps. And laughing. Ivey smiled himself as he remembered it again, not letting it show, but thinking to himself what might have been said just before the picture was snapped. He almost laughed himself, knowing his dad and thinking that if it was something that had made them both laugh, then it was probably not something his mother and the rest in the room would have wanted to hear. And a drawing—a political cartoon of his father as a mama hog lying in the mud and afternoon sun with six or seven piglets marked with names of local politicians and lying in a row feeding off it. He smiled and looked on. As he did, he was reminded of another piece in the newspaper about a statement Ben Ivan made when asked about running for office; he had answered, why he would want to be a local politician when he could own one. Ivey shook his head again, and looked on.

On the wall were three or four pictures of Florida Gator football teams sitting in bleachers, all the players looking strange by today's standards, some of the pictures signed, most of the players white. Crowded around other photographs were plaques, most of them brass, some just letters of some sorts—different sizes, different colors. And glassed certificates; things that probably meant something to Ben Ivan at one time like citizen awards from Rotaries and Chambers, Growers Coops, and city councils declaring some day, or scholarship, or some other reason for a presentation to the King Pin, as the articles would call him—the purveyor of the rolling plains of central Florida citrus, it said.

Then there was an old long and low console, set against another wall and holding a television screen in the middle and a Hi-If in one end. The other end had been altered at one time or another and held, as Ivey opened it to see, Ben Ivan's assortment of aged Scotch whiskeys for when he was with someone. Ivey had forgotten that about him. And the bottles of Kentucky sipping whiskey for when he was alone.

As if he was called, Ivey's attention, having somehow drifted toward his mother, returned to the room and back toward Addie, who was now sitting and looking at the magazine she held across her lap. He looked at the blond-haired Addie Hayes—a stereotype of southern legacy from Richmond, encapsulating all that was established and a hundred years old. She would look at Ivey as though there was something to say, pause, then look back in the magazine pages as Ivey sat and stared at the family room wall in his own home. Mostly male things, Addie called them. But they were things he liked and she allowed—things they both liked at one time. On the far wall hung Addie's University of Virginia diploma and her certificate as president one year of Daughters of the Confederacy. Then beside hers, and on the rest of the wall, were Ivey's college Diploma and his Doctorate from the University of Virginia in Charlottesville, where he met Addie. There was a picture of a group of rugby players, hair mussed and socks half down to their mudcaked ankles, with Ivey standing in the middle looking like he was hollering something at the camera. There was also a picture of Ivey standing with John Kennedy, with each of them in an open-collar knit shirt and Ivey laughing at something that had just been said.

"Your mother looks to be getting back into her daily life okay after the funeral," Addie said without looking up. "That's the way some do these days." Addie took off her tortoiseshell-rimmed glasses, ran her finger through her blond hair cut all-one-length, looked at her glasses as though checking if they were dirty, then put them back on. "Have you decided anything else about your need to go down there to do whatever you need to do?"

"I talk to everybody a couple times a day. I think one of the worst thought-out things I've ever done is when I gave out my telephone number at school. Everything's going right along though. Sometime within the next couple of weeks, I need to go down again and sign some things

Johnson Crews has for me. You met him, didn't you? The attorney?" She didn't answer as he stood up and walked toward the fireplace. He looked into the now tiring flames, fixed his stare, and remembered again...

"We've come a long way from this, haven't we?" Martha asked. "All this was good at one time, but Ben Ivan gave us better, did he not? He gave us better and wanted us to use it. But this, in all of its... well, this was his place to come. It wasn't mine. No, oh no. It wasn't mine; this was his. I knew when we left all those years ago he could never really leave it behind. He was part of this old house and that old lake out there. I mean, even from when we first got to where we could afford to move, he could not have sold it. No, we had to keep it around. Some people love an old dog or something like that. But Ben Ivan? No, it was this house he loved. He would come out here sometimes by himself, just him. Isn't that right, Tommy-boy? Sometimes he would invite his friends—those men around the Co-Op he always enjoyed being around so much. The fruity gang, I use to call them. He never liked it, but that's what I called them. What else do you call a bunch of old men who grow oranges, grapefruit, and tangerines for a living? Men driving around talking to each other through those squeaky radios in their cars. They would come out here, play cards, drink expensive liquor, he would say. And be himself he would say. Most of the time, it was just for the day, but sometimes they would spend the night, sometimes a whole weekend. Tommy used to keep me informed and up on what to expect. Didn't you, Tommy?" She continued again, and before he could answer. "I don't see what he ever saw in it, but it was honest. He never hurt anybody and he loved it. Oh, how that man loved it."

She half turned and looked at Tommy. "You'd come out here sometimes when you didn't want to, wouldn't you, Tommy? I know you did. You'd bring him home sometimes on Sunday afternoon. Sometimes, he would be that way, and you would have to put up with him like that. He'd be all red-eyed and smelling like some distillery somewhere. He told me a man needs to enjoy himself sometimes, to get away sometimes. And that he did and did it right here in this old rundown house— this old house not big enough to cuss a cat in, as Tava would say. The house would probably have been eaten up with roaches if so much liquor hadn't been poured on the floor and the stench killed them all. But he was all right. And I knew where he was."

Martha looked across at her youngest son Rip watching what she was saying. "I bet you think I'm forgetting about his trips to the Keys, aren't you Rip?" Rip didn't say anything but continued to look straight ahead and then down into a glass of something he found in the kitchen. She stood up, pushing down on Mary Celeste and Rip by their legs as she did. Ivey pulled back his chair as she looked to walk in front of him. She walked over to the front window, speaking to the outside, but loud enough for them all to hear.

"No, his place was here... You might think this old lady is going on and on and talking out of her mind. But I know what I'm saying. This and the groves were Ben Ivan Hayes. Oh, he would go off... He would go to the Keys or someplace. I've heard all those tales—that truck driver's gossip, that smut. I heard what people said. Nevertheless, it wasn't true. None of it was true... He was away being by himself, he would say... And I believe him... It wasn't very often, but he would go. Sometimes, he wouldn't even tell me he was going. He would just get up and go... I thought this place was all he needed, and I was right most of the time... but... I know he went down there and I will say until my dying day, it was down there where he went and fished."

Martha looked hard at her son, Ivey, then at her daughter, Mary Celeste. She looked as though asking for approval of what she was saying. Neither said anything.

"It was that Wiley Trace he went to see," she said as she started back to the sofa. "We both knew Wiley from years and years ago." She turned and looked at each of them as though checking to make sure they were listening and agreeing. "And then... after Wiley died, Ben Ivan would still go down there. I know what people who don't know any better would say about that thing... that— that woman. But they were wrong. Every one of them is wrong—excuse my language, but lyingthrough-their-teeth wrong. He even brought me pictures one time of a fish he had caught. You know, one of those 'hanging fish' like they sometimes have at fairs or sideshows or places for people to get their picture taken. You know, an old fish made out of cardboard that you walk up and get your picture taken beside and it looks like you and a big old fish. But his was real. There was ugly blood on it, and big black numbers scrawled on its side. Your father was like that. You boys know that. If anyone could do it, he had to do it, too. I saw other pictures, too—pictures of great long strings of fish, all hung side by side and laid out nicely in a row. You, Rip, and you, Ivey... you two probably know what kind of fish they were. I just know they were something I never had to face him bringing home... I know that's what he did. Fishing, I mean. Yes, I know for a fact that's what he did."

As though there no one else was there, she looked and spoke directly to Ivey. "And that place down there, that place he always went. I know he owned it. So, you get it sold, you hear me son? There's something wrong with the paperwork or something on it, Johnson Crews tells me. But you sell it, you hear, Ivey. If anyone still lives there, you get her gone, you hear. We don't need any of that kind of person around anymore."

Her eyes left Ivey as though she had said what she needed to say. "But that's enough about that. It's just us now, and we have to go on. God is with us, but we have to keep the groves going and by God himself, we will. Ivey, you've got to do that, you hear. Don't let us down, Ivey. We'll help, but it's up to you to do it, Ivey."

Addie put down her magazine, lifted then pulled her legs up under her on the sofa and patted her skirt down over them. "That doesn't answer me. Do you think you can continue with just telephoning, or will the time come when you need to spend more time there?"

"That bothers you, doesn't it?"

"Ivey, we can't continue not talking about it like it doesn't exist. Like it's something other people deal with but Addie Hayes and the scholarly, in-control, Sunday School teaching Ivey Hayes are above or something." She looked away as she said, "I mean, let's admit it; we quit having a marriage a long time ago."

"What does that have to do with anything?"

"If you're going to move down there, I, for one, have a lot to do with it. Maybe moving is what you need; maybe it's what we both need."

Ivey took off his reading glasses, as though lessening any formality, and stared at her. "That's what you want, isn't it Addie? Me with a reason to spend time away—away from the school, away from you. You with your new job—your tasting independence and liking it. That's it, isn't it?"

"What did that lady think in that Carver short story... she woke up one day and her life was already over? Maybe we both have a little too much of that going through our minds right now. Maybe we're both getting of the age that we need to change ways, alter directions a little."

"Taking a mid-life inventory and not liking what you find... is that what you're trying to say? I don't think I can say that, Addie," Ivey said as he walked again to the fire. "There are things I would like to change, but we're okay; I'm okay."

"You're changing, Ivey. Mister do-nothing-wrong, mister alwaysin-control, but mister searching in your eye for something that obviously isn't here. You're changing around me, Ivey, around the children, changing about the school. You don't even talk the way you once did. You're looking so restless, so out of sorts. So 'looking and acting like you're in the wrong place of late'—that there's some thing or some place else that you're looking for. Maybe for the good of both of us, you just need to move down for a while and see how you like it. Maybe that's what you need."

"I thought about it—strictly from a business viewpoint, I mean. I don't think I was thinking about it in a personal way. But then, I don't know, maybe I was. The first thing that came to mind was you, Addie. I would worry about you and your staying here and getting along."

"You've taken care of me for a long time, Ivey. Maybe it's time for me to do a little of that myself now. Maybe I need a little quiet, a little time. I'm old enough to admit that."

"You're talking like going separate ways, Addie. Or am I missing something? It's gone, is that what you're saying, Addie. I'm right, aren't I? I mean, what was there at one time."

"We're not talking about something we don't both already know. Ivey; you're the best friend I have. That's something we can never lose."

"And love? What about love? Is that something that people just outgrow? Is that what you're telling me now?"

"Isn't love, as somebody else said, caring for, and worrying about?"

"I can't believe we're having this conversation," Ivey said as he sat down, then just as quickly standing back up. "I mean, praise God, I know what love is."

The flames dancing in the fireplace slowed their burning, as they and the conversation almost came to a stop.

"People change, Ivey. I change. You change. I have a job now and new responsibilities. You have all those responsibilities that your father has left you and that your family thinks only you can take care of. All those things the Lord has arranged for both of us. We all change. The children are here, but they'll always be here for you. Ginny is going off to school next year, of course. Mark and I are getting along okay, considering. If you have to spend more time down there, you go ahead, okay?"

Addie stood up and walked over to him. She stood in front of Ivey and looked directly up into his eyes. "You do what you need to do, Ivey. I'll understand. God will understand."

Ivey stared, too. He said, "With all the things going on that you talk about, Addie, I'll always be where you can find me. Don't you ever forget, Addie, that there's one person in this world who still loves you and who always will."

"I know," she said as she reached and touched his hand. "But you go do what the Lord needs you to do. I'll do the same."

## Six

Ivey drove his own car back to Florida. With the exception of quick trips to a conference, an out-of-town game of the kids, or a retreat somewhere, it was the first time he had been on the open road and alone since before he could remember. Now it was a long drive—a long drive alone—and, as the miles measured by, a road he knew he might not drive again.

The morning after he arrived, Ivey pulled his '72 Cutlass convertible into a parking space in front of a residential-looking office in a nostalgia area of Orlando—down the street from the law offices of Tanner, Leigh, and Crews. He had bought the old convertible on a lark earlier that spring—one of the few things he could remember buying that he didn't need, had no reason what-so-ever for owning, or where the only logic behind doing it was that it was something he simply wanted. His justified it to himself by the fact that he personally knew and had seen others about his age (John Davies in Math, Tom Bunyan in Earth Science) owning older convertibles (or newer Porches). His decision was also helped by seeing the car parked near Hume Hall where the Admin people parked. After asking around, he found that a bookkeeper owned it—an older lady down in accounting.

Apparently, the lady had driven it since new, and surprisingly, wanted to sell it. It had been her husband's car—he a collector and keeper of cars in mint conditions. He was gone—had died quite a few years ago now—and older cars have special needs, she said on the telephone when he called. She had repeated to him what her collector husband had said: they need to be owned by someone who knows what they are and can appreciate them for that reason. Foreign cars with better gas mileage fitted her needs now, and she was overly pleased to sell to the right owner. For some reason, Ivey found himself wishing he had done some of the materialistic things he had passed on before: the memberships, the subscriptions, the rehab that time that he didn't put money in—all the I-told-you-so lessons throughout the years. So Ivey bought the car. Addie immediately questioned it when he did—even more so when he wrote a check on their debit checking account, paying for it outright and driving it home immediately.

She accepted it in the same way she accepted his running every morning, his worrying about aging, what appeared to be a layer of fat settling around his middle, and him joining a record club of all things (where he regularly forgot to send in his selection each month). That and his rediscovery of cotton pants and pleats—this time with names over the hip pocket—and his buying of even more shirts with button-down collars. She took it as one of Ivey's play things—silly maybe, but controllable. She gave him her usual unheeded spiel about him working too hard and about how he deserved to have something he wanted but had no earthly reason to own. Addie told him he should at least get the faded-bronze-color Cutlass (that had a dirt and what Ivey called an agecolored tan convertible top—a drop-top, he called it) painted, and get the car a new top. Or at least get it cleaned. But the old and the aged were perhaps part of the life toward which he found himself drifting, not knowing how to stop. Or even wanting to stop if he could have.

He walked up the sidewalk—the broken-up concrete walk where roots from trees pushed up four-foot sections of concrete that were now twisted around and laying at different elevations and angles. But they were all a part of what Orlando was those years before he left—before he thought he knew better.

As he walked, he remembered the conversation he had had on the telephone with Mary Celeste—10:00 at Johnson's office. He looked down the street and on both sides for her dated blue wagon. Luckily, it was nowhere to be seen. He looked behind him, past a few more of the old houses, and back at the car to make sure it was okay parked where he had left it. He looked at the narrow street and at the parking spaces that were not wide enough anymore. He walked past a house and suddenly remembered a girl who had lived there all those years ago who he had dated two or three times. She probably lives somewhere else now, he thought, and has kids getting out of school. Maybe she was even a grandmother. No, she could never be a grandmother. The world could change, but as he looked back at the dirty gold convertible again, it was still a new car, sitting up at Holler Oldsmobile's outside showroom, people looking at it on display, its top down on an early spring Sunday after church.

Coming out of his reverie, Ivey saw the street sign again—the 1642, hanging from a black metal sign by little brass chains and blowing lightly in a weightless morning breeze. He turned at the sign and walked up the narrow sidewalk, up the brick steps, and toward the wood-stained front door—a door with a cut-and-beveled glass oval in the center. Over the top and scrolled in green-gilded brass letters was the firm name: *Tanner, Leigh, and Crews.* He opened the door and stepped inside.

Sounds from the outside were shut off, leaving only the quiet of soft stereo music as he walked from the bright sun of the Orlando morning into the ambience of the law firm's reception and waiting area—a room conditioned against the mid-morning heat of the outside and colored in light grays, a darker green, plush Berber carpeting, and authority. A dark-stained mahogany desk belonging to a looking-the-other-way receptionist sat in the center of the room. The business-only lady at the desk turned and smiled, acknowledging that he was there and saying she would be with him as soon as she could get off the telephone, the receiver partially wedged between her cheek and padded shoulder. Ivey glanced to the left and the right as he waited, seeing matching sofas on either side and lightly stuffed and colonial-stripped Queen Anne chairs sitting on the sides of each of them. A large vase—Chinese, old, and knowingly expensive—divided magazines on an early colonial coffee table that was sitting perfectly centered in front of one of the sofas. Copies of current architectural and business magazines were stacked in two descending piles, as though they were placed there by a decorator for display only—to be looked at, but not to be disturbed. Breaking up the scene was a fax machine on a small table beside the desk, a computer on the corner of the receptionist desk, and a laser printer making a soft hum from the credenza behind her. Matching Chinese figurines were set around, perhaps looking out of place for a busy office, but adding to the Chinese and old American south decorum and rich appointments of the room.

His glance moved from the surroundings to the receptionist as she finally got through with her telephone call and looked up to speak him. A young girl with her hair pulled loosely back and tied into a bun, and still wearing the coat to her tailored business suit smiled brightly as she spoke. She looked like something ordered from a Brooks Brothers catalogue—set out front and only to be removed when next year's model arrived.

"Good morning, may I help you?"

"Yes—Johnson Crews, please."

"You must be Mr. Hayes," she said without waiting for a reply. "He is expecting you." She stood up from her desk, moved around its corner, and walked in front of him.

"Ms. Hayes-King is already there."

At least she remembers names, he thought, and didn't call me by my first. Mary Celeste has been here before to know where to park without being seen. That's like her.

"I'm Helen Forrest-Brown." The receptionist offered her hand as she walked up to him. Ivey smiled inwardly, thought better of saying something about her name, then shook hands with her.

"She must be early, or I'm late," he said with a smile. "It's probably the latter."

"Pardon?" she asked.

"Ms. Hayes-King."

"Yes, she's already here." She looked puzzled as she stepped out in front of him. "She's with Mr. Crews, so I'll walk you to his office." A perfumed scent followed her as she stepped in front of him—an evening scent, something Addie never wore, for sure nothing emitted by any of the women around the school, never the women teachers he knew, and for sure none of the students. It was a big-town aroma, a center isle of large department stores, and a fragrance that, if Addie had ever worn, it was many, many years before.

A narrow-looking, wood-floored passageway led out of the receptionist area, past back offices and presumably upstairs to the offices above. The hallway looked to be sided by offices, conference rooms, or working areas, with voices drifting into the hall as he and his guide passed closed or barely open doors. As they walked to the end of the hall, she led him into a stairway curving from the first floor to the second floor above. Glass blocks surrounded the stairway—something very apparently revised from the original and separating it from the out-of-doors and the morning sun, but adding light and a freshness to the stately-but-old decor.

"Mr. Crews has spoken of you," she said as she started up the steps. Ivey's look followed her and the tightness of her skirt, the outlining ridges of younger cut underwear moving with her as she ascended the steps in front of him. He shook his head a little to get his mind back on why he was there.

"Your offices are quite nice," he said, making friendly and proper conversation. "It always surprises me what one can do with an old home. It adds a degree of closeness to a business, don't you agree?"

"It's nice," she answered. "But we're really busting at the seams here. We're working on getting us new space down in the CNA Tower— maybe right there in the building you were in Tuesday."

Tuesday, he thought. How did? …why did? They must be really watching me.

Miss Forrest-Brown interrupted his thought again. "This is Mr. Crews' office on the right."

She led him into a large, dark-wood and Persian-rugged office where Johnson walked from behind his desk to greet him. Ivey walked quickly to Johnson Crews, shook his hand while giving his best and most correct, nonsensical, business chitchat and only then saw Sol Weinstein sitting with his back to them and the door. Mary Celeste was standing at the window and looking out at whatever was below. She turned as he entered but only nodded his presence.

"Hello, Sol," Ivey said as he gave the accountant his hand. He looked back at Ms. Forrest-Brown, but she had already gone. Sol stood up, a stack of wide green and white computer paper that was in his lap and which he now pressed against himself allowing him to only slightly bend as he stood up.

"Don't stand up," Ivey said.

"It's no problem," he answered. "Johnson and I were just going over some of your figures."

Ivey walked toward Mary Celeste, meeting her as she walked toward him. He hugged her without speaking.

"Coffee?" Johnson asked as he waved his hand toward one of the chairs, at the same time retreating behind his massively large desk. The desktop was covered with stacks of files—six or seven stacks, each one four or five manila-folders high.

"Please," Ivey answered. "Black, with a sweetener, if I may." He sat down but continued looking around the office.

Speaking to the intercom, Johnson said, "Mr. Weinstein, Ms. Hayes, and I would… err… just bring a pot of coffee," He let go of the button without hearing an answer. "On second thought, she's playing phone receptionist today with two of the other people out. Let me go and get us a pot. It'll be a lot quicker."

Ivey started to say no, but Johnson spoke before him. "You just give me a minute, and I'll be right back." He was not wearing a coat but a long-sleeved, blue-stripped shirt, white collar, and a pair of dark gray suspenders. He wore the same tasseled loafers Ivey had noticed the last time he saw him.

"This looks to be a busy office," Ivey said.

Neither Sol Weinstein nor Mary Celeste answered or looked. Johnson spoke as he walked back into his office, "They're brewing up a fresh pot of coffee, so it'll be here in a few minutes."

"How is it staying out at the lake house?" Johnson asked. "Has Tom Ripington got you everything you need?"

"It's fine. I remember staying out there as a boy. I don't think things have changed all that much since then."

"No, Doctor," said Johnson. "Just a career, a wife, and couple of children." Both Johnson and Sol laughed—almost as if on cue.

"You know what I mean," Ivey said. "It's almost *too* quiet if there can be such a thing. People have a way of forgetting how quiet the world can be sometimes—when there's nothing around to make any noise. It's given me time to read some of the volumes of things you sent me."

"I wish I could say there's nothing to worry about here," Johnson added. "I mean, I'm assuming you're talking about Summer Tree. But worry sometimes brings out the best in us. Or, maybe that's just something I've read somewhere before. Or maybe something someone taught me."

Johnson looked at Ivey and saw from his glance that the small talk needed to come to an end.

"Sol and I have been discussing and going over the information we have, and though we've discovered some setbacks, we think we can help you work things out."

A yet different person entered the room carrying a silver tray holding a glass coffee pot and four what looked like china cups. He looked at the person—Beava. Yeah, Beava something, he thought. I remember the name. The cups were set on four china saucers, a small creamer in the middle and five or six pink sweetener packets tilted against one of the cups. She sat the tray down on the edge of Johnson's desk and poured each of them a cup of coffee.

"I saw you earlier with a throw-away cup, Sol," the new face said as she walked past Sol Weinstein. She looked to be about the age of the woman at the front desk—the hyphenated lady. And tall—striking was probably the word. "I'm Beava Leigh," she said, stepping over to the side of Ivey. The business-suited woman with blond and short-cropped hair thrust her hand toward him.

"Are you the Leigh in Tanner, Leigh, and Crews?" Ivey asked, taking her hand.

"In a way," she answered. "Aaron Leigh is my father. He's semi-retired now." She looked at Johnson, as though expecting approval, and then went on. "I'm an attorney first, daughter second. Moreover, when he's in a good mood, I've been told I'm a pretty damn good one. Attorney, I mean."

"I never said that," came Johnson. "I mean, err… I mean… "

"Glad to meet you then, Ms. Leigh," Ivey said, with a chuckle to himself. "Thank you for the coffee." He wanted to say something about charges, and coffee, china cups, and attorneys pouring coffee, but decided not to say anything.

"It's no problem. Besides, we've been looking forward to meeting you for some time now. Being a little short on help today, I volunteered before some kind of sexist rank was pulled on me." She smiled, looking at Ivey for a reply, but he said nothing. She picked up Sol's throwaway, then turned and walked away from the four of them. "She's a bit of fire—that one is," Johnson said as she left.

"She's a nice lady," Mary Celeste said, entering the conversation. "She's been seeing Tom Ripington of all people, don't-you-know." Johnson immediately looked at Ivey, as though looking for his reaction, while Ivey looked back toward the door, as though to look at Beava again.

"No, I didn't know that," he said, setting his cup down. "But I've had a lot of surprises of late."

Ivey leaned back, looked at both Sol and Mary Celeste and then at Johnson. "So tell me what I don't want to hear. As I remember, that's why we're here, isn't it? Tell me how things are going with Summer Tree and what it's going to take to make sure all the gears are greased and all the bills are being paid."

Sol answered for Johnson. "Summer Tree's financials—and here's a copy for you of this month's and this quarter's statements—are a problem, partly because of Consolidated Realty; that seems to be the culprit. A problem, but solvable. As you are no doubt aware, Consolidated is a subsidiary company to Summer Tree for direct ownership of property. A different pocket, Ben Ivan called it, and it's taking a pretty good loss. We've already brought Mary Celeste up to speed on it. Some of the other things—the other parts of Summer Tree—are walking on perhaps too thin ice but seemingly all right: Sunny Acres, Sunny Acres Morning, Citrus Management."

"What kind of thin ice?"

"Well, Citrus Management Inc. for one," he answered. "That's a management company Ben Ivan formed to provide management to absentee owners. You stop me now if I start telling you something you already know."

Ivey didn't speak, so Sol Weinstein went on.

"He would grow, pick, and sell; do all the dirty work. You know, for investor types or family groves or whatever. For it, he would get a healthy commission. That is, if things sold as they should."

*"And...* if they didn't?"

"If they didn't, the quarterlies would show the way they do now."

Ivey scanned the room, then fixed his stare on Johnson Crews.

# Seven

It was late in the afternoon when the elevator door opened on the third floor to Mary Celeste and Sutton's Winter Park condominium. They had lingered at the grove house with her mother and the others, talked and mingled until they made a reason to get away.

Mary Celeste pushed open the door to the condo, then fiddled with pulling out the key while Sutton walked across the condo great room—entertainment room, she called it—and opened the door to the screened balcony. Mister Tutu and Daisy—two Lhasa Apsos—darted in as the screen was pushed back, both, as if synchronized, running toward Mary Celeste, then just as quickly back to Sutton. They turned, each jumping to lean against one of Sutton's legs, as he smoothed down the hair on the backs of their heads and fingered behind their ears.

"We need to think up a better place to leave them, Celeste. They go stark-raving mad being left alone like this." He watched as they both turned and ran toward her. "Maybe something permanent on the porch—something with one side as protection against the rain or whatever. Especially with you going to be gone as you are. Maybe we ought to just go ahead and do that."

"You seem to think that all that's going to happen now, don't you?" She put her purse in the corner of the sofa and turned on the cut-glass table lamp, throwing more light into the darkened room. She pushed off one shoe with the other, then set them both at the edge of the off-white Vinyl sofa. She leaned back, her toes outstretched in her pantyhose and moving as if they themselves were walking. "I told you all along what's going to happen. I told you if anything ever happened, Ivey would be the one—the one to push all the buttons and pull all the cords to save us all. I told you, didn't I?"

Sutton only nodded. He stood tall, his tortoise-shell glasses wedged under lightly permed long hair that was pushed back on the sides and away from the receding hair line in front; his hair was lightly curled and tufted toward the ends. His tie hung loosened, and his Oxford buttondown was pulled open at the collar.

"But Ivey Hayes is a piece of cake," she said, "southern and boring cake. He no more cares about the business or anything Daddy was into than he did back when Daddy all but offered to give it all to him twenty years ago. As long as Mama is taken care of and nobody is owed any big debt, he won't care a thing about it. Ole, don't-make-waves-and-leaveme-alone Ivey Hayes. But in a few months, he'll be all through with his obligation—Ivey Hayes and his doing right and putting out his appearance of old-south pomp and whatever. He'll find some way out; you can bet the farm on that. He'll go back to Virginia—to his books, to his faculty lunches or whatever, and those tight-sweatered and loose-headed Penelopes all around—and we'll never see him again."

"I've got to hand it to you, Celeste. So far, you're right with everything you've said. You get on in there and get things going, just like they ought to be. You know what we need. We'll be all right. Just like we've planned."

"All right? Listen, we'll be in great shape. That little matter with your San Palo buddies—we'll get them paid off and won't ever hear from them again. You just don't go getting yourself hung out there to dry like that again. You let flying in that little airplane of yours remain your only hobby. I'll take care of you this time, but next time, I just might not. But you know that, don't you?"

"Well... next time, we'll have a little more staying power, honey. A little more cash flow, a little time, if that's what a man needs."

Mary Celeste walked over to the closed sliding door and looked through to the screened porch and the third floor view beyond. She looked at the view of open green fairways and probably the last golf cart of the day making its way past a raised bunker and then on to a slightly undulating green in the distance. "Think about now and what their money can do for us. I've got a string going from the money men through the merchandiser, to the sales people, and all we need is the merchandise, baby. Maybe now they'll all go together."

Sutton walked up and stood beside her as she spoke. "That's the first time I've seen Ivey in years. However, I agree with you; I can't see where he has changed all that much. A little grayer around the edges, I guess, but still the same Joe Exercise and Ivey-league-looking Ivey Hayes."

Silence fell between the two of them. Then, "Are you sure he's going to be all right?"

Mary Celeste turned and walked away from him and toward the black lacquered table separating the stark white walls of the room from the foyer. In the foyer beyond, hung a Soho Gallery and two New York gallery posters, advertising art showings back in '74 and '78. She playfully reached toward one of the dogs, causing it to run and slide into the foyer and onto the black and white squared marble of the floor.

"I'll take care of my brother. No, don't you worry about that. Selling the land in the Keys might be a little tricky, but I can take care of that. Getting your buddies to talk about forgetting what you owe and then to still put up a pile for a major chunk of the development "ain't no cake walk," as they say. But all that will happen. Especially, if we can get Blum moving on it and keep Johnson Crews happy. Then we can get it out of just being daydreams."

Sutton walked over to a wine rack hidden behind two bi-fold doors and picked up two stemmed wine glasses. He put his hand on a bottle of wine, then looked at Mary Celeste.

"White or red? A chardonnay or—"

"Red," she answered. "...Especially, if we can tie in with him if he wants to develop it. Blum, I mean. So far, he's got those offshore dollars needing to be spent and me in my role as expeditor as well as investor for his great island in the sun. It's his way onto an island screaming to be developed—our own little Key in the Keys."

"Exciting, isn't it?"

Silence lay between the two of them before he went on.

"And Blum seems to be the man with the plan, doesn't he?"

"He's walked down this road before. He knows how to take a piece of sorry land and turn it into a producing gold mine. He's got a history of that."

"Speaking of Keys, honey. Listen, that was a little surprising, wasn't it? I mean, your mother saying what she did about... how did she put it? About that thing in the Keys, she called it. I mean, yips! I damned near laughed when she said it."

"It's no laughing matter, Sutton."

"I know. It's just always been hard to categorize Ben Ivan Hayes. I mean, what he has done. You know what I mean. But that woman person—the one still sitting on the property. I bet she's wondering what that island is going to be called now."

"The Coquina Key Club we finally decided on—close to what it's called now. Except no one but the locals and old-time boaters know it's even there."

"Yeah, Coquina Key. You're going have to share with me some day the real story on all that Ben Ivan did down there. The mystery man, I mean. I know he had something going with that lady that everybody seems to know about but nobody will ever admit to knowing."

"That may be what we have to watch out for," Mary Celeste said, almost in a whisper. "With Ivey, I mean."

"You don't mean that lady?"

"No, I don't mean that lady. I'm talking about the lady's daughter. That's the one I worry about. The goody one. I don't think they've seen each other in all these years, but Tommy Ripington tells me it was a real he-she thing at one time. You don't ever know about those fires. I mean, as to when they can flame up again."

Sutton laughed. "Excuse me if it seems funny, but somehow I can't see Ivey Hayes getting involved with any little island chick, either."

"No one could see my old man, Ben Ivan Hayes getting involved either, but that's what happened. It happened so much that Summer Tree Corporation—Consolidated Realty technically, I guess—has ended up owning the biggest part of the whole dang Key. I still can't help but think that this was part of his whole plan."

"Ben Ivan Hayes giving his own fat-self out for property?"

"No, *giving* of himself," she answered. "The street says that he fell for her, hook, line, and sinker. And in this case, that old analogy may have been completely right."

"You don't think Ivey will step into the same thing.... will he?" Sutton asked. "Surely, he knows about his dad. Probably more so than you *or* I. Surely, he remembers."

"By the time Johnson Crews, Sol Weinstein, and I get through, and once it sinks in how much Summer Tree really owes, and how the Hayes name and Martha Hayes and all that which is the mother-lode of society is about to end up in some debtor's court... and then, how valuable that piece of property is... he'll learn and make sure it sells. And I mean sell sure and sell quickly. He'll make sure it sells. And when it does, The Coquina Key Club group will be the buyer."

"You're a smart business lady, Celeste. That's what I've always loved about you."

"Just don't you get us all stretched out tight again. This will get us what we need for right now, but you let me make the deals. You just bring them to me. I'll do the dealing."

Sutton walked over to where Mary Celeste had, a moment ago, been looking out on the now-completely-darkened fairway. He looked out but didn't have to turn around to know that Mary Celeste was still there behind him

# Eight

Ivey stopped by the big house on Coventry Circle that night after talking to Johnson Crews. Like a college-aged son in town and in need of a good meal, he called his mother earlier and talked long enough to get an invitation to see her and to revisit Tava's cooking.

It was a private meal —just he and his mother. They talked over a casserole of thin strips of fried steak, yellow rice, and whatever else Tava did to the dish. As if she didn't already know, they talked about what he was doing and about how long he could continue at the school while still getting even more involved with the groves. And they talked about what he thought overall about what Ben Ivan had left. They talked about whether Addie was ever going to visit, must less move to Florida. (They both knew that she would never do that.) When they were through, Ivey took their plates to the kitchen as he always did, excused himself, and stepped out the back door. Lights were on in the apartment over the garage.

Ivey walked past the fruit trees in the back yard and toward the painted white steps and the wooden handrail to the upstairs. He had been up those same steps many, many times in the past, mainly in those trytest-and-explore years some thirty years before—those times when his independence required counsel from his barely older uncle Tommy Ripington. The trip up the steps was not just another memory; it seemed as though he had walked up here the day before. He hadn't, though. Apart from one time during one of his rare visits, it had been a lifetime ago.

Tommy's dog stood at the landing. Odie, thought Ivey, yeah, that's it. Odie's tongue hung out as he waited for Ivey to get to the top step— waited to point his head up to be patted, rubbed, and spoken to.

"Come in," Tommy hollered before Ivey knocked. "Door's open."

"You still never shut or lock the front door, do you?" Ivey stepped inside, allowing the screen door to shut gently behind him but keeping a hand behind him to prevent the door from slamming. Tommy stood next to the table in the kitchen tossing letters from the day's mail into a small stack in the center. His shirt was unbuttoned, open, and hanging from his shoulders as if he was getting undressed as he walked into the room. Ivey looked at Tommy's exposed stomach—flat and looking like something Ivey had probably prided back in college, but which had now somehow disappeared, despite his daily running.

"No need to," Tommy answered, referring to the unlocked door. "Besides, I can hear things better if it's open. You know, back when Ben Ivan was not in town. Sometimes, when Martha calls for something—or Tava. He looked at Ivey with an almost surprised stare of wishing he had said something else. "With only Martha there now, except Tava, of course. I still keep my ear peeled in the direction of the house. You know, just in case. Ben Ivan and Tava both asked me to do that. You never know, Ben Ivan used to say."

Ivey stood staring, his own thoughts mirroring Tommy's. It seemed like those years before—years when they were both young and had all those plans... Who would have thought? he mused. Dad gone. Maybe moving back. Addie and the kids. The world sure can change.

"I came out tonight to have supper and some quiet time with my mother," Ivey said. He looked around the room as he spoke, the room looking the same as when he had been there last. A single bed was set against the far wall. As before, the sofa was set under the large window looking onto the stairs, with a narrow coffee table sitting in front of it. Florida Sportsman and a sun-faded copy of Playboy both lay in disarray on the wood-stained top. Two doors hung unnoticed and led off from the one large room to a bathroom and a walk-in closet. On the other side was the kitchen: a compact room with all the built-ins and appliances anyone could ever use to fill the space. In the center of the kitchen sat a rectangular table with four wooden chairs neatly pushed under it. On one of the walls hung a diploma from a trade school Tommy had completed before Ben Ivan told him to give it up and join him full time. There were ten to twelve pictures, some framed, others just pinned to the wall—all pictures that Ivey had never really seen.

"You want a beer?" Tommy asked walking over to the refrigerator. He reached in and took one out for him. "You're old enough to come up here and drink one if you want one."

He smiled as he walked over to the single shelf on the wall. Books were stacked on the shelf—old books, books from growing up, Chip Hilton and sports hero books, Florida history books, a book titled "Indian Tribes in Florida," and one more of mostly pictures, called "The

Seminoles; Rising From the Glades." Then, beside the shelves, were the pictures. The first one he walked up to was a picture that Ivey thought he had made out correctly from across the room—a picture of Tommy and Ben Ivan, both down on one knee and six large fish of some kind laid out in front of them. Another was a picture Martha had taken of Ben Ivan, Tommy, and him the weekend they drove to William & Mary for his own graduation. Ivey looked at it closely as he walked up to it. They both had flattop haircuts and looked so young, even considering when the picture was taken.

"You think if we'd known then what we know now, we would have changed anything, Tommy?"

Tommy didn't answer, returning a smile instead—a smile that had a question behind it.

Ivey looked quickly at the other pictures—pictures of a little girl sitting on a dock with a "lab" beside her, she holding up a fish, and an older woman smiling broadly and squeezing the little girl around her shoulders. He thought "Emily Trace" as he saw the woman and looked quickly at the other pictures, as though looking for someone else.

"Tell me, Tommy," he started. "Tell me what else you remember about Wiley Trace."

"I thought you'd be coming up here asking" Tommy said, almost relieved that he was right. "What else you want to know?"

"I want to know everything—everything and anything you remember."

"I think I told you everything before," Tommy answered. Quiet fell between the two of them, it seeming that even Tommy was needing to think about what to say. Then, Tommy broke the waiting and the silence. "Ben Ivan went, he fished, he got into a deal with Wiley Trace, Wiley's boat burned, Ben Ivan gave him some money for a new boat, and they ended up owning all that land—owning the whole island together."

"Do you think the land can be sold? Anything special about that?"

"Sure it can. Ben Ivan always said that if somebody out there wanted it, and if they wanted it deep enough in the pocket, they could buy it. Of course, he said that about most everything."

"If it can be bought, why hasn't somebody already done it?"

"The Traces. That's the reason. Miss Emily; she wants to sell it. She would sell out right now and move to some place nice. But… "

"The daughter?" Ivey asked.

Tommy stood and stared at him before answering. He started to smile, but then did not. "Don't talk that da-burn way to me, Ivey. Is that what you call her now? 'The daughter?' When are you going down there?"

"You know who I mean. And, soon." Ivey stood up from his chair, walked around a minute, and then sat down in another. "You know what I have to do. That's valuable land."

"Pride is what you'll find. That's what you will run into from her. She's eaten up with trying to conserve things and put them back the way they were. You know, one of the original swamp-loving types, Ben Ivan would call her—has a save-the-manatee license tag on her car." He looked at Ivey expecting a comment. Not getting one, he said, "And if the da-burn truth be known, I don't blame her. If the world would slow down a little, well… it wouldn't blame her either."

"I figured you'd think that way," Ivey said. "But Genna… do you think she'll ever change?"

"She'll never change. When you see her again, you'll agree with me. She'll never change about the land—about anything else either." He again looked for a comment from Ivey, but got none. "Besides, she won't ever change with what I've heard about what some people want to do with the property."

"Such as?"

"Such as, a group checking around and asking a lot of questions, checking county records, utilities, those kinds of things. They want to put up timeshares, maybe a hotel. You know, all that "frou-frou," Ben Ivan called it. They'd build swimming pools, widen the dock, and build little palmetto-covered huts on the beach. You know, generally tear the life out of everything on the island. At least that's what Ben Ivan said before he died."

"Are they still around?"

"Yeah, they're still out there. No one has heard from them recently, but they're here. At first, it was a group from Orlando, now a group from Ft. Lauderdale. Something tells me that it's all one group, though. Least that's what I'm hearing."

"Any other interest in it that I should know about?"

"No," Tommy answered. "There was an Indian group some years ago—Seminole Indians thinking about what they could do with it. They were talking about bingo, gambling, and all those things. They raise their heads again from time to time, but nothing's going to come of it. I hear they're waiting for a south Florida governor to help them push it through."

"So, that Florida group—the timeshare group. Is that the main interest?"

Tommy nodded as he picked up a beer, looked at Ivey, smiled, and put it down again.

"Do you know any of the group? The Orlando part, I mean. Did my dad know them?"

"It's some offshore money, as I understand. They've done other fun-in-the-sun things, Ben Ivan would call them, and done some things in Orlando. They've picked up people to work with them. But other than that, and as to specifics, I don't know for sure. I can guess, but I can't name names."

"You don't know anything firm, anything concrete?"

"Just what I've told you. And it wasn't your dad they were going through. No, they were trying to deal directly with the Traces, Ben Ivan told me. I guess with him gone now… All I know is what Miss Emily tells me, and what I hear from here or there is that the people want to buy quickly now, move in, and get their things started."

Tommy stood and moved away from Ivey, suddenly getting the urge to get busy with whatever he could find to pick up or put away in the kitchen. Ivey sat and watched him as he moved.

"Tommy Ripington, you and that packing house grapevine know exactly who it is. I just don't want to be surprised one morning when somebody calls that I don't know, and he wants to meet about some property I supposedly don't know anything about."

Tommy looked at Ivey and held his glare as they looked intensely at each other.

"I don't know who the lead person is, but you keep your eyes on Johnson Crews, you hear."

"Johnson Crews? I was with Johnson Crews, yesterday. If he was representing someone, don't you think he would have said something about it?"

"From what I hear, he may not be representing," Tommy said. "He may be, as Ben Ivan would say, in an ownership position."

"He can't do that," Ivey answered. "I know enough law to know there are rules against that sort of thing."

They both became quiet, both looking at other things in the room or out the window. Then Ivey turned to him. "Beava Leigh. Is she involved?"

"Some things I know may not come from the packing houses," Tommy said. "You know what I mean."

"Was Ben Ivan Hayes involved in the deal? Tell me that then."

"No," Tommy answered. "That's one thing I know for double sure." Ivey looked at Tommy and, without taking his eyes off him, walked over to the window.

"I'm surprised my dad didn't get involved with it somehow. I mean knowing him—and you knew him better than I."

"He talked like he liked it just the way it is—the way it is now, 'the way it's setting,' he would say. But you know what? He would always say that it could be bought. But then, every time he'd say it, he would laugh… laugh like he knew something no one else knew."

"And he never said as to what he knew?"

"Never did?"

"And you don't know?"

Tommy walked into another room, but Ivey waited until he returned and gave his attention back to him. He said, "So tell me this, with all the miles and miles of oceanfront land that we're talking about, why did he pick Coquina Key? Why did he get so involved with the Traces?"

"He just liked them; that's all I can figure."

"Or that's all you're going to say."

"I think you might be right," Tommy said.

Silence again fell between the two of them before Ivey broke the quiet.

"Tell me about Genna Trace then. Whatever happened to her husband? I mean, I assume she was married. I mean with the little girl and all."

"She was married to a guy named Riggs. Digger Riggs, they called him. I don't know what his real name was. Anyway, they split up years ago now. It must have been right after Katy was born. Ben Ivan said she had Katy late in years. Said she was waiting… But as far as Riggs, I don't know where he went off to. Ain't nobody seen him that I know about."

"She never remarried?"

"No, never has."

Ivey walked over to Tommy as though he was going to speak, then turned and walked back to the table. "Do you remember when I used to know her, Tommy? It's been years and years ago, now. Naw, you probably don't remember that, do you?"

"Sure, I remember the worst-kept secret there's ever been. Maybe except for one. I thought there for a while I was going to see a lot more of her than I actually did. I told you that before. You know what I mean. I mean you and Genna."

"So tell me. Does Genna ever say anything to you about me?"

"She doesn't have to. But you can tell, though. Yeah, you can tell. Your dad would say things loud enough for her to hear when he was talking to Miss Emily. I mean things like when you graduated, how proud he was of you, those kinds of things. When you went back to school, when you got that doctor thing, when you started teaching at that school. Then you married, then the children. He kept a running tale going of what you were doing. He never talked a lot about you getting married the way you did, but she knew. She's kept up with you all along."

"He went down a lot then, from what you say. I mean, all those things occurred a long time ago, but he kept going down a lot, didn't he."

"Yeah, he went and took me along sometimes," Tommy said. "Then he went on his own. He did it by himself a lot more than when he took me. But when he would ask me, I always went."

"How often did he go?" Ivey asked, knowing Tommy was full of answers and wanting to talk.

"Oh, he would go a couple, three, maybe four times every year. Sometimes even more. In fact, last year it seemed like he went down every month."

Tommy got up again, looked, and then walked back to the same window. Ivey followed him with his question.

"He must have really loved fishing," Ivey then said, almost as a question. "And a lot more than anybody realized. Or that's what he wanted people to believe. He and Wiley Trace must have been close after all the years."

"Yeah, they were close. But many, many times Wiley wouldn't be there. He'd be off somewhere with a charter somewhere or whatever.

Wiley would take off in the boat, by himself or with charters, and go God knows where fishing. He'd get those big-time charters and off he'd go. "

Ivey picked up and tilted his first beer, then saw that it was almost empty. He set it down and took up the new cold one. He looked at the bottle of beer in his hand, twirled it around as though he was looking at it, tilted it up to take a few swallows, then stared back on Tommy. "After Wiley Trace was gone, what would he do? I mean, I can't picture him with the patience to take many trips out. Were there other people around that he knew?" He almost chuckled, then went on. "I think I know the answer, but I'm still going to ask."

"Just Miss Emily," Tommy answered. After he spoke, he looked down and with a look like he wished they weren't in the conversation they were having. "She was always around. But Ben Ivan, he went to fish. You can be rest assured of that."

"Did I say anything? No, I was just asking to see if there was anyone else I should know about. Now that you bring it up, though, did he have any real reason to spend time with Miss Emily? It's Emily Trace you're talking about, isn't it?"

"They were just friends, Ivey—I don't care what you ever heard, they were just long and close friends."

Ivey looked the other way and breathed out heavy, as in relief, as in putting together the puzzle he'd known was there all the time—or after hearing the answer he'd hoped to hear. He got up and walked closer to Tommy, stopping and standing a few feet from him.

"So, what has Beava Leigh asked you? What have you told her? Better yet, what do you know to tell her?"

"I know enough to tell her what I want her to hear, if you know what I mean," Tommy answered. "That's all I know. Nothing else."

"The reason I'm asking, well, you know the way things are, tax problems and all that. Tell her to bring things out in the open if she knows something about the land or if somebody wants to buy the land. I'm not going to cry wolf or turn people in if there's something strange about the deal. Or shop her people's price to somebody else or anything like that. You tell her to tell whoever she needs to tell to get in touch with me, you hear?"

"I hear you," Tommy said. "But you go do what I told you now. That's the important thing. You hear? I'm not going to tell you again. You might be boss, but… "

# Nine

Sutton and Mary Celeste King walked down the hallway on the fifth floor of the Ft. Lauderdale office building. It smelled as though burning cigarettes were ground with crushing heels into the blue-green carpet, then watered and left to set.

They traced their way past nameless, non-descriptive doors. They walked under age-yellowed and stained acoustical tiles, on to the wood-looking double doors at the end of the hall, and into suite 505. As if proud of whatever was going through his mind, Sutton pushed open the door, then stepped aside in a gentlemanly fashion, allowing Mary Celeste to enter before him. A younger-looking Spanish lady sat behind the large, dark-stained desk in the reception area; she watched for the lights on the bottom of the telephone to go off so she could ring through for whoever was holding on the other line. Sutton didn't stop at the desk, only smiling at the lady and leading Mary Celeste down a short hall to another pair of double doors.

In Blum's offices hung a large aerial photograph of a guitar-shaped island surrounded by a variety of indigos and blues—hues of varied depths of waters and differing shades of color. Mary Celeste looked at the wide expanses of green, the bottom shallow, and the deep. Then at splotches of bleached-out aqua that she would later find out were shallow reefs around the island. She and Sutton stood without speaking, staring at the blown-up photograph until each had assured themselves that they knew what they were looking at. It was Coquina Key.

On a sidewall hung a rendering—a blueprint drawing stuck up with plastic pushpins and showing a three-story condominium. It looked to have thick solid shingles—probably concrete or some type of white tile like they use in South Florida. It showed a light-colored exterior, covered with tiny dots representing stucco or something looking like it belonged in the Keys. What must have been a stairway curved around from the first floor, past the second, and up to the third. A hand-sketched, impressionistic drawing depicted a "V"-shaped man and a similarly shaped lady standing at the base of the stairs as though they were just leaving, both with imaginary tennis racquets in their hands.

"Mrs. King," Clayton Blum said as he stuck out his hand and walked toward her. Her husband stopped short as the man passed him by, and he watched as Blum greeted her. The man's smell—reeking of cigarette smoke—kept Mary Celeste backed away from him, even as he came immediately in front of her.

"It's nice to see you, Mrs. King. We've spoken so many times on the telephone. It's so nice to finally meet." He looked at the cardboard model on the table and waved his hand toward it, presenting it to the two of them. "This is it," he said, sounding almost as though he was showing off one of his children. "This is a seller if I ever saw one. What we are seeing here now is one of the mid-rise, three-floor units. Sutton, Mary Celeste—it's okay if I call you Mary Celeste, isn't it?"

She didn't answer.

"Anyway, there will be three units on each of the floors—nine units per building. There will be eight three-story units, and that will give us twenty-seven units for our first phase—mainly two-bedroom, but three-bedroom units are in the middle of each floor."

She stared as he continued, staring at him almost as much as she did at the model. He was a short man, mostly bald, with thin hair that fell straight on the sides and looked wet, though it probably wasn't. As he came close again, carrying the cigarette smell with him, she could also smell something that reeked like an old hair cream she used to smell on her father. She stood, trying to place the smell, before he went on.

"Johnson Crews and I have talked in detail, and we all like what we want to do. Anyway, we will do the Boatel—don't you love that name? It will be three stories, too—not big, but ample. The clubhouse and recreation building will be on the south end of the Key. The actual land area to be used for the amenities is not very large, but, with careful planning, we can do what we need to do to support the condominiums, and it still won't seem cramped. Then—" He walked over to the aerial on the wall. "Then—and getting back to the timeshare condominium units—we'll put our one- and two-bedroom units in clusters of twos and threes, facing out across the gulf or back toward the mainland Keys. Ocean units, of course, will be more expensive. And—"

"You've done quite a lot of work here, Mr. Blum," Mary Celeste butted in. "One thing else. How about density, ecology, permits, and all of those other pain-in-the-rear kind of things?"

"This is a go project, Mary Celeste. It's almost a done-deal project. With the work we've put into it, with what the powers-that-be have said, it's a big-time go. In fact, our sales people have already told me that we'll have pre-sales even before we put the first sign on the Key.

"And... and... I almost forgot to tell you, Sutton, things have been going so fast. We've found the man we want to spearhead our sales team. An important cog in this project, if I must say so. We were wanting the best, and I'll be damned if we haven't found him. Excuse my language when I get excited, Mary Celeste. What's more, he knows the key like the back of his hand... even lived there on Coquina Key at one time. Can you believe that? Digger Riggs is his name. He's been working over in Naples for the past year or so. Sold real property before in Lauderdale, West Palm, Boca, and those places. Upper income properties—buyers who have been looking for something like Coquina Key."

"Digger Riggs," Mary Celeste mouthed to herself. And then aloud, "The name doesn't... I mean, I thought there was only that one family living on the key. I mean, how... "

"Digger?" Sutton said, seeing Mary Celeste mouth the name.

"Yes," Blum said. "It's apparently a well-known name around these parts—played football at the University of Miami some years ago. Even turned pro, then got hurt. I remember him well." He looked quickly at Mary Celeste. "And that's right; he must know Coquina Key," he smiled, and then just as quickly frowned. "He was married to our Miss Trace— the one living there now. But it apparently didn't last long. That happens you know. His daughter is still there even now. I mean living with her mother. I think he has as much interest in the project as we do. I mean, wanting the best for his child and all."

She looked at Sutton and said, "And probably, if he's like most men, needs to make some money to pay child support." She didn't look away from Sutton, just motioned with her head for him to sit down at the table. She pulled out a chair in front of the model and joined him.

"Your plans are impressive, Clayton," Mary Celeste said. Again, you've done a lot of work, and it shows. However, getting down to where the tires hit the pavement or whatever, what I understand is that what you plan to do is to take down the property as we discussed. You don't mind if I reconfirm that, do you? A token five hundred thousand down and in an account which we choose, the remainder with sales, and three points over prime on the unpaid balance. Two penthouse units will be cut out for me and held at construction cost. And... all site improvements to be by your companies with construction loans to you by mine."

"That's right," Blum answered. "Sales will be no problem. And to start, to get a permit won't be any trouble at all. The county people who know such things say that the Keys will love another employer in the area. Those people down there and in the surrounding areas can't live on just the fish they catch and the sunshine. No, they need employment, and we'll be able to give it to them. Not a whole lot, mind you. But enough to help us get things approved."

"And then, whatever percentage you work out with the real estate people—" Mary Celeste said.

"Digger Riggs, you mean."

"Yes, whatever percentage you work out with Mr. Riggs will be between you and your Realtor. Then, as we agreed, you will pay us three percent of all sales over and above the land purchase price and on top of any other sales cost."

"You're right again," Blum said. "The only thing you have to do is get me clear title to the property and you'll be a rich woman. And I'm talking a perfectly clean title to all the property."

"I can do that," she answered. "But I'm already, as you say, 'a rich woman.' Cash, though, will make sure I stay that way." She looked at Blum, then spoke to both of the two men. "The property has to sell. There is no way anything that large and that prime can stay there the way it is. And the only way it can be sold is with me or my brother approving it. So, what does that tell you?"

"That tells me that when it sells, and if you play your cards right, you can end up with title," Blum said, in a way reconfirming.

"That's right," she said, narrowing her eyes as she said it. "And I know how to play my cards right. Now, as I understand, you propose to handle the sales and marketing, and Johnson Crews will handle all of our legal needs. And financing... besides my investment, we understand that a prime investor has been located. A deep pocketed one."

"The one you recommended," Blum said. "If that's what you mean."

"Let me put it this way," Mary Celeste answered. "My partners on that end are one of the reasons I'm involved. They have the serious dollars. Land closeout, construction money, everything. All we have to do now is finalize the sale of the property."

"My sources tell me that the present owners—especially the daughter, that Genna Trace lady—say they will never sell. But are you still assuring me that this is not going to be a problem when I approach them?"

"Put it this way," Mary Celeste said. "If you have an outstanding loan—a sizable outstanding loan—and it's called due, what do you have to do? I'll tell you what. You have to pay up. But what if you can't pay up? Then you have to see what you have, lose it through foreclosure, or make some money and get on with your life. That's what that little tree hugger is going have to learn pretty damn quickly. And, any way it happens, sale or foreclosure, the process and the proceeds will have to come through me."

"And your brother? He won't get in and foul up anything?" Blum asked, now with his glasses fallen down on his nose.

"Forget a bunch of my brother. He is so eaten up with his holierthan-thou world, with getting away from his musty life and time-warped wife, and with raising money to save the good old family business that he'll sell just as soon as he hears the figures. Sell and give to the poor. The only thing we need to watch out for—I mean *will* watch out for—is that Ivey Hayes must never know that I've had anything to do with the buying or developing of the property. If he does, it could queer the whole thing. Do you understand?" She looked at them both for nods. They both nodded their heads in agreement.

A tap on the door caused them all to stop. Mary Celeste looked at the door, then both Sutton and Clayton Blum, as if maybe someone might have been listening. The door cracked open, as if answering her question, and a voice came sneaking in.

"Can I come in?"

"Sure," Blum answered. He pushed himself away from the table. "I want you to meet these people anyway." He stood up as the man walked in—a large man, middle-aged, tanned, his hair maybe too long—and a glad hand reaching out to Mary Celeste.

"Hi! I'm Digger Riggs," he said, smiling a broad and toothy smile that seemed to be permanently etched onto his face. "And you're Mr. and Mrs. King. Clayton has told me about you. In fact, he tells me you may be interested in being one of our first Coquina Club condo owners."

"Yes, we've talked about it," Sutton answered. "We'll see how things go; then maybe we can talk about it some more."

Digger wore a white knit shirt—upon which, when he came close enough, the others could read "Naples Bay Club" scrolled across the top of a crest of some kind—khaki pants, and loafers with no socks.

"It's going to be a wonderful development," he said. "I'll make sure I get in touch with you when we start to break ground."

"You do that," Mary Celeste said. "But we'll keep up with you, too. We'll all be interested in how things go." She looked at Sutton, then at the ever-smiling Clayton Blum. "We'll all be interested, won't we?" It was a question that needed no answer. She stood up and leaned over to look at the model again. "This is going to be quite a change to that part of the world, and, from what I see and from what I understand, change will be good. Let's get it going."

# Ten

  Ivey drove past the entrance to Pennekamp State Park, past signs on the side of the road and on both sides of the highway advertising diving and displaying lists of tropical water things to do—signs designed to make people look, to show them some place where they could jump into their visions, and to help them remember why they were driving down the two-lane in the Florida Keys.
  He read them all as he passed—the dive shops, craft shops, and all the things that were there to attract the tourist dollar, especially during the winter months when the deep-pocketed tourists were in season and out and about. As he drove, he saw even more signs—for more dive shops, snorkeling, jet skies, and anchorage. There were charter fishing signs, bait and tackle signs, cut bait, live bait, *Snorkel the reef—boats leaving twice a day.* He was finally back in the Keys, he remembered— the Keys he now knew were still there, but now hiding behind the signs.
  He drove down the highway, with the Atlantic Ocean and the Straits of Florida on one side of the car and Florida Bay and the Gulf of Mexico on the other. On the left, he saw more tourist signs... *Theater of the Sea - 10 miles.* Across from it, *Ten Thousand Islands and Backwater Cruises.* He looked through to the gulf when there was an opening— when there was a vista without something man-made blocking it. Dotted islands lay in the quiet water like so many planted gardens in the middle of a sedated ocean. Ivey looked and remembered navigating through and around them—through water not more than a few feet deep, inches in spots, and all within a curvature of land that by some map-makers pen called itself Florida Bay before the waters opened out and became the Gulf of Mexico. His mind mentally started counting the islands that were visible, only to quit at a dozen and remember Wiley Trace telling him how the Indians claimed there were over ten thousand of them— some not big enough to warrant a second look, much less inspire a flatbottomed-skiff pilot to divert in order to walk up on their shores. That was true; their only reason for being there—and for being named, if they were large enough for a name of their own—was to serve as mating and

fertile areas for beginning shrimp, crustaceans, and nameless beginners of the food chain. This was true for all but the one he could not yet see. The one, unlike the others, where maybe things could start again, thought Ivey. (Was that asking too much?) The one inhabited island called Coquina Key.

There were small motels, set back from the road; some he recognized by a remembered name, but many of the buildings were new since the last time he had been there. Most, whether he recognized them or not, stood when he and his dad drove that same road. Seeing a few of the motels or restaurants, it was as though he really had not been gone at all—Sea Cove, Golden Grouper. Some were new, like Lorelei and Ramada, with signs out front advertising rates, boat rides, and their own restaurant—all famous for sea food. His eyes caught them as if he had just gone up the road that morning rather than a lifetime before.

Hidden back from the road in scrub pine and undergrowth he would see a house, a nearly forgotten motel, a bait shop. Missing were anything over two stories, brick, columns out front, and front porches. He saw conch houses: the concrete-block three-roomers—the places where the people of the Keys slept when they had to rest, ate when they had to eat, or used for those celebration times when they had caught something, found something to their liking, or found a reason to spend one more day in paradise. Or it was a place to drink when the only reason was another sunset, another watercolor brushing of the sky, another breeze blowing in a non-caring aroma and in that certain unexplainable mystery of it all. He remembered the saying, *Just another day in paradise.*

Mile markers appeared—numbers indicating where to find the road, where to turn in. He approached a concrete bridge—a short one, one that looked familiar, one over a cut from one water to the other. And another sign—*Cut 57,* it said. Then another—a new name for a key he remembered as something else from before. He forgot what. But the Key was the same.

The rows of single-story, yellow-painted stores thinned out. The motels and the houses sitting back away from the road were now becoming more at rest, and without the hollering signs. As he went on, he saw that, in their stead, were open dunes—sand hills partially hiding the water, palms, and pines growing on angles, the pines growing taller, and under them wild grasses stretching all the way out to the road. And sea oats, blowing and waving with the wind, but only partially muffling the sound of the water, the birds searching and cawing, and the cry of the beach. Toward the water on the gulf side were banyan trees with their backward roots going up and away from the ground and forming shelters for backing-up tides. It was all a scene—a scene he could get used to again. *Don't let some Developer get it! he thought.*

He looked through the loneliness on each side of the road. Then, for the first time, he saw no cars behind him. He looked and saw a condition, a way of life, and a visible air now surrounding him. And off to the right, far out on the Gulf side, he saw a stretch of land, far enough away to be a dark green outline against a yet darker sea—an island by itself, something he had seen before, maybe something he was looking for. He saw a sign— a new sign—and a few old gas pumps borrowed from an Andrew Wyeth painting. He eyed a yellow-painted storefront that ought to have had old men sitting on the outside enjoying the warmth. He let the car drift maybe too far to the right before whipping it back.

There was no need to signal to the few cars behind him as he pulled onto the shoulder and watched them pass and continue their way to Key West and to all the world that found itself further on down the two-lane road. He drove on slowly to the place that stopped him, the store, and the dock behind with boats for hire. He pulled into the place in his remembrance and slowed next to a sign—the hand-painted sign on the store: *Billy Earl Bearclaw, Dive and Snorkel, Sport Fishing, Keys Information.* Then a different sign nailed to the post of the larger sign: *Coquina Key.* And the multi-colored sign he had almost forgotten. The big, funny-colored fish that Genna liked. It had to be the only fish in the world like it.

He pulled past the store, to the side, and to an area surrounded by a chain-link fence. Strips of green and white vinyl weaved through the squares of the fence, the fence surrounding a cleared square of land with fine white stones and shells paving an open area for parking. A sign on the fence told him to park there for Coquina Key. He pulled through the gate, toward the side, and stopped.

He laid his arms across the steering wheel, leaned forward, then sat looking at the wooden dock in front of him and the few boats tied to it. There were two or three outboards, all painted the same blue color, and one speedboat, also blue but with metallic flakes in a fiberglass body. A pontoon boat—a party boat—bobbed gently with the waves.

"Going to Coquina Key?" a voice called from the store.

There appeared a squatty-built, black-haired man walking toward him—a man with too small a T-shirt covering his belly.

"Yes, I am," Ivey answered, almost scared, but the only thing he could say.

"Park here, five bucks. Five bucks for the boat taxi and I'll have you there in under fifteen minutes." The man shared a wide tobaccostained smile as he got closer. Ivey pushed the "Up" button on the dash, then watched as the top slowly wound up, the whole time buzzing a motor's tune. He fastened the chrome hooks securing the top, then reached into the back seat and pulled out his canvas overnighter.

The man walked up to Ivey. "I'm Billy Bearclaw," he said. He took Ivey's bag and pointed to an old wooden inboard—a teak-finished launch with a dark blue painted deck, wooden sides, and with shinny chrome fixtures that made him think of Fitzgerald or Bogart or some boat as old as the sea would still allow. The same color blue dressed the hull, but a wraparound windshield and chrome-reflected darts of sunshine bouncing off of it made it different—something someone named Billy Earl Bearclaw might have liked to use.

"I'll have you there in fifteen minutes," he said again. "Your car will be all fine right where it is. I lock things up just in case. That is, of course, unless Miss Emily calls me and tells me to leave it open. You know, in case somebody is either coming in or going out. Have you talked to Miss Emily yet?"

Ivey shook his head no to the question then followed his driver to the boat. He smelled what was probably some decaying fish somewhere at the water's edge or in the washed-up weed beside the old dock. But the natural scent of whatever it was mixed with the smell of the salt and made it okay.

Billy stepped into the boat, took the overnighter, and set it down in the place that Ivey remembered as aft. He turned and offered Ivey a hand. Ivey stepped down and settled back into a rolled and tufted vinyl seat. Billy buckled up his safety belt and started the engine. Ivey looked at Billy's maroon-covered safety strap, reached for his own, and fastened it around him. Billy backed up a few feet with the boat's motor churning the water behind them as though it was a salt-water eggbeater. He cut the steering wheel hard to the right and pushed the lever forward. They headed out and toward the open blue-green water around Coquina Key.

The boat captain was quick to speak again. "Sure seems strange the way people have been going out there of late." He almost hollered above the sound of the engine. Wind blew through, and straightened, nearwhite hair as it blew over Billy Bearclaw's copper and age-worn skin. Ivey watched his lips to make sure he was hearing him and understanding what he was saying. The wind shot by, carrying its own roar as it did.

"You don't take many people out?" Ivey hollered.

"Sometimes. Usually, I go out to pick people up—people who tie up out there then come into the mainland. I rent them one of my cars— older ones but okay for getting where they need to go. Get twenty dollars and up. Then I have to take them back. Sometimes they'll stop in the store and buy something, but Miss Emily sells for the same price. The past couple of weeks, I've been taking people out, waiting an hour—I wait for twenty dollars an hour—then bringing them back. Must be interest in buying the place, I hear. Least-wise, that's what Miss Emily tells me."

"I didn't know it was for sale," Ivey said. "But then I bet a lot of people wanting to go out there suits you just fine, doesn't it?"

The driver stared coldly at him. "It makes me more money, if that's what you mean. People talking about building something—making something for a lot of people to go to."

"Both your taxi service and your store should do quite well, I would think."

"They would," he said. "But it'll never happen. Not in your lifetime and definitely not in mine. And I'm the first to be glad it won't." "Why do you say that?"

"That it won't sell? Hell, Genna Trace won't have it, that's why it won't. Miss Emily would sell. She'd sell quicker than you could put the paper down in front of her. That's just because she would move somewhere else—someplace with not as much work and all. I can't much blame her, though. Naw, it's a shame, but I can't blame her one bit for that. But Genna now... Genna is another story. She'll die on the island, that woman will. That's one tough Indian lady, and I ought to know. You'll probably meet her. She's already come back from work today. Went out about an hour ago."

They both looked straight ahead and at the wide green island getting larger in front of them. Finally, Ivey broke the silence.

"Is there anyone else on the island?" I mean, full time."

"Miss Emily, her daughter, and granddaughter Katy. Oh, the Lab, Mango. That's all. You'll see them all. But I thought you must know that. I mean going out there and all. Just that little suitcase thing." He stared hard at his new fare then back to the water in front.

"I do. It has been a long time, though. We were friends a long time ago."

"This is a surprise then? Nobody told me about nobody coming to go out. So a surprise makes it all make sense."

Ivey only smiled into the noise of the engine. They approached the island, the water getting both clearer and lighter as they got to shallower water. They rounded the "C"-shaped key on the southerly end and entered clear and almost quiet water. "Backwater," local conchs would call it—fertile water where life was going on but water looking separated from both Florida Bay and the Keys, water seemingly tucked in and hidden on the lea side of the gulf and hugging the opened side of Coquina Key. Ivey looked mesmerized as they got closer, and Billy put the lever into neutral and drifted the last two feet to the dock. The quiet of the white-stuccoed building and the silence of the dock made it seem as though Billy had cut the engine even before it was needed.

Their boat barely touched a black tire bumper on the side of the dock. A loose rope lay tied to one of the pilings and in a small curl on the dock. Billy reached out with a piece of what looked like a broom handle with a hook on the end, retrieved the rope, and pulled it toward him. He held the boat steady while Ivey quickly tossed his overnighter onto the dock. He took Billy's hand, then stepped onto the rubber step on the side of the boat and onto the dock. He stood up, turned back to Billy, reached in his pocket, peeled bills off his loose dollars, and gave them to him.

"Thanks," he hollered to the boatman, louder than he needed to with the engine now idling. "Can I call you to come pick me up?"

"Sure," Billy said. "Miss Emily or Genna... one will call me for you. I come out here a couple or three times a day, anyway."

Ivey stood watching as the boat crawled slowly away from the dock, the engine still coughing and churning the water behind it. As it straightened out after turning from the dock, Billy pushed the lever on his left forward and the boat headed back toward deeper water. Ivey watched him as he left. Almost as though afraid to do so, he slowly turned, scanning the water, the dock, and the adjacent beach. He looked at the Tiki hut—a hut sheltering a grill and a long picnic table. He looked at the squatty and brightly painted little concrete-block buildings—each building holding two rooms, if memory served him correctly. And the green and manicured grass running from the dock, past the rooms, and to the office further on. His eyes dropped to a sign stapled to a white-painted wooden standard on the end of the dock—a sign that said, *Manager, Inquire at Unit 1.*

He walked to a driftwood board and saw a handwritten note—a saran-wrap-covered and faded index card—that said *If We Missed You, See Us at The Manager's Office.*

He looked, feeling worried that he had not called, but had driven all the way down and now didn't know what to do next. *Where do I go now that I am here?* he wondered. *What do I do next?*

He started slowly up the dock and toward the buildings. The view in front of him and his memories meshed—the same water, the same beach, and the same little bungalows as all those years before. He smiled to himself, trying somehow to log his feelings so maybe he could tell somebody how it was to see everything again. He looked at a small beach area beside the dock, it partially washed away, but with clean white sand, with everything neat and in somebody's order.

The air smelled like something circulating from a fan after blowing across salt and across everything just washed—something clean and un-touched. He pushed pulled, straightened, and tucked in his shirt, and pulled up on his khaki shorts, running pinched-together fingers down the front as though there were creases from traveling to be pushed out. He looked again and it all looked the same—a new dock, a longer dock, but everything else the same. Except for people. There were no people.

He walked slowly toward the side, looking down into the water. He saw the sandy bottom and faded green shoots of underwater flora as he moved closer to the land.

Ivey looked down—not at anything in particular, but to somehow collect his thoughts—to take in what was there, to remember where he was and why he drove all the way into the Keys. He prayed, *Lord, are you sure all this is right?* His concentration was suddenly interrupted by a woman's voice from somewhere in front of him. He looked up and saw her as she stepped from the building, across the thinly grassed yard, and onto the dock.

"Welcome to Coquina Key. May I help you? I'm Genna Trace."

# Eleven

Nearly three days went by—days with time being somewhere else and for someone else—and were then gone before Ivey realized time had passed at all. They were days filled with remembrances of what he had somehow forgotten. Or had forgotten even existed. Recollections brought back to life by Coquina Key itself—things filed away somewhere until now, but never asked for.

He barely remembered Emily Trace as anything other than an older lady—a pretty lady he remembered—and as someone he didn't know enough about. Genna's mother. Then, in later years, she was the one to whom he would not admit that there was someone else there with a quick smile and a laugh, a hug, and almost talking eyes. Both Genna and her mother were hidden behind all the hushed and quieted rumors of the island—the island where only a few ever went. No one but his own father.

He also met the new Katy and remembered again the unending exuberances and the unspoiled or faded truths of a seven-year-old. And her dog Mango—the big black dog that Billy Bearclaw supposedly found clinging to a board from a shipwreck and floating in the Gulf stream. But then, Billy Bearclaw was full of stories. Some even true. Whatever his story, Mango was little Katy's shadow and slept only when Katy was at school or when the island was asleep for the night.

Mostly, they were days of living again where the sun was a constant reminder of where he was and what he was doing. He took quick and constant glances at the place—the cottages, the dock, and all that was the island. It was clean and clear. (Anything that was not was okay, too, and just part of the color of where he was). He experienced again the smell of salt and the sea and the constant but changing views of the trouble-quieting waters. And—he only now allowed himself to admit— there were again days with Genna Trace.

What was doubt before he got there—even questions without answers—now turned into soul awakening and a near euphoria. Maybe it was due to seeing those he had not seen for all those years. Yes, it probably was, he thought. Those who, like himself, had lived their lives, had done whatever and all they would ever do, and had probably made whatever impact on the world that they would now ever make. That was true of Billy Bearclaw, after Ivey finally introduced himself to Billy and his remembering him from all those years before. And Miss Emily. They were all in the same fraternity of spent dreams that they had come to terms with.

Maybe it was the idea of just being away from Deerfield, away from classrooms and schedules, away from doing whatever someone else was demanding. If only for those few short days, it was away from having to decide what to do about Summer Tree. Even if that was a part and portion of why he was there. Nevertheless, that part would take a while. Coquina Key just wasn't a place to push.

After that first surprise at seeing each other, a polite social hug, each telling lies about nearly forgetting the other, each with phony surprises that the other even remembered them, they reassumed the roles of long lost friends with years and years of trivia and happenings to pass on to the other.

Ivey remembered and remembered well. It was a constant task not to forget the hidden-from-himself truth of who he was, what he was, and why he was there. It was hard not to think back through all the talk of kids and places and school. How is Tommy? How long can you stay? To think back to the special oneness they had once shared and to what maybe—he found he thought about it a lot when she wasn't there—what could, or maybe could still be there between them. *(It was all right; they were just friends.)* His discipline wouldn't let him think that way for long. No, he enjoyed where he was but tried to think about, occasionally even talk about, business, the school, the children, even Addie. Oh, he still loved them all, loved them all dearly—those who were always there. But now—and he knew it was only for a short time—it all seemed so different, with an unconventional color on everything he saw, one he had forgotten ever existed, one that cast itself onto a completely different, clean, and much richer canvas.

Genna was working every day. Ivey couldn't believe anyone would drive all the way back to Miami and the Gables twice a week—that far to work only to turn around and drive back home again. But then, everyone didn't have a place to go home to with a gulf for a backyard, Florida Bay and all the mangrove-laden islands, standing egrets as neighbors, the blue-to-green-to-nearly-clear shades of the water, and the life that quietly called from everything he saw. With everything new and alive, he also felt the solitude—an active quiet that made everything he brought with him dissolve into just being real, dissolve into anything and everything that the sun-warmed days could provide.

When Genna would get home each of those days, he would smile—impersonal but at the same time graceful, and do it all as the image he felt he had to provide. But when she was home, and it was only she and her quiet surround, he would look at her as part of the sun and the blue of the over-the-water sky, and the gulf and the life it gave out just by seeing it. He would think little questions, then answer them himself— things like the way she looked before, like how she had gracefully changed—aging as if mellowing but not losing any of the island strength and beauty that were, and, he now saw, still were Genna Trace. He could not help but search his mind for a better word for aging, for living through days he envied. Only cold words came—nothing that could describe where he was and what he was seeing. In the same way that she had stood out as a teen, then a college freshman, she now also stood out, and maybe even more so, as a single parent, as mother, as teacher, as the mysterious woman from all those years before. Now, just as the tides and the skies, she was a part—the main part—of Coquina Key.

Alex Roan stopped by in a State of Florida, Dept. of Natural Resources boat the first day and left something for Genna. He seemed disappointed that she wasn't there. He left some papers with Miss Emily, and then walked with her to meet Ivey. He was the first to stick out his hand when they met, a meeting that somehow didn't make the man seem comfortable, even though he was the one who had come to the island. He looked sincere when he said to her that he had heard about Ivey. Billy Bearclaw must have already told him that an old friend—an old beau of Genna's—was on the Key. But, in his mind, he still questioned the need to drop something off for Genna, or did he just want to meet whoever Billy Bearclaw was talking about? Couldn't Billy Bearclaw bring it out on his next trip?

Regarding Miss Emily—Genna explained her request to drop any mother names years before, especially when Ben Ivan or others were around. Even more so, if it was the name Ben Ivan called her. And probably, the best she could remember, it must have been about the time she first started noticing herself getting older. The Miss Emily name made her take on another person—a person with time that had stopped sometime before things were plain and gay and happy. It also put them more on the same level. Miss Emily liked that. Miss Emily was nearly as glad to see Ivey, it seemed, as was Genna. She shared her remorse about Ben Ivan at first, but befitting her, she didn't let it stay around. There was too much of life to see, she would holler without speaking, too much outside to take advantage of to waste time pouting when that would do nothing at all. Wiley was gone; she had gotten over that. Now, Ben Ivan was gone. Silently, or at least admitting it only to herself, maybe that was even harder.

As he sat on the end of the dock, it was so easy to see his dad being there and there for whatever reasons people wanted to pin on his visits. He had a rough agrarian presence—so different from the Keys, the water, the sun, all that was easy and not-to-worry. But in the same way that opposites more times than not seem to do, they somehow found their way to fit.

Ben Ivan shut down the engines of the wooden-hulled powerboat after cutting the wheel hard right. He was three to four feet from the dock but let the boat slow, then come to rest just touching the rubber bumpers.

"If there's a man alive who can drive this lumber yard, it's me," he hollered as the boat carefully touched the dock. "Hey, that man can drive." He laughed as he said it to the only one there to hear him. He stepped starboard and threw a rope to her as she stood on the dock. "Here, Miss Emily, you pull me on up there and tie me off now. Not too tight, mind you. You know what the lady who runs this marina told me."

"Yeah, you just tie it off too tight with a storm coming or if the gulf's at low tide. You tie it off without any slack and you won't be able to bellow like Tom Paul Jones or act like somebody who maybe knows something."

"If you're going to be lying about navy captains, Miss Emily, you better be talking about John Paul Jones. I don't want him raising some angry arm from the bottom of the ocean, grabbing hold of *Carefree VI,* and scattering me on rocks from here to the Dry Tortugas." Ben Ivan laughed his from-the-bottom-of-his-stomach laugh, a howl capable of being heard all the way back to his room in the blue-painted bungalow at the Coquina Key Boatel.

Emily Trace tied off the bow, then the stern, carefully leaving at least six feet of slack, two more feet than she was figuring the tide to rise. She then untied two bumpers from cleats on the dock and carefully put them between the dock and *Carefree1,* making sure the boat was secure.

Ben Ivan jumped onto the dock, the handle of a cooler held by one hand, the piling grabbed by the other. Emily stood in the direct line of his walk as he secured himself on the dock and freed his arm to put it around her. Both of her hands grabbed his one as if his arm was quivering cold and held it tight to her body as if to make it warm.

"Miss Emily... I don't know which is better, when you first get on a boat and head her out to sea with a salt spray cooling you in the face, or getting back on terra firma again." He squeezed her tight to him as they walked off the dock and toward the round picnic tables behind the rooms. "But as long as you, Miss Emily, are with me, any of it is so good I can hardly stand it."

They walked to the first of the three concrete tables where Ben Ivan put the cooler down on one of the benches beside it. Emily let go of his hand to continue past him and to walk into the office to check with Genna. When she returned, Ben Ivan was sitting at the table, staring at the gulf, turning his head back up into Florida Bay, and waiting.

"Genna spends most of her time these days studying, it seems like," Emily said as she walked up to him. "That or writing something out by hand—poems, little lacy love things."

"She's doing all right, isn't she, Miss Emily?"

"Oh yeah. College life and the university seem to agree with her. She's in her junior year now. One more and she will probably be teaching somewhere. If I know Genna, it's not going to be far away."

"Has she got something special yet? Somebody who might have a say in what she does when she gets through? I know what I was doing hasn't worked. Or hasn't worked yet, shall we say."

"Why, no. I go on hinting and all but taking her by the hand to make her pay more attention. Someone is always out and dropping by here on Saturday or on Sunday afternoons, but she writes her drippy little poems and studies. That and worrying about the ecology, she calls it. Worries about the water, the fish, the air, everything. Maybe if more people would be that way. She worries enough for everybody... After she gets through with that, she studies some more. And *reads.* Anything and everything. If it has words on it, she reads it. Cereal boxes, anything. It's good for me, though. Her sitting in the office there and letting me escape for a while, I mean. She likes to keep busy that way, she says.

Gives her a chance to have peace and quiet, she says. Imagine a daughter of mine liking peace and quiet. With just the whirling of that old fan and the few odd telephone calls—which are too far in between or are just a scrambled call on the ship-to-shore. Nothing comes in on the radio to warrant its constant crackling anyway. But she keeps it on, keeps it low. Guys call in on it from time to time. I mean, besides the boats calling in to see if we are still here. She'll cut it even lower if it's somebody who could be personal and not even answer them."

"She says nothing about Ivey?"

"Nary a word," Miss Emily said. "Have you heard anything? Besides your talk, I mean?"

"Why, no. I've done everything I know how to do, but it seems like everything I'm involved in, anything I know anything about at all, sends him running. But do you mean am I through working on Ivey? No, not by a long shot. It'll be someday, you watch." Ben Ivan fiddled with folding some all-weather gear into a canvas carry-on he had carried up from the boat, then the cooler. "Let's talk about something I know something about. Here, put these blues in with your cut bait. I want to steak this snook, though. Let's grill out tonight, okay? You or Genna cut up something for a salad, and I'll throw four or five potatoes on the grill and clean the snook."

She nodded as she opened two tall bottles.

"Ain't nothing a man needs more than a cold beer, a little grilled fish, and a pretty lady," he smiled.

The cotton, wide-brimmed hat Emily was wearing got pushed back to the back of her head as she sat on the bench across from Ben Ivan. He immediately stood up, started walking around the table to sit beside her, then sat back down where he was already sitting.

"You can sit here beside me," Emily said in a tone meaning he could get up again if he wanted.

"I know that, Miss Emily. But I want to sit across over here, so I can look at you. How can a fellow look at a pretty lady properly if he's sitting right beside her? You tell me that, now."

"You sure do run on sometimes, Ben Ivan Hayes."

"I know. I just don't want Genna or anybody walking up to think the wrong thing."

"I thought that was what the lady was supposed to worry about," she answered. "Are you scared of me all of a sudden? Are you scared of lady-folk? Is that what you're saying?" She almost laughed after she said it.

"I'm not scared of nothing. I told you that. Especially whoever would think any differently of either you or me. Genna... now Genna, I think, understands. But anyone else... I don't care if they do or not. I just don't want you to be worrying none."

Ben Ivan picked up his beer, finished it, and then put it back on the concrete table. "I got in touch with an electrician I know in Key West. I told him to come up here and put out flood lights at the bases of these trees, flood lights on the water side of the units—two or three of them ought to be enough—and to make sure all the lights are working on the dock. He told me he would need some help, so I told him to offer twenty dollars to Billy Earl Bearclaw. He has to see him anyway. So, when he comes, let him do what he needs to do. I trust the fellow."

"We don't want to brighten things up too much," Miss Emily said. "Leastwise, not until they finish painting."

"I'm going to keep this place fixed up, Miss Emily. Don't you be worrying none. You hear?"

"I'm not worrying, Ben Ivan. I'm just rattling on."

Ben Ivan reached across the table and took her hand. "I like the hat you're wearing, Miss Emily. You look good in a new hat. But then you've always looked good in hats."

"I've always worn hats. It's just you've never noticed."

"You just keep on wearing them," he answered as he squeezed her hand. "You're something this old orange farmer needs. You go on wearing them, you hear. Yeah, you go on doing just like you're doing. And Ivey. Give the boy time. He'll come running on home. Just give him time."

## Twelve

Miss Emily only spoke of Ben Ivan those few times—once with Genna just in passing when she first knew Ivey was there and again during the first time she and Ivey talked. Then she barely spoke of Wiley either.

She went into his father's death when Ivey asked, and he was only told some of the details of the lingering sickness. There were things Tommy had all ready told him—things he knew his mother would sometime say when she saw the time was proper. They were the details that only Ben Ivan, Tommy, and the doctors even knew about. She shared how both of them—Wiley and Ben Ivan—both loved Coquina Key. They both talked about it as if it was some woman, some flirting lover, always there, but showing a different side every time you thought you knew her. Wiley even said that he thought that the hardest part of ever dying would be leaving the Key. And to Ben Ivan, and now to Genna— especially Genna—it was life itself.

Maybe the biggest surprise of the time he spent that visit, and for sure the biggest change to the island, was Katy. She and Mango, and Mango's hanging around as though he was listening to everything being said. "Katy Trace," she would proudly announce to the world when she was introduced. There was no question about her taking the Trace name back after Digger left. It was never even discussed. Katy's hair was like her mother's, kept cut straight and layered just to her shoulders. And full; it fell dark and rich. It only took an allotting of Katy's entrancing smile for Ivey to remember the specialness of a little girl and the gleaning she could pick out of any day for the making of sunshine. Or what she did to a grandmother, polishing her world with smiles from when she first stepped off the boat after school onto her own island and until only the pink of the sky told her it was time to go inside. It didn't take long for him to realize that Katy did that to him, too. Like her mother— and he was finding it was her grandmother as well—everything about their world was right. Only the days were not long enough to rightly croon the song they loved to sing.

As he hid the real supposed reason he was here—from himself, as well as from Miss Emily, and sometimes even Genna—he was kept free from any needs, schedules, or responsibilities. Since being back on the Key, his lot was to live days without hours or minutes or, for that matter, reason. He did take the responsibility each day of riding with Miss Emily into Bearclaw's store to meet the school bus at two fifteen. After the first day, he did it on his own. He would finish with his fishing, or reading, or whatever else he was doing so he could be there to watch her step off the bus. He would watch as she came running across the shell and asphalt drive in front of the store, hollering out life and tossing waves and shouts of energy as she both ran and floated like rose petals thrown on the tide.

After FECO had reached the point where it was taking every minute she could give it, and with her "time in grade," Alex Roan called it, Genna turned her teaching into only Tuesday and Thursday classes and a literary workshop on Tuesday afternoons. The rest was FECO. That first Tuesday that Ivey was there, she held one of her workshops and invited Ivey—something he turned down but later wished he had not. He had already set his mind to check some things in Miami instead—Summer Tree things that made him feel guilty. He would go some other time, he told her. There was not any reason to hurry, he told himself. He would have a chance again.

It was after he had mistakenly turned down the invitation, and after the third day, that he allowed himself to remember. He remembered that he had come to find out about Coquina Key, about having to sell it, about there really being no other choice in the matter. Nevertheless, everyone in Gotha, on Coquina Key, and probably back in Virginia, knew that, down deep, Ivey wanted to find a reason to leave Coquina as it was.

He set aside the next morning for a trip to Key West and for a visit to the courthouse—though he did wear shorts, boat shoes, and a 'Cursillo' T-shirt with a large likeness of Christ. He found the property in the Monroe County property books and reconfirmed what he already knew. The ownership was listed as Summer Tree. There were no liens filed on it—there was something legal about approval before sale—and all the utilities were in and functional. It was all as Johnson Crews had described. His real estate and legal knowledge were well honed in the classrooms of Virginia and even more so by Ben Ivan Hayes himself, when Ivey would listen. They all told him that everything appeared governmentally and legally right to sell. But there were those other things—those things not showing on any land books. Those Ben Ivan things, those "gut" things, he called them. He could now see those things as things he could not or would not see before. Those were the things, as hard as he tired to forget, that were there. He could get involved in something else—something seeming so important any particular morning or evening... time running, fishing, with or without Genna, or just time spent for no particular reason. But there were things he would ultimately have to face. The Lord would be with him—that was not the question. But they were things, he, Ivey Hayes, would have to face.

As Ivey left Key West, the sun burned down on the narrow asphalt highway. It stayed in the forefront of his mind as he drove past waters on both sides and through a sky without cloud or thought of rain.

Miss Emily would move. He could see that. She was past the age where most people are slowing down anyway. She should be where she enjoyed life all the time instead of daily working, cleaning, and worrying about making the few bucks that the boatel could make. He imagined Miss Emily sitting out on the dock with a line in the water, and little Katy sitting beside her and doing the same. How could anybody ever think of leaving all that was there?

But people are forced to move when what they are moving to is a better place overall. Even his own children. Their life wasn't structured for that—for that kind of a change, for having things sold out from under their everyday lives, then moving. If they had to, though, they could do it. If I go back to teach at W&L, Ivey thought, they may have to do it. On the other hand, to move to Orlando full time. A fresh start in a new place may be all that Addie needs anyway. Commitment and a new set of challenges. Maybe that's what she needs. I can give her that. The only question is, to Lexington or to Orlando? *Is that it?* But the children ought to be involved, to understand. A place is part of one's world, a major part. Addie knows that. There's too much to lose for her to be the way she is.

He pictured them as he drove. And he pictured Coquina Key. Like a double exposure on a film... Addie and the mother—the mother who was a part of him as nothing else or anyone else could ever be. He tried not thinking about her for a while, but she always came back, in his mind, in his speech—about something she had said, or something they had done. He had thoughts about what she would not like, or even what she would or wouldn't approve of.

He pulled back into the parking lot beside Bearclaw's as though he had never left. He stepped down to the boat he had brought in from Coquina Key, untied it as though he had done it many times before, waved to Billy Bearclaw, and headed back to the island. He watched the island getting closer and larger as he rode. The sky behind it formed a palate upon which to set his thoughts again.

Lord knows, he was not any college kid anymore. His half-century mark had been met and passed, like just another mile marker. This marker, though, was real and rang through his mind and body as if it was supposed to be felt, not just experienced—as if it was a page in a book. This one was real and would never occur again. Anything lost, or put off, could never be brought up again. He didn't like to think about it, but what he was—that supposedly learned professor of letters—was probably the most he would ever be. One day, he mused, you can wake up, and your life has already been lived. There are no more steps to make, no more curves to take. That is, unless you do something drastic.

Maybe the involvement with the Hayes family, his family, and the Hayes groves was what he needed. Maybe that was what he needed as well as Summer Tree. He would choose, but for the time being, he would enjoy where he was and who he was. And maybe, he could rationalize to himself that what was hidden so deep in his mind was all right. As long as it remained only as friendship.

Ivey tied up at the dock, went to his room, and then immediately returned to the dock, almost as if confused about where to go. He dropped his sunglasses from his nose, letting them hang freely from the cheap red cord he had bought for them. They were an old pair of bifocals that Addie had tinted for him and something that had become part of his uniform since returning to Florida. Especially in the noonday sun. He propped himself up against an extended piling with one tennis-shoed and sock-less foot dangling over the side of the dock. He opened the book he had brought with him and straightened out the dog-eared page marking his place in the book—an almost-worn-out copy of Eudora Welty short stories.

As quickly as he opened it, he closed it, put the book beside him, and watched as Genna walked from the manager's apartment in front and toward him on the dock. She walked toward him—young, vibrant, intelligent, and carrying herself that way. He could see it... all that was

Genna Trace. There was that first afternoon when she still didn't know who it was, and he had turned around to see her for the first time. Then the next time, when he had stood there trying to think of something clever to say until she had gotten within speaking distance and had stopped, him only able to stare. This time, she walked up to him, did not speak, but welcomed him with a gleam from her eyes.

She had changed into shorts due to the day and due to the still-hot sun. The maybe-too-thin high school and college girl was gone. And now, a woman with years in the sun, years working, years as a mother, stood in front of him. The woman who could work in an environmental lobbying office, who could charter fishing trips and work the deck like the pro that she was, but the woman who still taught a class and wrote poetry to read in a workshop of college-aged people stood in front of him.

She stood in shorts that were clean, looking even ironed, crisp, and fitting, like the ones maybe placed on a mannequin for a summer beach display in some downtown Miami department store. A thin white top, thin like gauze, hung from her shoulders, falling ever so slightly from time but firm and solid from the outdoors, from fishing, running, working in the boats and around the property. All that he thought she would be. That and her soft chestnut tan and, today, a new pair of white tennis shoes that she wore without socks. She carried two long-neck beers between the fingers of one hand, the other hand free.

"You're probably used to some wonderfully French sounding wine or something with only a splash of water and a twist of lime. But we have beer. So beer she brings."

"Beware of Greeks bearing gifts," he said.

"Or Indian ladies toting long-necks," she answered.

She handed over the two beers, crouched down on the dock, then let her legs dangle freely over the side. She raised her legs, took off her shoes, and placed the shoes beside her.

"Tell me what occupies an English professor's mind on a day like this, doctor. Some lacy-edged poetry filled with Dickensian excesses, or are you more into New Wave minimalists and first person expressionists?"

Ivey answered, "I ran this morning—late morning, and that's it, I guess. That's probably the only constructive thing I've done all day. No expressions, just a run down the beach and through the sun and sea gulls."

"How far did you run?"

"Two miles. It's the same as I run every day. It's not much, but it's my contribution to health and well being. And you?"

"Sure, I run," she answered." I've been laying off the past few days, but I ran even before it was fashionable. Don't think that I'm some kind of health nut, though. No, I have this ingrained fear that if I ever stop, I'll never be able to run again and would add fat until I was the size and shape of a giant egg, then explode into piles of flab, aches, and running shorts. I even run in the seven-mile race across the bridge every year. Keeping in shape for that is another reason to keep running."

"That's commendable," he said. "It sounds like you outdo me, but maybe tomorrow we can run together."

"Sure," she answered.

"But maybe now we can walk. Take me on your island tour."

"Sure" she said again as she pulled her legs up, crossed them in front of her, and stood straight up. She reached down and gave Ivey a hand to help guide him in the right direction. "I'll start us off walking one way and come back from the other—a neat trick that an island can teach you. You can carry your beer with you. We make the rules here."

They walked off the dock, across the grassed "backyard" and onto the sand that serpentined into the water. Genna laid her tennis shoes at the edge of the grass instead of wearing them and did not put them back on. Ivey took his off and did the same, now with each of them carrying their beers in their hands. He looked at her as though wanting to say something else as they walked but succeeding in holding back what he had to say. Finally, he did.

"Listen, I have to be getting back."

"And why, might I ask?"

He stared at her, both of them quiet before he answered.

"I just came down to see what's here, check some things," he said. "And to see you, of course." He smiled as he said it then quickly wondered what she was thinking. "With my dad gone, and everything left in disarray, I just needed to see what's what."

"Did we pass your 'what's what' test?"

"There was no test involved. I just wanted to know what people talk about. I mean… you know what I mean."

"You mean you wanted to see if there was anything here worthwhile," she answered slowly. "Something you could sell or trade off if need be."

"You make it sound so callous. You wouldn't believe how much mystery has fallen around both your and Coquina Key's names. Every time anything is said, somebody quickly changes the subject or says, 'Yeah, that's something we've got to get into.' You know how lawyers seem to know everything—or just about—to find out the answer to life's questions. So, the only way to solve the mystery was to drive down and see for myself. Okay?"

"Okay. Are you pleased with what you see?" she asked. "I mean, on your own answer to life's questions?"

"Sure, who wouldn't be pleased? It's wonderful here—too wonderful—like a little Eden hidden out here in the middle of the water... not far from the Florida mainland, not far from the Keys proper, but away from everything. This is the best kept secret in mankind." He looked ahead and into the mass of water in front of him, the light waves only touching against the beach. He turned his head quickly away and again stared straight into glossy Indian-colored eyes. "But about loans, and deeds, and all those other horrible things, we'll just have to take them one by one and solve the problems when they come up."

"I have a feeling you would just as soon not talk about it," she said. "I mean, the whole time you've been here. Miss Emily and I both knew that you or someone would come—that sometime, someone would have to do something. We're both glad it's you."

Genna reached and placed her hand over Ivey's and squeezed—a quick squeeze—then let it go. Ivey used his same hand and took hold of Genna's outstretched and reaching hand. They walked on, as they had the last time they had walked along this same sandy beach.

"Seriously, I do need to get on back. My Protestant work ethic is crying at me to get back to accounting, lawyers, accounts payable, and all those horrible things that have a way of shooting up a perfectly good life."

She grinned and joined him staring into the water in front of them. She sipped down the last of her beer, then took the bottle, turned it upside-down, and put it in her pocket. She took her free hand, put it with the first, and continued their hand-to-hand walk.

"But listen," he shifted weight and leaned toward her as he spoke. "You *tell* me."

"Tell you what?"

"Tell me what occupies an English professor's mind while she has one foot in a sun-washed heaven and the other staring at students and at narcoleptic eyes all day. You're the one who's still the college professor. I'm checked out to being somewhere between a few days off, an extended sabbatical, or a never to return again."

"Okay, if it's my turn, and if you promise not to talk about that other again… As far as teaching, I think it's nice to teach, to have good students, to teach something. I like teaching. Besides, it pays for me to do everything else that I need to do."

"I met your Alex Roan, who must work with you in your conservation efforts. He seems like a nice kind of chap."

"He's a good friend, Ivey. Probably my best friend. When times haven't been what I've wanted them to be, Alex has been here for me."

"Did I hear a little romance in your voice?" Ivey asked.

"I haven't got time for that now. It's crossed my mind, as I'm sure it's crossed his. But that's where it's stayed—crossed off my mind." She laughed. "If truths be known, he's even more into conservation and preservation than I."

"Do you have a chance to write any more?"

"Just for the sake of writing—things for the workshop. I had a couple of short things and one poem published in one of the little magazines. That's all I've ever published. Besides, "publication is the auction of the mind of man," or so Emily Dickinson says. I write some things for myself, mainly poetry. But I have always enjoyed writing without worrying about publishing and worrying about all those big business clouds that somehow form around whatever you do." She turned to Ivey, squinting as she first looked past him and at the sun. "And you?"

"And you what?"

"Do you lead by example? With writing, I mean?"

"Oh no, nothing," he answered. "But I think I might have seen yours."

"No," she laughed. "No one has seen anything I've ever done."

"It was a piece of poetry. I forget in which magazine it appeared. I kept it, though. It was a piece by Genna Riggs. I wasn't sure, but something told me it was yours."

She looked back toward the water and away from Ivey. She could tell he was staring.

"That was from my married days. I'm surprised you recognized it as mine... with using Riggs like I did."

"I remember the last line... Let me see... oh, yeah... *'...and the sun kissed the clouds and all that was real goodbye... then only tomorrow to return to the palm, to the willows, to the lonely's sigh...'*"

He paused, thinking the rest of the poem. Then they both completed it in chorus... *"...and the brooks and the rivers and the tide will love... then hold, and warm in their hands, a lover's cry..."*

"That's it," she laughed. "Gosh, is that not horrible?"

"No, it's not horrible. That's how I knew it was you. I mean, the sun and sunsets and Genna, all wrapped up in one. It all had to be you."

"That was years ago, Ivey. I feel honored, even amazed, that you even read it, much less remembered it."

"You forget that reading and writing is what I do."

Silence, then the call of two birds skimming over the top of a lightly breaking wave, fell between them.

Ivey continued, "I guess brooks do flow into rivers and rivers into oceans."

"And oceans form into unrelenting waves both beautiful and alive," Genna said.

"And the sun returns to the palm and to the willow. And the weeping willow cries; it cries until the willow's love comes back." He flashed a quick look at her, then joined her in staring out into the nothingness—both of them as though in thoughts they didn't want or need to share.

"So tell me; tell me about Riggs."

She quickly twisted her head and looked toward him. "Do you mean about the institution of marriage? You know about that. Or do you want to know about the son-of-a-you-know-what?"

"Listen, you've got to learn to speak up, Genna. Don't sit there with things pent up inside you." He laughed as he said it. She didn't. "I think, for some reason, I can correctly assume that the marriage wasn't one of your favorite things in life."

"I think you can well assume it never even made the list for consideration," she answered. "That, my dear Ivey Hayes, is what you may assume."

"Are you okay with it?" he asked. "Is it something you can talk about?" He looked directly at her then back into the sand at the water's edge. "But listen to me rattling on. She's probably thinking I ought to leave well enough alone."

"I can talk about it now. It was all about fashionable biological clocks hollering my age and those horrible reasons seeming to be popular today. And I fit all those reasons. I was the career girl, as they politely call most unmarried women, and pretty much to grips with teaching, with what conservation things interested me, and doing what little amount of creative writing I was doing. Then, and at about the same time, I was starting to notice my age and those things you wish would just disappear—those which never do. I mean really notice. But about the time one starts to think about such things and gets thoughts about how they need to make sure they experience all things possible in life so they don't accidentally miss one, I started getting the big rush, so to speak, from Digger."

"Digger was his first name?"

"Oh, yes, Digger Riggs. Mister football, the protagonist of some cheap pulp-grade novel, and the cause, or maybe the curse, of every college girl's dreams. And some fickle college professor's dreams. He was big and good-looking, a good catch, and any girl's security blanket for the future. If you don't believe me, just ask Mr. Riggs. Mister Damnthe-torpedoes, full-speed-ahead. Give him an hour of your time and he would tell you all about every football game, every girl, and every yard he ever made."

"What was the main thing that came between you? I mean, after you were married? Again, if you don't mind me asking."

Genna looked at Ivey, at the near empty bottle he was still carrying and that was getting warm. She took it from him and put it to her own lips.

"No, I can talk about it now. It's all behind me now. You see, Digger—and I'm still not sure if he got the name for the way he played football or for the way he seemed to get under people's skin—well, Digger had grandiose plans about making uncountable buckets of money and a conviction that fulfilling his dream was his reason to be on this earth and that he was duty-bound then, and maybe still is, to do anything he had to do to step on whoever he needed to step on to make sure it happened. Listen, he even had a plan to use the property you're sitting on right now to build some kind of timeshare condominiums. Are you believing that?" She continued before he answered. "Condominiums... little cracker-box apartments bringing in all kinds of people, all kinds of additional water lines, sewer lines, telephone lines, general riff-raff—all those things that can tear at the very heart of, if not destroy, what they are supposedly there for. That ass! Then, by the time everything would have been done, the water, the beaches, all that's here—all that would have been gone. Well, he tried, I cried, and then he tore off one night to find his million someplace else."

"That's a shame," Ivey said.

"The only thing good coming from the so-called marriage was Katy. And I'd do it again if that's what it would take to get a Katy." She fixed her stare on him again. "I love that child, Ivey. And as long as I live, she's going to be right here with me. She's going to be here on this Key and right here with her mother. I'll do everything it takes to make sure of that. Do you understand what I say?"

"You've got custody rights, don't you?"

"You have that part right," she answered. She seemed relieved, almost as though he had changed the subject. Then she said, "I've got her, this land, this dock, those five rental units, a loving lady who calls herself Miss, a dog now called Mango, and Katy. Tie it all up, and that's who I am."

They walked on, both looking out to sea and feeling the sun falling on them.

"Speaking of your mother, I've been wanting to ask, how did things go when she heard my dad had died?"

"I remember it well, Ivey—too well. It was sad. Tommy called here early one morning—early before any of us were even up. My mother took the call. You could tell who it was and what he was saying just by looking at her. That, and by a phone call at that hour in the morning. You get a call that early and you have to think something is wrong. Anyway, she shared what Tom told her then went back to bed."

"She went back to bed?"

"She went back to bed, and that was about what I saw of her for that day and most of the next. She and Katy share the same room—I have the other—and for the next few days I took Katy to the school bus stop in the morning, and Billy got her in the afternoon."

"She didn't come out and say anything?"

"The second afternoon, she told me she was getting one of Billy's rental cars and that she would be gone awhile. That's all she said and then walked back into her room. The next day, she was gone. Billy

Bearclaw said she took one of his cars. I worried, oh how I worried. She seldom or ever drives; then it's to Marathon or such; never on a trip on the open highway. It was late that night before she got back. She went all the way to his funeral, but she has never said anything about it."

"I didn't see her, but I don't think I would have known her if I did. Besides, there were a lot of people there."

"After that, and almost as if it was a miracle, she was up the next morning, smiling, with a full breakfast on the table. She joked around the kitchen, cracked funnies, and was her old self again. The only thing she ever said after all that was that she had to get on with her life, then all kind of trite sayings about life being worth living."

"Tommy tells me they were very close friends." He stared at her eyes as he said it.

She again turned to Ivey, this time looking at him seriously and straight in the eye. "And close friends was all they were, Ivey. If you ever hear anything else—about her doing anything to keep Coquina Key and all that—think nothing of it. We've had long talks about Ben Ivan, and all she would ever confess to is friendship. So, I've let it sleep."

"They were good friends to each other," he added. "Let's both leave it at that. Okay?"

She stopped again but did not look at him as she spoke. "You can tell I was lying."

"Yes," he said. "I know you were. I hope at least it was after your dad was gone."

"It was. She would have told me if it had been any different. She made sure of a respectable length of time. And your mother?"

"No, I don't know that she really knows anything. She made a remark one time, but for all I know, it was kept quiet. I try not to think about it."

"It can be hard when one has to worry about one's own mother."

His hand felt warm, almost cramped from her grasping, but he continued. "Both mothers, Genna. I hope this is the last that will ever be said."

"It will be. No one else knew or even cares. Except Tommy, of course. But he understands."

"That Tom really gets around, doesn't he?" Ivey said.

She stopped and pulled him back to her so they both stood there at the very edge of the water. "But Ivey, I suppose I know more than I want to know about what's facing you, what's facing this island, what's expected of you. But you tell me... What do you plan to do with Coquina Key?" She quickly spun her face away toward the water. "There, I've asked you."

"Me do? Listen, I don't think I've got, or want, that much input as to what happens. Or not as much as you think."

Genna straightened up, looking surprised at his answer. "You know nothing can be done with the property without your approval. I mean, you've taken over Ben Ivan's holdings, have you not?"

"Yes I have, for what they're worth. I know about some long-ago loan between Ben Ivan Hayes, or Summer Tree, and Wiley Trace. That, and we have to give approval if the property is sold."

"And the loan," she said. "You don't know the details of the loan? The one between the company and my mother and me and you as owners of Coquina Key?"

"I know there was one. And the actual agreement is probably filed in something I haven't taken the time to read. Tell me what you know, and I may be able to avoid it all together."

"The best I can find out, the loan was for a little over a hundred thousand dollars. It covers monies my dad borrowed from yours over the years. Any paper work on it is supposed to be in your hands."

"Well," Ivey said. "If all that be true, I really—and excuse me if I'm sounding presumptuous—but I really don't see you with that kind of money lying around just to repay loans."

"Of course there isn't that kind of money. Anyone can see that. Not anything close. What I get from work and two hundred and thirty-two a month Social Security for my mother is it."

"So, why do you have to worry about the loan then?" he asked. "Why do you even bring it up? If you can't pay it, you can't pay it."

"But you could force the sale of Coquina Key to pay back the loan. At least that's what I've been told."

"Who told you that?" he asked.

"I asked one of the law professors at school after I was told by that lady. He said, yes, with that amount owed, you could, I believe he said, 'call in' the loan."

"I hope that nothing like that or anything of that kind needs to be done, even if it is financially feasible. Who told you that? What lady?"

"That Miss Leigh person. She's with some real estate concern in Orlando. She seems to think it's imminent and that the land needs to be sold before it goes to the courts. That real estate man from Ft. Lauderdale said just about the same thing. I get the feeling that he's working with her, but they're both asking questions. Surely you know about that?"

"A little bit more each day, it seems. What real estate man called? What was his name?"

"Some man Miss Emily talked to. There was not a need for me to pay it a great deal of attention at the time. We get calls all the time from people, people just asking about things. Nevertheless, this person, he told her he was going to send her something. A proposal or something like that."

"You don't remember his name?" Ivey asked.

"Brown, Brun, Blum—or something like that."

"I've got no guess as to why anyone was here," Ivey added. "I mean, you would at least think I would be kept abreast of any interest being shown. Oh, I don't mean from you and Miss Emily. I mean from my people in Orlando. Like I said, whether I want to or not, I need to be getting back."

"Will you come back again?" Genna asked.

"Yeah, I'll be back. You can be sure of that. Maybe next time, I'll have some answers."

## Thirteen

Ivey walked out the front door of the Gotha house, his mind on anything but Tom's truck, which was now parking at an angle and at the corner of the yard. He looked at the truck, toward the side yard, and didn't see anything. Then Tommy's voice—what he was listening for— came as he stepped around the corner.

"Welcome back. Came out to let Odie run a little and make sure everything is still okay. You've been gone a long time. But you know that. You got all the way to Coquina Key, didn't you?"

"You don't hide coming right to the point do you?" Ivey answered. He looked to make sure the front door was shut as he left, then pushed on it to make sure it was locked. "But what makes you say that?"

"People go looking at orange groves, they take a day. If they check on fruit or a packinghouse, maybe two. But, now it's over five days. "That means something else got done. Is that good or bad? Probably Coquina Key."

"Yeah," answered Ivey

"Yeah, what, da-gum it?"

"Yeah, I got all the way to Coquina Key and yes, I got to see old friends I haven't seen in more years than I like to think about."

Ivey looked at his watch—he had time—then at Tom, then walked over and propped himself up against one of the two rough-sawn wooden columns.

"So what you think about his hideaway? Did you fish?"

"I borrowed a rod and reel from Emily Trace one morning and fished what must have been a couple of hours. I didn't catch anything though—anything I would tell anybody about… one sting ray and one damn cat fish, the best I want to remember."

"You met little Miss Katy then, huh?"

"The damn cat fish gave it away, didn't it?"

"Ben Ivan said the worth of fishing is in its peace. The peace and the quiet, he would say. He would say if you catch anything, that's a bonus." He laughed as he hadn't done since before the funeral. "That's what he said, anyway. But I know better. Anything he ever did was a contest— first to market, more groves, bigger fruit. Oh, that was Ben Ivan Hayes all right. That was your daddy. And fishing... he and Wiley competed all the time. Over anything and everything, they did. There was nothing that Ben Ivan wouldn't do, and I mean nothing, to beat Wiley Trace."

Ivey looked at his watch. "You got time for a beer?"

"Never saw a time I didn't, as Ben Ivan would say."

Ivey pulled open the screen door again, found the correct key on his key ring, and opened the door again. He walked back into the lake house with Tommy following.

"Was it what you remember?"

"It's beautiful, Tommy. You know that. Coquina Key looks like some poster for a South Seas island somewhere. As far as remembering, I don't guess I saw it before the way I seem to see it now. That's really some place, isn't it?" He opened the refrigerator, took out two cans and gave one to Tommy Ripington. They each flipped the tabs on the top of their cans on their way to the living room.

"Miss Emily all right?" Tom asked. "I worry about her some. Don't know why; just worry about her, I guess. Genna says she took it kind of hard.... when he died, I mean."

Ivey turned on the sofa and looked toward the door. He crossed one of his legs and comforted himself in the corner. "Yeah, she's all right. But it still seems strange... I think it's fine now, don't get me wrong, but, you know, I think it's something special, the way you remember and seem to keep in touch with those people."

Tom sat across from him, placed his beer on the wooden corner of one of the tables, and nervously twirled the can around. The last time Ivey was with Tom, Tom was calm and relaxed. Now, despite being in the same friendly environment and having a beer in the late afternoon, Tommy wasn't that way. Something else was on his mind.

"Miss Emily is close to us, Ivey," Tommy said. "Ben Ivan and me. Genna too, of course. She's special. But especially Miss Emily. And Katy. You know, I was the first to ever take that little girl fishing— fishing right there on that dock. I didn't teach her about damn catfish though—that was Miss Emily—but I enjoy that one. First time I have ever been much around children like that. Ben Ivan—he wouldn't take me much, or as much as I thought he should have. But when he did, I enjoyed myself. I really enjoyed myself. How is little Katy? Has she grown any?"

"Don't know if I can answer that," Ivey answered. He shared Tom's smile as he did. "But she's as rambunctious as they come. I can attest to that. I would give anything for just one hour of her energy."

"And Genna—she still writing poems and driving all the way back to that Miami twice a week? Someday, she's going to quit all that."

"That she does, and that she is." Ivey looked around the room, as though looking for something. "At the way you seem to know everything that's going on, you probably know that I came back primarily to talk to you."

"And you know that I came out to run the dog so I could talk to you."

"So tell me then," Ivey said. "They say they got a call then a note from a Mrs. Leigh. I'm assuming it was Beava. Am I correct?"

Tom did not answer, but only stood up and walked to the kitchen. He reached for a cupboard door, apparently out of nervousness or just needing something quick to do. He took out a glass, filled it with his beer, and then sat the empty can down on the kitchen table.

"Could'a been," Tommy answered.

"Are you still seeing her?"

"Yeah, I still see her sometimes. She came to see me while you were gone. I don't see her much, though. Naw, I don't do that. Why?"

Ivey left his stare with Tom and his nervousness and then continued. "Why do you think she called? Called Miss Emily and Genna, I mean. And why is she calling Emily Trace in the first place?"

"Beava has a client, you see," Tom answered. "You know, like Ben Ivan used to have clients when he was trying to unload some property. People gonna' buy something, he would say. And having a client, good or bad, is all part of it, whether you like it or not, I suppose. The trick is in having him something to buy. That's what he would say. Anyway, he's a client who's trying to buy some property in the Keys. I told her Emily and Genna wouldn't sell, but she wanted to call anyway. Ben Ivan said you never know until you hear it firsthand. He always said that. Anyway, I know that Miss Emily and Genna still don't want to sell. But maybe they need to sell."

"Why do you say that?"

"Wiley's been gone a long time now, Ivey. And now, Ben Ivan is gone. It's just those two ladies out there all alone. Billy Bearclaw can help some, but not too much anymore." He finished his beer, picked up the can that was still on the table, drained what was left into the glass, bent the can in two, and took it to the kitchen. "I'm saying they might need to sell, now. Not that they will sell. Naw, I ain't saying that by a long shot. That's a horse of a different color, as Ben Ivan would say."

"You didn't tell Beava anything else?" Ivey asked.

"No. Not anything special-like. She asked about the water and beaches and those kinds of things—things ladies always ask about. You know what I mean... But anything I told her she could always see for herself anyway, I figure."

"I'm not accusing you of telling her anything she shouldn't have heard. Listen, I don't think there's anything at all that everybody doesn't know about anyway. If there's anybody who doesn't know something, I think it's me. Everything seems clear as a bell—not good, but clear and simple. Then something happens that tells me something else I didn't know—something just out of the blue. Has she said who her client is?"

"Which client?"

"The one looking for beachfront to buy?"

"Foreign people, I think. She never has told me who, though. She will sometime, but she hadn't yet. Way she talks, the client may be foreign—South America or somewhere like that. Yeah, maybe Central American people. Maybe money needing to be spent. Laundry money, Ben Ivan would call it."

"What makes you think that way?"

"I said about the trees going right down and almost into the water and clean white sand in between, but she says her client wasn't interested in the beach or the sand. They just want waterfront. You know, something with a view maybe. Ben Ivan said the only thing a view is good for is seeing more of what's yours already."

Ivey did not respond but waited until Tommy spoke again.

"She was interested in the dock, though. And utilities. She has asked me a couple of times about the utilities on the Key. Anyway, I figured if it was for anyone with any good intent, they'd be concerned about the beaches."

"I agree with you," Ivey answered. "It's strange, though, isn't it? And a good question. I mean, what they do for power, sewer, water, and all those things out there. I've never paid it much attention, but everything anyone would ever need is right there."

"Ben Ivan used to talk about that. He thought as if it was some miracle or something. There was a man name Flagler back in the twenties or whenever and built that railroad into Miami and developed all that land in south Florida. They probably taught you all this in school. Anyway, they put a railroad into the Keys, too, but a hurricane got it. It was just after that that he bought the island, they tell me. He brought in a pipeline from the mainland and everything. You could do that back then. He was going to develop it into some place for vacations and all that. Anyway, according to Ben Ivan, he had all that work done, and then dumped it. You know, dumped it like Ben Ivan used to do when something was not any good to us anymore. He apparently lost interest in it and sold it off for about what he paid for it, Ben Ivan said. But he left everything—all the improvements he had done. I mean underwater pipe and underwater lines and everything. There's still a little lift station thing, he called it, with a wire fence around it. I know Ben Ivan had to put those in sometimes up here when he would develop something. I would go and cut the weeds from around it. Ben Ivan would make me do that."

"Who bought it from him?"

"Some of those tribe people, they say. One of those Seminole tribes bought some—that live around Coquina Key. There's some money in those people, Ben Ivan would always say, even if they don't show it. They're the ones who sold to Wiley Trace in the first place, he being one of them and all. He didn't pay hardly anything for it, Ben Ivan said. Ben Ivan said he stole it. But he said he owned it enough to borrow on it and all that. He worked himself a deal, then worked a deal with Ben Ivan. They got it all in writing and everything. You know he was Indian, don't you? Not Ben Ivan. Wiley Trace, I mean. Wiley Trace—you must have met him one time."

"Yeah, I remember him. Wore his hair long, even back then. Back then, it was long and black as an ace of spades. I guess I had heard or saw all that at one time. But I didn't know all the details. Interesting isn't it?"

Tom answered slowly. "Interesting and strange when it happened. But now there's nothing strange to it. The Traces own it—at least on paper, but they can't do a thing with it without Summer Tree approving. That's something Ben Ivan made sure was attached to the paperwork."

"People talk about that as though it's a problem," Ivey said. "And I can't see why it would be. If they want to sell, that just alerts us to let it be sold and we call in what's due. Then, if we want to sell, we call in the loan or whatever and sell. But tell me… when did all this happen? I mean my dad getting so involved and all."

"A long time ago, Ivey. Back when you were just getting married probably. Or the best I remember… He kept it quiet for years and years. I knew, but he kept it quiet from everybody else. But then he told me a lot of things. I guess he wanted me to know just in case. Leastwise, that's what he said. He never wanted Johnson or those to know anything about it, though. No, he just up and told me about it—back when we first used to go down there. He got some other attorney to work it up— somebody down in Key West. Your mama had a copy of it at one time."

Ivey looked first at his watch then to the clock on the stove. "Gosh, we've sat here talking until it's time for dinner, and I still have to drive into town."

Ivey and Tom both stood up, Tommy checking his own watch, and started for the door. "Have you got time to eat with us? You know Tava. She always fixes enough for a couple of armies."

"No, I wasn't invited. But I couldn't go anyway."

"Sounds like Beava Leigh might be lurking in the brush somewhere."

"Don't know what that means, but if it means am I going to see her tonight—Yep, I am. She called and invited me over to her place… It's not very far." Ivey started toward the door with Tom walking slowly beside him.

"So Beaver Leigh is better looking than your sister, my mother, or me. Is that what you're saying?"

"I'm saying you better hurry. That's what I'm saying. Martha sure doesn't like to be kept waiting. You should know about that." "I well remember," he said, as he opened the door.

They walked outside, Ivey shutting the door behind them. He stopped and watched Tom as he quickly clapped his hand on the side of his hip and called the dog. Ivey watched as he walked on, his own mind turning in the sense of pity—the sense of regret—that seemed to call out loud whenever he saw Tommy Ripington. He didn't know all there was to know about him, ole taken-for-granted Tommy. He and Rip, Rip his blood brother, but Tom, he being so much closer. Most of what he did know he had learned from their quiet talks—chats over a beer during those rare times when they could get themselves alone—or from what he could see during the times he was there or was around to even think about the boy who was now a man. Tommy was the one who was always there, whether it was in the house or in the middle of a Summer Tree grove somewhere—like the ways of Ben Ivan Hayes or the fruit on the trees, if you looked around.

Tommy the person, though—the brother of his mother with things—Ivey could tell had never changed. He was the one who missed the Haitian lady of whom it was said he couldn't know—the lady he still had to see each day, though. Ivey knew that much.

Tom got in his truck and Ivey into the old Olds convertible. Ivey watched as Tom opened the tailgate, slapped it, and let the dog jump in. Tom closed the tailgate, walked around to the front, and got in himself. He waved as he left.

Of all the people to miss my dad, Ivey thought. He pulled away himself and toward the hard-packed road that was the start into town, still thinking about Tom. Tom probably misses him the most. Maybe Emily Trace if all I've heard about is true. Surely, Mother's going to have a difficult time for a while. Especially with Dad gone like he is. All that will probably never be known. Rip, Mary Celeste, and me. Yeah, him being gone is going to be hard on Tommy.

He reached down and turned the window crank, making sure the window was up as high as it would go and was secure, then visually double-checking this. He followed Tom's lights back to the two-lane that ran all the way into town.

# Fourteen

The back of each of the rental units abutted its own concrete patio. "A little class to the place," Ben Ivan said after it had all been done. The terraces consisted of symmetrical concrete squares in the fresh cut St. Augustine grass—grass that someone from Bearclaw's cut once a week. Each of the patios held a white plastic lounge chair, matching straight chairs, and a small circular table—a weather-worn platform, large enough to hold two glasses, two bottles, and an ash tray that was Miss Emily's specification for those times that she decided she wanted to smoke.

A couple of glasses of iced tea and the brown depression-glass ashtray, still holding some of the late afternoon rain, now filled the table between Genna and her mother.

"It appears that unit four will have the place all to itself tonight," Genna started the conversation, after sitting herself down to talk to her mother and to view whatever the late afternoon would allow. She had arrived home at her usual Tuesday time. She had changed into shorts and a t-shirt—an old one saying that she had run in the seven-mile race in 1986, one she had worn at times when comfort outweighed fashion. She had quickly done the things she had to do before joining her mother and the last afternoon.

The *Out To Lunch,* a Hatteras from Wilmington, North Carolina, called in to Miss Emily. The pilot said that, if he hadn't called in by three, he would be tying up in Miami. Miss Emily picked up the cellular telephone Ben Ivan had bought them and sat it back down on the table. An occasional call on the ship-to-shore could be heard mutedly coming from the open window of the office, one boat calling another, or some fisherman somewhere in Florida Bay or in the Gulf calling out for someone else. For the time, no one was calling Coquina Key. She would have to get used to that.

The sun was beginning its change into a darker and lower glow, a round object over the nearly flat gulf, appearing as widening light-reflecting and sphere-changing colors and hues on the ground and over clouds that lay around it. It sat surrounded by hanging gray and white floating figures of animals, of old men with puffy cheeks, of things that those watching wanted to make out as disappearing pictures in the sky. Genna watched closely what she saw and whatever she herself wanted to see in the clouds. Those figures that would appear—despite looking to be forming what she thought was both full and right—would then, like the others, disappear as if they had never been there at all.

Miss Emily had checked in the only guests for the evening—three men and a teenage boy. They had left a 28-foot Trojan tied up on the end of the dock, walked up, rented two units, then seemingly disappeared. They wouldn't be seen again until sunup the next morning.

Miss Emily walked barefoot and wore a brightly flowered dress, the dress light and almost see-through—a habit she had picked up from Genna. She lit a cigarette—her worst habit, she said—then looked over at Genna. "Is Katy turning in early?"

"She has a new thing—this homework craze she's going through." Genna smiled, almost laughed, but looked straight ahead and not yet back to her mother. "I can't understand for the best of me this latest struggle or where she ever came up with it. She's determined that she's overloaded with homework—homework for a second grader now—and is about to break under all the efforts now pushing into her world. There's one thing good about it, though. I hope with all the slaving she's doing, she might be learning something."

"She'll drop it all in a heartbeat and fish, though. That's good… You had a lot of little 'almost' problems when you were her age— problems no one else in the world could have possibly endured, you thought, but worrying about studying wasn't one of them. You could always do your homework, clean fish with your dad, and read half a book before supper. Katy isn't going to be any different… you watch."

"I know that," Genna said, staring at her. "I just want her to know that things may sometimes be tough. Sometimes, what you look for, work for, may never happen. You take what you have, and make the best of it."

Miss Emily reached for the ashtray and snuffed out her just-lit cigarette with a frown, as if she wondered why she had lit it at all. "When is he coming back?" she asked.

"Who?" Genna said, looking at her mother as she asked, then quickly back to nothing. "Probably within the next few days, I would imagine. He had some business of some variety in Orlando. He didn't really say what. Oh, I can in all probability guess, but he didn't say." Genna turned her face into a cool spraying breeze, her hair blowing very gently away from her face, her eyes closed as though that made the breeze feel that much better with it brushing against her cheeks.

"You enjoy him being here, don't you?"

Genna paused before answering, her eyes squinting, closing as though hiding concentration. "I've known Ivey a long time, Mother. A long, long time."

"I remember long time. You're not telling me about longtime. For years around here, I think the sun came up then went down around you and your young Ivey Hayes."

They both stared into the sunset, the reddening of the sky creating crimson blushes on each of their faces. Genna spoke again, slow and quietly, almost as if speaking louder would be a sacrilege to the late afternoon—to both the time and the place. "It was good to see him again, Mother. It has been such a long time. So much has transpired in both of our lives. He with Addie. He and his children. He with his work. He has been blessed with a very fortunate life."

"And you with your work, your child, your Coquina Key. You've not done half bad either, lady. I bet he's thinking the same thing about you."

Genna looked again at her mother—a pleading look, almost a begging one—her eyes trying to say something before she quickly turned back to the western sky and to the performance they were both watching.

"You be careful, Genna."

"Meaning?"

"He's a married man, is what I mean."

"I know that, Mother! Don't worry about that. That of all things, if that's what you're thinking. I can't believe you said that. I can't believe that came out of you, of all people." Genna stood up nervously, walked to the edge of the patio, and pointed her toe toward something in the grass, as though it was the reason for her rising. "I'm not even thinking like that."

"I know you're not Genna, and that's what worries me."

"You said it first, Mother. Ivey Hayes is a married man—very much a married man."

"I watch him, Genna. I watch the way he looks at you. He had that same look about him when he was a wet-behind-the-ears high school kid coming down here to dive in the summers, him roostering around here and looking for some henhouse to alight in. You can't hold it against him, Genna. But he definitely has that look about him." Was it a look like his father had, she thought?

"Like his father had when he was around you? Is that what you're trying to tell me? ...father and son, goose and gander, all those trite analogies?"

"I have never hidden anything from you, and you know that. Don't you go starting that Ben Ivan stuff again. You also know that Ben Ivan never did anything, anything at all, while your father was alive. Admit it now. You know that, don't you?"

"Everything was on the up and up while Daddy was still alive. No one could ever say anything about that."

"Ben Ivan was a nice man to have around; you know that, too. He loved it here. He took care of things: fixing, mending, and buying stuff when it was needed. You know he did that."

She looked around, as though pointing with her eyes at the concrete dock, the patios, the outdoor lights, and the table between them. "We needed him, Genna. I cringe to think where we would be if he hadn't been around as much as he was. Besides, I liked him being here. You did, too."

"And Mrs. Martha Hayes. She was never considered? Was she just a wife for the weekends when he stayed at home?"

Silence fell between the two of them and stayed there until Emily finally spoke again.

"You need someone, too, Genna. It gets hard. Oh, it gets so hard. I'm not going to be here forever, you know. You're going to need someone who can do-for. And you had better admit it. I see you around or not around anyone who comes by here. I see you around Alex Roan when you two go out every other year."

Genna walked to her chair, sat, stood back up, straightened the way the chair was sitting, and sat down again.

"There's another Mrs. Hayes now—besides Martha Hayes. Mrs. Addie Hayes, Mother. Besides, as bad as it seems, people are out there waiting and wanting to buy Coquina Key. And you know what that means. It means we're going to see ever more of him. Something is going to happen, and Ivey is going to be in the center of it when it does. He's going to watch out for his share first, but also, and hopefully, ours."

"You've got that right, lady. Summer Tree can do the proper paperwork and sell this out from underneath us without thinking about it twice. You know that. Not a blinking of an eye. But if things go like I hope the hell they will, in a few months, this place could sell to someone worthwhile, someone you will approve of. We could all be off to God-knows-where, but God-knows-where without all the upkeep that this place gives us."

"From talking to him, I don't get the feeling that he will sell."

"Well, I know this. Last year was one of our best years ever, and it barely paid us *anything*. When it gets into big expenses, we need bigtime help, Genna. We need serious cash-flow help. Bills and money and all that—Ben Ivan took care of that when he was here, and he's gone."

"Is that what you're trying to tell me?"

"That's what I'm saying, professor. That's exactly what I'm saying."

The sun was almost gone as they continued staring into their common and graying western sky. Only pink streaks remained from the shine of the sun, leaving Genna and Miss Emily almost in darkness. Floodlights switched on by a sensor Ben Ivan had installed, giving a new light across the patio.

"Like they say, people have to do what they have to do," Emily said after a long pause and after enough time to even forget what they were talking about. "They have to be extremely careful with what they do, but sometimes there isn't a choice, Genna. You know what I mean, don't you?"

Emily reached over and touched Genna by the hand. Her daughter put her other hand over her mother's and squeezed it. The sun was gone but left them staring, searching, and reflecting into the quiet gulf and through the darkness that was getting deeper around them.

Genna looked to the cut-glass table clock sitting on her office desk; it was 10:00—time for the office to Coquina Key Boatel to officially close. The windows were cracked to let in the evening breeze as it blew in from across the water. Windows were open, as was the screen door.

The breeze was almost a chill to the sun-impacted Coquina Key, to the office, and to Genna Trace.

No one was coming. Experience told her that. The telephone was quiet—no call from the people in number four as the light had gone out there over an hour ago. From the telephone or them just tying up at the dock, it had been years since anyone came much after eight in the winter, nine in the summer. Nevertheless, just in case, she would keep the outside lights on along with the bright spotlights on the end of the dock. If anyone was going to come, on clear nights the lights could be seen for miles away. But they would probably call.

She had already called Billy Bearclaw to see if he was bringing anyone else out. He told her probably not and considering the hours—he would see her in the morning. Then:

"Night, Genna," came a voice over the radio.

"Night Genna," sang another more sugary voice.

"Night, John Boy," came another.

Genna smiled, shaking her head as she turned down the volume to where it was barely audible. The radio stayed on overnight, just in case. They could hear anyone if they did try to reach them—an awareness learned out of force of habit, something from what Wiley had done, something both had involuntarily mastered.

Miss Emily had already turned in. She did that with the sun these days. But she also got up before the sun in the morning.

Genna checked the front door by walking up to it and pulling on the lock. She threw on the safety catch as a secondary lock. She knew there was no need for the one lock, let alone another. She did it anyway. She switched on the night light, giving the room a mustard glow. She turned, surveying the office—something that had not changed in all the years, but something she did as a check before leaving... the counter where the few to stay would sign in, the windows to make sure they were cracked open but closed enough in case of rain, and the pictures on

the wall: *Carefree I, Carefree VII,* and *Carefree IX.* This time, though, she walked over to the wall with the pictures—pictures of boats, some known and named and some unnamed. And pictures of men with their fish. It was one of the things that Ben Ivan talked them into doing. Genna had looked at all of the pictures so many times that she didn't even see them anymore when she was in the room. However, in the yellow light, she looked again.

There was a picture of Miss Emily and Katy—one she had taken of them with an Amberjack that Katy had somehow managed to catch off the dock. They both stood mugging and posing like grand victors, standing taller than they could, flexing their muscles, and smiling cockily into the camera. And a picture of Katy, three years earlier, with a little pinfish— her first fish—and standing with Tommy Ripington. Katy loves Tommy, she thought. He being so big, with so much patience, and the one who taught her to fish and who baited her first hook. She touched the pictures as though doing so somehow said that she approved of them—that in touching them, she could feel the warmth that each would give off. Then an older picture—probably some twenty years old now— of her Dad and Wiley Trace, standing with Ben Ivan Hayes. She stared at the picture of them, both of them now gone, both of them such a part of Coquina Key, a part of her life, Katy's life, and her mother's life. Then a picture of Ben Ivan alone, him holding up a fish no larger than a baitfish, but him with a full grin, one of his laughs from ear to ear, and mugging to the camera. She smiled back at the picture, then looked at the one next to it—a picture of Ben Ivan years before, standing with a thinner and younger looking Tommy Ripington and a youthful and shirtless Ivey Hayes. Near that picture was a picture hung in a way designed not to stand out and almost hidden—a photograph of Miss Emily and Ben Ivan. It was a picture neither one of them wanted taken, but one Genna had taken and hung on the wall with the other pictures of life at Coquina Key.

She took her eyes off of it and looked to where once stood a picture of she and Digger Riggs—Mr. big-time, Mr. come-with-me-while-I-catch-a-falling-star. She was so proud of him then… him young and going to be such a part of them. Besides all his plans for Coquina Key—all his plans to build a place back on the highway, a dive shop, bait shops, and place right there to book rooms for Coquina Key. Always talking big… talking about not destroying anything, about booking charters, renting rooms, building more, all-day fishing trips for *Carefree X,* his plans for a boat-in party site with live bands and reggae music. She stared at the wall, the picture gone and only an unfaded space left behind. She wanted it that way —just an empty spot on an empty wall… nothing to take its place… an empty and lonely space, a void showing absolutely nothing for where he once stood.

Then there hung a picture of the old dock—the wooden dock with eight lobsters lying flat on the wooden planks, all arranged as to size and carefully positioned. A very young Genna Trace and Ivey Hayes, both tanned and skinny in early sixties bathing suits and goggles pushed up onto the top of their heads, and both standing behind the morning's catch. They looked at each other in the picture, Ivey looking like he was about to speak. The picture stayed flat in an office drawer during those other years—those years until Digger left—but she often thought about what he was saying. Maybe it was one of the few things she had forgotten, but there were only a few. She took the picture off the wall and moved closer to the light.

We were so young then, she thought. So not-a-care-in-the-world back then. I've put on weight—not much, but some. I was so skinny then—maybe too skinny. But so was Ivey. It was a skinny world back then, but probably neither one of us noticed. We've both put on weight... not much, but some. Running probably keeps his weight under control, too. I figured he was a runner. Ivey looks good now... He carries it well. He looks good as a man... a man; let's see... probably 50, maybe 51 years old now. Then, Ivey always looked good.

...And Addie Hayes—I wonder what she's really like. He's been married what must be twenty-five years now. He's changed in many ways... changed a lot. Teaching classes all day. But talks about reading heavy literature. A business mind wishing he were teaching English, I guess. He ought to know better than that. But I can understand him getting into all that... I wonder what he does read... Probably period pieces... Galahad and doing right. Maybe better romance things. I wonder how his memory is. It can't be very good. He has to have forgotten. Maybe it's just not that big a thing to him. No, that's not true... anybody as caring as he... then going off the way he did and never coming back, never calling, or anything.

She carefully hung the picture back on the wall.

...I know mama goes on about her and Ben Ivan. I know that Ben Ivan did a lot around this place. I know the legal grasp the Hayes people have on Coquina Key. Surely, he won't sell it out from under us. Ivey wouldn't do that. I guess I need to come right out and ask him what his intentions are and get some kind of definitive answer. Maybe he came just to see what he thinks it's worth. Maybe that's what's in the back of his mind—that he wants to go back up north and sell this out before he goes. No, he could never do that.

Genna looked back at the picture of her and Ivey on the dock... Maybe he wants to come back again. What if he thinks he can start things up again after all these years? No, he wouldn't think that way.

Ivey is too experienced—too worldly—to ever think that way... Surely, that's not what's on his mind. I can take care of myself. I'm not some eighteen- or a nineteen-year-old schoolgirl anymore. I can keep my mind where it needs to be. I'll watch out for Coquina Key. I'll watch out for what's mine and what's Miss Emily's and what's Katy's. I don't care what it takes.

She straightened the pictures on the wall again, touching each one, moving them just a little to make sure they were straight.... We'll do all right, she assured herself. I need to keep my head about me. We'll all do all right.

Genna walked to the open front door and pulled on the door to close it. The radio sounded as she did.

"Bearclaw calling Coquina Key, the Bearclaw calling Coquina Key. Come in, Genna... Bearclaw to Coquina Key."

Genna leaned against the desk holding the ship-to-shore and picked up the mike.

"Coquina Key... go ahead, Billy."

"I'm bringing you out one, Genna. I know it's late, but keep the lights on for us. You hear? Copy?"

Genna looked closely at the microphone, then pressed down the long black button on the side.

"Is it a single Billy, or do you need a double?"

"Just one, Genna."

"For the one night, Billy? Copy?... Come back, Billy."

"You'll have to ask him when he gets there, Genna," came the answer. "It's Ivey Hayes."

# Fifteen

It was a little past ten—nearing hot-noon, Miss Emily would call it—when Genna came out from the office. Ivey went to the same unit as before—the one where Ben Ivan always stayed. But he and Genna had sat and talked away much of the night. Now the morning was nearly gone.

Genna was hurrying that next morning when Ivey saw her. It wasn't that she was moving so fast; it was more as though she was making sure something was going on—that she was doing something all the time. Ivey saw her from his unit #4 window; she was talking to herself, arguing at times out loud. She moved quickly, as though she had some kind of time limit to do whatever she was doing. Very unlike Genna and very unlike Coquina Key, Ivey thought. Weren't they going to take a trip when he got back? *Doesn't she remember?*

He had work to do, but most things could wait. Besides, those first few mornings he had spent in his room with a cellular telephone wedged into a hollow between his cheek and shoulder. He talked endlessly while looking at maps and site plans showing acreage and computer reports and endless numbers. He talked to Sol Weinstein on yield and pay back. But there was more to the world, and Genna was teaching him that.

Even with the air conditioner on, he heard her through the propped-open door as she walked from the office to the picnic table behind. She carried and set down a cooler, the whole time volleying words back and forth with her mother. Something was funny between them and they laughed, Miss Emily even raising her voice to a high pitch giggle. Genna did the same.

His time there told him that it was as it was before. It really had not changed that much. The concrete dock was new where a wooden one had sat before. It probably docked the same number of boats. The patios were new, probably some new lighting, but everything else looked as he remembered. Maybe it was him. Maybe he hadn't changed. No, it was the Keys—Coquina Key. No, it hadn't changed. It was almost as though he fell asleep and woke up back most of those nearly thirty years before.

He thought through what he needed to wear—running shorts he could get wet if needed, even swim in, and a V.M.I. t-shirt that looked presentable for what it was—one to wear to block the sun if needed. All the same type of things. Yeah, names had changed on t-shirts, shorts were cut a little different, but everything was just about the way it was back then. He looked down over legs that were finally not as red from the sun, and at his white-soled boat shoes—the only thing he had worn since getting there. The other things could have been the same things he had worn all those years before. A hat. Yes, a hat, just in case. He picked up his sweat-etched and dark-blue Boston Red Sox cap, put it on, and moved to the door.

Genna walked to him as he stepped out and into the sun. She wore those same loose-fitting khaki shorts she had been wearing earlier and a man's blue long-sleeve oxford button-down—two or three sizes too big—its sleeves pushed up past her elbows, the back ballooning out as though it was a sail, its front unbuttoned then tied in a tight bow above her waist. Ivey thought, why do some women have a way of looking so sexy wearing men's clothes? The top of a bathing suit showed from under the shirt.

"I packed a cooler," Genna said as she stopped walking toward him and waited for him as he walked from his room. "There's not much in it." She turned and walked beside him back to the table.

He hung the zipper bag she had been carrying on his shoulder and took the cooler from her. "Is there anything else we need? Cold drinks or something? Can we stop some place or.... or—?"

"There's no place or… or no place to stop at," she answered. "That is, without going all the way to Bearclaw's. I brought part of a head of lettuce, a little this, a piddling of that, a bunch of fixings for a conch salad. We're okay. I even put in a half dozen long necks and an unopened bottle of white wine from the grocery store—guaranteed to be three days old."

"That beats my usual picnic or tailgate lunch of Kentucky fried, stale potato chips, and diet drinks."

They walked down to the dock, past the boat that was still tied to the dock where they had tied it not long before and stepped next to it and into the latest *Carefree*. Beside it on the dock was a dark green canvas—something with a tubular aluminum frame.

"We got a Bimini top, which I haven't had the chance to put on," she said as they walked up to it. She nudged it lightly with her tennis shoe as she spoke. "Billy Bearclaw came up with it somewhere, somehow, and gave it to us. Something probably thrown in on some trade he was making. He's good at that. He gave it to Mother, and she has had it stored in the Tiki Hut for a while. But it's for this boat."

Ivey picked up a corner of it, as though looking to see how it would go on, then set it back down. "He bolted some lugs of some kind on the boat for it while it was over there one day," Genna said. "Something to fasten to, he said. Says it's self-explanatory, which means neither he nor I know how to put it on."

"He's a good man to have around, isn't he?" Ivey stepped into the boat, turned, reached, and picked up the cooler. He placed it tight under the boat's deck and wedged it into the bow. He put his hand on it and shook it. It didn't move.

"It probably seems that way. Actually, you hear Miss Emily or I say something about him, because he's our contact to sane regularity—our contact person to society. We—he takes care of everything out here. I mean, repairs and fixing and lifting and all those stereotypical masculine things. He helps when he can, but our honey-do list is really Genna-do and Miss Emily-do."

Genna picked up an end of the sun-blocking Bimini top and pulled it toward Ivey. She walked around to the other end and picked it up as Ivey picked up his. He held it overhead and walked it the few steps across the boat. She climbed in behind it and took the other end. Genna slipped hers onto the lug on the side as Ivey did with the other. He fastened pens into the lugs then pulled the back side of it out as it opened into a canvas cover over the wheel and part of the way to the stern— bright green with open sides.

"We make a pretty good team, Ivey. That'll keep the sun away if we want. Will it not?"

She patted the Bimini Top then grinned as she untied the bowline from the cleat on the dock and tossed the loose end of the rope onto the seat behind Ivey. She moved forward and sat beside him, Ivey having ended up sitting at the wheel after looking up and pulling again at the top. He pushed the top back into a folded and corrugated position, like in his convertible, leaving the boat open to the sun.

"You drive if you want, Captain," she said. "I know the waters out to where we're going and there's no problem. I'll show you once; then you can come out any time you want."

Ivey put his right hand on the controls, put the lever in neutral, then pushed the black rubber button of the starter. The motor started immediately, the water churning and rolling the water behind them. He looked at the other boats around—the renter's boats, the run-around wooden boat that Miss Emily used on the crab traps—then looked to see that everything in the boat was in a place, tied down, and secure. He looked at Genna as if to say he had checked, and everything was okay. He cut the wheel and headed out toward the open Gulf.

They headed west by northwest, not needing a compass and following the shoreline of the Keys on one side and island landmarks on the other. They passed boats going out to sea, others going seemingly nowhere, and others just leaving docks and tiny inlets. They passed the backside of shops, passed restaurants and motels along the road, and passed various tie-ups for boats. They passed cuts and bridges in the Keys themselves. Genna leaned back and brought her legs up tight against her; her gold-rimmed sunglasses, carried on a tubular plastic chord attached to the frames, hung around her neck. The glasses seemed to sparkle as they reflected back rays from the peering sun.

The "vee" of the hull cut through the light waves and the slight swells of the gulf. Occasionally, the *Carefree X* hit a wave, splashing a watery spray and making a sound like an oar being smacked flat against the surface of the water. The air racing by carried a stifling smell of both wet and salt, but a cooling from the unaccustomed hot and burning sun.

Genna's hair stayed tied back for the first few minutes and until she reached behind her and removed the thin red cloth holding it in place. She shook loose her Indian-black hair, letting it fall into the wind, the constant gusts whipping it straight and full as though they were both teens again and racing somewhere on a Saturday afternoon. Ivey took off his baseball cap and put the bill under his leg to keep it from blowing away. He took a free hand and ran his fingers through his own hair, causing it also to become free and letting the wind flow through it as it wished.

Genna looked at him and smiled.

After five or so minutes of wide-open running along the edge of the Gulf, Genna grabbed onto a handhold, leaned up in her seat, looked far out to sea, and then back toward the shore. "Bear hard to port," she said over the sound of the motor. "Almost all the way to your right and you'll be heading right toward it." Ivey did as she said, cutting the wheel and holding it on line five or six additional minutes until he saw a little island approaching on the starboard side. He remembered it when he saw it again. It looked to be but a big pile of shells with a few trees stuck around. It stood maybe three hundred feet long and not too much wider. As they neared it, he cut the power and let the boat drift on toward the beach. He could make out a stand of mangroves, then probably two or three trees of some type on one end, and three, along with more mangroves, on the other. Shorter-height wild plants lived at the edge of the waterline and formed a narrow green ring around the island. And palms—a couple were scattered about, tall, angled, all looking as though they were maybe planted there in order to be some deserted island for a movie. Mingled with the palms were tropical almond trees, fragments of their orange-shaped fruit laying untouched where they had fallen. The area between the trees was flat, sea oats growing from it and clumps of green, wild-growing grass in amongst what looked like deep and clean dry sand.

"We can anchor here off of the beach," she said after he cut the engine. She leaned forward, pulled out the cooler, then reached behind it and pulled out a coiled line and a small anchor. She dropped it over the side, then watched it as it fell through the shallow water and buried itself in the sandy bottom. He listened but heard nothing after the motors died—an almost eerie kind of quiet with no sound of wind or waves or anything or anybody else on the water. They floated to a stop at the shore.

To his right, he could see land in the far distance—the Florida mainland and what he had now re-learned was mainly mangroves and foliage. Behind him were the Keys—a broken green line, not that far but seemingly as though miles away. He looked at Forgiving Key and listened again to the absolute quiet hanging around in the realness of both time and tide. And the hot but soul-warming sun. They were all a part of what he saw and what he prayed in thanks was still there.

The only sound interrupting the quiet was the rhythm of near-quiet waves gently rubbing against the sides of the boat—waves hitting in a steady syncopation. And smell—a clean aroma of warm sand, clear water, and undiluted air being carried over the water, pushed along in a slow breeze.

"Where's all the noise?" he asked. "It sure got quiet all of a sudden."

"This is it, Captain. Forgiving Key—the Key that civilization, pollution, and mayhem have yet to find. The only thing here is water to swim in, sand to get between your toes, fiddler crabs if you look for them, and maybe a solitary crane from time to time. Your own little deserted island. Surely you haven't forgotten so fast."

She looked at Ivey and smiled, her hair now pulled back and tied, her face now waking up to the little hidden island in the Gulf. He looked into the water as though there was a story there for him to read, the water blue, green, and surprisingly shallow. "Those summers we would ride out," Genna said, "emptying the crab cages and re-baiting them. Just like we do now. You remember."

"I remember," he said slowly. "It's all coming back to me now. Funny how things completely escape one's mind when we don't use it."

"This is the place where Miccosukee chiefs would come when they would have to be alone. They would row all the way out from Florida Bay, build a fire, and communicate with their fallen elders. Do you remember being here now?"

"I think I want to, if you know what I mean. I mean, as things happen, things come back to me. Of course, this whole trip has been that way. When I cut the engine and first floated on up, it was like I was here one day, left, lived a whole lifetime, then somehow came right back." He stood up and looked over the island. "It's something. Where does the name "Forgiving" come from again? Did you ever tell me?"

"Besides being the hideaway for the chiefs, legends say it was a place where the Indian people would come when there had been an unsettled disagreement between two members of the tribe. That, or couples would come after there had been a dislodging of their vows. They would be sent out here without food or fresh water and not allowed to be picked up or returned until there was peace between the two. The island would somehow take away anything they needed to have taken away, forgive them, and then send them back on their path again. Furthermore, they would never have to think about it again. They say it's still true today… or that's what some of the Indian women say."

Genna stood up, sat back against the side of the boat, and swung her legs over and onto the outside. She stepped down into the shallow and sun-warmed water. She pulled the legs of her shorts up higher, then tightened the knot on her oversize shirt.

"So does that answer your inquisitiveness? Is there any more Indian folklore that your psyche is craving?"

"No, it all sounds logical to me. If there was a problem, time and tide as they say took care of it, and it was never heard from again. Pretty darn logical, I think." Ivey stepped out of the boat behind her, then walked to the front while pulling on the anchor line to make sure the anchor was firm and holding. He straightened the edge of the new Bimini top as he did.

Genna continued, "Legend also has it that one young buck would not admit to wronging his lady. He left for a while, and then tried to come back. He supposedly thought he was justified in leaving and then returning, but she did not. The woman decided to wait the scoundrel out until he admitted he was wrong, apologized, and then convinced her that he would never leave her again. They came back out to get them after a few days, then a week, then two weeks, but they would never agree. She knew what she had to have, and he thought he did, too. He's buried under those trees on the north end, and she's buried on the south."

"You're talking the pinnacle of stubbornness there, Indian lady." Ivey looked at Genna walking around to the other side of the boat and getting out an old bedspread to use to sit on the sand. "So, what activity does Forgiving Key hold for the afternoon? Or is a word like 'activity' taboo on the island?"

"That's part of why people come here. There are no activities—nothing in the world to plan for or to care about. This is about it. You can swim if you want. On this side, it's not deep for a good ways out. The bottom is about the same depth until you get out to where the color changes. With the bottom almost level, there are few breaking waves. That allows for nice swimming."

They did not go for the shore but stood together in the shallow water. The two of them walked along the edge of the water, then deeper, the water up past Genna's knees, both of them looking down and into the water as they walked.

"There goes a crab," Ivey shouted.

"Go on out and get in one of my traps, brother crab. You don't need to be in here this close to us anyway."

"So besides spinning yarns, she talks to crabs."

Genna slapped her hand down, splashing water up on Ivey.

"I'm sorry," she said, nearly shrill. She put her hand up against her face. "I didn't mean to splash that hard."

Ivey laughed and ran the few feet toward her, splashing water feverishly as he did. She turned as he got to her and immediately dove into the clear and shallow water. She came up with her sunglasses draped and twisted around her neck. Her black hair, now shining, was pushed

~ Coquina Key ~

back straight and away from her face, her hair joining in back and past her shoulders in a water-wrapped braid that gathered on her soaked blue shirt. Ivey dove in behind her.

He came up beside her and stopped. They stood, as though surprised when they really weren't, and looked at each other standing in the water, Genna with a full smile across her face, her fingers combing her hair straight back again.

"I wasn't really planning on going swimming," he said.

"It was too tempting," she answered. "And too hot. I should have known."

"The water is great, isn't it"?

"It is."

She stood, hesitating and looking like she was searching for what to say next. "That's enough impromptu swimming," she said. "I'm glad I was wearing a suit, even if it was under a shirt."

"My shorts are wet, but that won't bother me. I figured they would get that way... but I still apologize."

"For what?" Genna asked. "You never apologized before."

"For getting your clothes all wet."

"As I said, you never apologized before. But then you never worried about clothes before."

"You mean..."

"Surely, you haven't forgotten about—"

"Out here?"

"Out here. Have you really forgotten, or are you just leg pulling?"

"Genna, some things I will never forget. If it's a case of not re- membering, of not remembering something that was real. Or is that just something from my hopeful imagination?"

"If you really don't remember, I'll never tell you if I'm really joking."

She smiled at him as they got back to the boat. She took the spread and two towels stacked there and threw one back to Ivey. They walked to the center of the Key, first through the small waves kissing the shore, then across the expanse of sugar sand along the edges. Genna threw out the spread on the sand then went to the corners, pulling them out and making sure the spread was tight.

"Forgiving Key, Forgiving Island," said Ivey. "Anything that goes on here stays here."

"Or so the Indian yore says. See, you have not forgotten."

Ivey stood up straight. "I think it's Miller time. You said you brought some, right?"

"Yes, and I imagine I'll be hungry before long, she said…Let me get us a place here… I will try to keep the sand where it belongs… there… then, this is all part of a picnic, is it not? If you could bring the cooler over, it's got beer, vino if you'd like, and our lunch.

"Forgetting, forgiving," she went on. "I can buy the forgetting part. I've tried to after all these years. It's the island's responsibility to forgive, though. Only with time will it forget."

Ivey looked away from the sky and the water and back at Genna. "Maybe the island has forgotten and forgiven me then. Is that what you're saying?"

"We'll never know," Genna answered. "The forgetting part is for we Indians."

"I know," Ivey said. "And the deciding on how we're going to get out of this Coquina Key mess is on me." He walked back to the boat, picked up the cooler, then walked across the sand with the two-handled cooler out in front of him. He leaned over and set it down at the edge of the spread, Genna pushing back the top when he did. She reached into the cooler and pulled out a long necked bottle of beer. She wrapped her hand around its cap, twisted it off, and gave it to Ivey.

"A cold beer for the captain, Mr. Hayes."

"And one for you, Mizz Trace," he said as he took one from the cooler and did the same. "A little cold beer on a hot day, a little water, a deserted island, and a pretty lady. For what else could a heart possible pine?" He took off his shirt, looked for what to do with it, and then looked back at the boat.

"The deck of the boat looks like our clothes line," he said. Genna took off her shirt and gave it to him. He walked over and hung both shirts the best he could against the hot surface of the deck then returned and sat down on the spread beside her—but this time closer. His arms were tan from the sun, his body a new tan—a shade between the red of the early sun and the rust color of extended time in Florida's sun. He leaned back on a cocked elbow, held his beer in front of him, and looked at all that was around him.

"Let me know when you get hungry," she said as she flipped down the top on the cooler to keep things cool. Then, "So tell me, Good Professor... Is traveling to Coquina Key to check on whatever you are checking on, a 'have-to-do,' or a 'want-to-do'?"

"It depends on when you ask the question. When I first came, it might have been a have-to. Now, it's definitely a want-to."

She did not answer, but just looked out at the water, at the trees together on one end, at the two alone on the other, at the boat anchored and moving ever so slightly with the water. He looked down at his suit— a pair of dark blue running shorts, the nylon almost already dry. He pulled his stomach in and his suit up a little.

Genna leaned back onto elbows bent so that she also looked out and across the water. He stared at her as she did, watching as he would have done—like maybe he did—all those years before. Now, Genna was a woman—a lady whose age had not escaped but somehow seemed only to have seasoned her. Years of working, years of living. A husband, even if he was gone. A child, seven years old. But she herself could not have planned the way she looked any better.

She spoke without looking at Ivey. "I had a student from Brazil a few years back. Everyone in Brazil must have money what with the way their children go off to school wherever they want. Anyway, she tells me that in Brazil, if you're at a cocktail party or the like and in conversation, and if someone asks what you do, they don't mean what you do to make money to live. I mean, Doctor, Lawyer, or Indian Chief. They mean what you do in the world. You know, what you do with your time besides working. Everyone has to work." She looked at Ivey. "Do you have time besides working?"

Ivey moved and propped up on his back and elbows beside her. "I told you, I'm boring. Between classes, admin responsibilities, my own children and their worlds, that seems to keep me busy. That would probably be in everyone's answer, though—that they keep busy, I mean."

She did not answer.

"I run most mornings," he said. "I have to run outside as we're not blessed at school with an inside track or sun-warmed beaches. So, with the weather, I can only admit to running most mornings. I'm not one of those polar bear types who dive into freezing water because it's good for them or because it's simply there. No, under about forty degrees and more than a sweatshirt can take care of, I find I wait."

"If you are anything like your father, you're a busy man, Ivey Hayes."

"During the fall and spring semesters, we play basketball every Tuesday night for an hour. I cannot imagine my dad doing that. It's just a makeshift thing that whoever shows up at the gym plays. But I find I'm even doing that less and less. I've got to make concessions to aging bones and what were, at one time, muscles."

Ivey crossed his legs in front of him and stood straight up.

"He gets up like he keeps in shape," Genna said as she squinted again into the sun. He turned and started to the boat.

For one of the first times, he looked like the Ivey Hayes of old as he walked back to her. Older of course, thicker, hair longer, but the same look in his eye—a look carrying on a conversation of his own with her own eyes, her own look, and almost not caring what else was going on at all.

"You smoked when you were in college. I remember that," she said. "But then we all did."

"It's been years and years. Still the dumbest thing I ever did. I still tell the youth about it whenever it comes up."

He sat down beside her again and looked out across the water—at the sea and the sky becoming almost the same color, erasing the seam between them.

Genna said, "Tell me what you're reading then."

"Listen to you ask questions. I sure would hate to be in one of your classes. Reading? I don't know when anyone has asked me what I'm reading. Ah, mainly class materials. You know—renewing and rereading. I try to keep something to read from outside the classroom, but then it seems to be the same old things. I read a lot of things, like Flannery O'Conner, Eudora Welty of course, Katherine Anne Porter, Faulkner, though he sometimes bores me to death, and Conroy now. You know... that crowd."

"Well, hot dang you-all, I swear, she laughed... You stay right there below the Mason-Dixon, don't ya?"

"And you there, Miss judge and jury of geographic savoir faire?" Ivey asked with a smirk across his face as he rolled over and stretched out on his stomach.

"I was the one asking questions."

"I've run out of answers."

"Oh, Browning, Dickinson; those you would expect. And yes, sometimes Dorothy Parker and the girls."

"All romantics, yes, but more so—I mean, firm in their convictions on what's right and wrong."

She turned and pushed the top off the cooler again. "I practice what I preach, I suppose... Would a late lunch be good about now? That's what we came here for, you know. Besides, that long swim of yours made me hungry."

Ivey kneeled up while putting out his hands, looking ready to take directions on what he needed to do. All he could do was sit on his knees and watch. She took a part of a head of lettuce out of a Tupperware container and tore it apart, putting the lettuce back into the plastic bowl. She took out a stack of smaller containers with celery, bits of carrot, black and green olives, one with croutons, and mixed them into the lettuce. She opened yet another container with meaty pieces of Conch (so the handwritten piece of tape on the top of the container said) and placed them in the salad mixture. She mixed an olive oil with something he was not sure of and poured it over the salad. She set out a plastic bag with round crackers of some sort in it.

"Lunch is ready," she said, then put a fork, a napkin, and a small plate in front of her and the same across from her on the spread.

"Looks great, but I stood there and watched you instead of helping. I'm not used to not helping."

"I'm not used to having someone around to help... and I love it. But your job is to open the wine and pour it." She reached over in the corner of the cooler and pulled out a bottle of a white wine and two wine glasses wrapped in paper towels. "That is what men claim as their domain, I understand. Wines, I mean."

Ivey turned and sat down where he had been sitting before. He took a corkscrew that she gave him and opened the bottle, pouring her a glass and then one for himself. He took the plate with the salad from Genna and gave her the wine. He situated himself comfortably, then took the first bite of the salad. "So she also prepares lunches to marry with the occasion. Why do things outside always taste so much better? This is just a little on the other side of stupendous. How in the world do you get chunks of conch like this? Do conches jump up into your crab nets? I've never seen it being sold... I mean, you can't possibly get all this from those round shells—those cornucopia-looking things set out in tourist shops."

She waited until she got through chewing, and then answered. "Some things are best being kept a secret... things for lady to know and man to have to only wonder about."

Ivey looked back at the boat, then to Genna. A minute passed before he said, "You've reintroduced me to Forgiving Key, and, even after all this, there's still one thing I want to do this trip to Coquina Key... The sailboat. The *Doubloon*. Is it still sailable?"

"That became one of your dad's play-things; my mom and your dad's plaything, I should say—in the late afternoon. You could hear them out there from as far as you could see, hoisting sail and pulling lines, cussing and hollering, jumping from one side to the other. You couldn't help but somehow hear them. Both of them. They were like music singing in time with the waves. A real classic."

"The boat or those two?"

"Both. You never see wooden boats like that anymore," she said. "We've kept it up through the years. It's in the water now, but, before long, we're going have to put it up on scaffolds —dry-dock it, with the tarp over it. We maybe should have done it by now. He maintained that boat like clockwork; probably replaced the sail every other year. But sailable? Yes, it's very sailable."

"When did he put the name on it? You do remember what a doubloon is."

"He had it named more years ago than I can remember. I know that." She picked herself up to stand on her knees and reach into her pocket. She dug around, as though sorting through change and then produced an antique, gold Spanish dollar. "Have you still got yours?"

"Sure I do... I brought it with me. I keep it as my good luck piece. But I didn't know that... you... I mean?"

"There were two of them. Your dad had one and my mother had one. Five or six years ago, she gave me hers. I still don't know why, but she did."

"There's probably a story there somewhere. My dad sent mine to me. Probably about that same time. I wondered why at the time, but he never said. I guess I'll never know now."

"You're right about that," she said. "About the story, I mean."

"Will you tell me some time? If you know it, I mean."

"You probably already know and are just asking that."

He let it get quiet again before asking; "I don't know. The story that sadly replants itself in my mind, no matter how hard I try, is about Coquina Key and Summer Tree and agreements and all that." He put the bowl back, wadded up his napkin, and put it beside it. "And who is searching for some reason as to how he can keep his business going—a business he really doesn't care about but one he has a new-found responsibility to keep active and out of the hands of the moneychangers."

"I'm not good enough at either to know how to mix pleasure with business," she answered. She put her plate down half eaten. He put his under hers, then picked up the wine bottle from the cooler and refilled both their glasses.

"You finish eating... I have no right to— That's something we have to talk about sometime, but let's not do it now." He looked out across the water again as Genna put the used containers and plates back in the cooler. He walked back and picked up the sun-block, which he had left on the spread. He thought about asking Genna to put some on his back but didn't. He poured a little on his hand and rubbed it on his back the best he could. He did the same with the other hand. "Besides, the water is too mysterious and moving, the breeze too clean... cooling."

"And guest is taken in by what he sees."

"You can never be too enamored, Genna."

She moved the cooler to the corner of the spread, then leaned back to lie flat in the sun, her legs stretched out straight, her head resting on a folded-over towel, her hair pushed back away from her face to catch the early afternoon rays. Ivey moved beside her and turned to lie on his stomach again, the sun still beating hot against his back.

"Yes it is, Ivey." She did not open her eyes as she spoke. "And I don't want to think about that other." Then they both got quiet. Ivey lifted himself to prop on bended arms and to look down at her. He stared and took in where he was and what he was doing. He looked at closed eyes. All these years, he thought. She probably doesn't even know she looks the way she does. Her coming out here like this. If it was anyone else, one might question whether she was just trying to be overly nice because of Coquina Key. Genna though... Genna would still be Genna if there were no question about it at all.

Ivey sat up and found himself staring again, still deep in thought...

...I can't see her primping and fretting, hair saloons, moisturizers, and all that. There are bound to be men at school, men somewhere. That one botanist fellow is all Tommy ever said anything about. And I'm here beside her. A whole lifetime has gone by, but she's still here. And that marriage. So many people are like that, though. They get with people, and then things somehow change. People change, but what they have between them doesn't. Or that's what they tell me. She could only be in here, though, not anywhere else.

He looked at her face—a permanent glow from sunlight that was bouncing off the water, her body strong, but her skin soft like someone who would answer to "Professor" and read Browning and teach Dickinson. She could never be anywhere else. She needs the Keys, he thought, the sun and the water. She needs Coquina Key. He looked over his shoulder, past Genna, and to the water behind her. She *is* Coquina Key.

An afternoon hour passed. It could have been longer. He woke after stretching out and falling asleep, the heat from the sun across his face waking him up. He looked to Genna. She had not moved, but her eyes were open and looking at him.

"You fell asleep, Dean Hayes."

"I did that, Professor Trace. Yeah, probably burned my back to a crisp. I remember doing that. I'm afraid I don't share your affinity for the rays of the sun anymore." Ivey put his hand back to his side, pushed himself up to his knees, then stood up. He wiped what might have been sand off his chest and off the top of his legs, like wiping away the sleep. He reached down and gave a hand to Genna. She took it as he pulled her up.

She stood beside him, but didn't let go of his hand. He ran his thumb across the top of her fingers—soft but firm, like someone who knew what she wanted. He did not let go. He looked at her as if trying to say how he liked being there with her, that he remembered the last time he was there… that look… he remembered maybe thirty years before, lying with Genna in the sun, on a spread, and no one else around… watching the sun setting to the west.

"It used to be a good sunset out here," he said. "I mean, I guess the sun sets the same everywhere, but across the water without anything in front of it, I still remember this sun."

"I thought you would if you ever came here. We can come back, you know. The sun still sets here every night."

"Yeah, well…" he started.

Genna let go of his hand, walked over, put on her shorts and top, and slid on her shoes. She threw Ivey's shirt to him. She moved the cooler off the spread, then folded over the spread to pick it up. Ivey picked up the cooler, and they both set their things in the boat. He walked out and dislodged the anchor.

He walked back to her and took her hand as if to help her into the boat, but she stopped. "Katy's been wanting to come again," she said. "It's been a while since she's been out, so this will be my excuse. Miss Emily will probably ask to come, too."

"You mean tonight?"

"Sure, tonight or tomorrow night. The sunset, I mean."

"Yeah, it's a deal then. We'll all get in the *Carefree* with the new Bimini top and ride out to watch the sunset. Unless Miss Emily wants to swim out."

"She'll come. It'll be fun," she answered. He squeezed her hand as she sat on the side then twisted her legs into the boat.

They left Forgiving Key and started their way back to Coquina Key. They took it slow as they cut through the water, watching, looking, and being a quiet part of all that was around them. Birds flew by them, called, and then dropped into the water as they spotted their next meal. Ivey watched the birds and listened to the gentle waves as they broke lightly against the side of *Carefree X*. He took in the smell of the salt that was caked on the runners in the floor of the boat and that was in the air.

When they were almost back, Genna broke the trance.

"Miss Emily is standing out on the dock," she said as she strained to see.

Ivey leaned up and also looked. "It looks like she's waving."

"It looks like she's waving for us to hurry in." Immediately, Ivey stood and threw the lever into a higher speed.

"I hate to think what she's signaling for. But we'd better go find out. There must be something bothering her for her to be out and what looks like waving something in her hand."

## Sixteen

Miss Emily stuck the edge of the letter-sized piece of paper between her lips to allow her to catch the boat's rope as Genna threw it onto the dock. She tied the rope off to a cleat while Genna jumped from the boat and took the paper from her.

Emily squealed to both of them as Genna read. "Something told me that old fart wasn't fooling around. Naw, I knew it somehow. You know how you sometimes just know things?" She didn't wait for an answer. "I told that old fool Blum on the telephone just yesterday that if he was serious in wanting to buy Coquina Key, to put it in writing. Put his money where his mouth is, I told him. Ben Ivan told me before he died that if anyone offers you over five million dollars for it, you get it in writing. You get a down-stroke, he called it, to make sure they are serious; then call a lawyer fellow he gave me the name of in Orlando."

"And what do you think that lawyer will do with it?" Ivey asked after jumping onto the dock and as he tied off a line.

"Hey, I almost forgot that we were with the man right here. The man himself. Did you know he was going to make an offer, Ivey? You know all about this, don't you? ...Pulling legs and teasing an old lady."

"I don't even know for sure who he is," Ivey answered. He took the letter from Genna as she finished reading it.

"Well, one," Genna said, as if not listening to the other two, "I have no guess as to who these people really are, Ivey. And two, you know what I think about selling to anyone—any way or any where. I don't know or care who they are. As Tommy Ripington would say, it just ain't a-gonna happen."

"What do you know about this Clayton Blum fellow, Miss Emily?" Ivey asked.

"Tells me he's from Ft. Lauderdale. Says he wants to build on it. Says he wants to build condominium units. Didn't say much, but that means time-shares or some such is what I'm thinking. You tell him, Genna. You talked to the man."

"If I have to… He's like all those others who have called throughout the years, though. The only difference is that this one, I admit, appears to be a lot more insistent. I talked to him twice, it seems like. We talked, I suppose, so I could find out what was on his mind. You remember that fool calling here. Anyway, that was an old habit your father taught me, Ivey. Anyway. I told him then that it was not for sale. Not for sale at any price."

Emily opened her mouth to say something, looked as though she had rethought what she was going to say, and closed it. She turned and started a slow walk off the dock and back to the rooms, with Genna and Ivey following behind.

"Is Katy inside?" Genna asked.

"Inside drawing pictures and sitting by the telephone. I put her in charge while I came out to find you."

"I knew that a group somewhere in South Florida was considering making some kind of offer. We can check it out, but it just might be official," Ivey said.

"This one isn't considering, honey," Miss Emily said. "This one already has."

"It is not for sale to either group as far as I'm concerned," Genna added.

"Here we go again. So, what do you plan to do about ever getting money then? About paying off what is owed? Tell me that, miss stubborn-as-a-mule."

Genna looked at Ivey until he felt her stare. "You have a point. Technically, our loan can be called in at any time they tell us. Is that not right, Ivey?"

They walked to the outside picnic table behind the office where Ivey and Genna both sat down, then faced each other. Emily walked on into the office and pulled three tall Coronas from the refrigeration and a Saran-wrapped saucer with cut lime wedges on it. She walked back outside to the other two.

"You're right," Ivey said as Miss Emily handed over the cold beers. "And right now, you're probably waiting on me to say it's no problem—don't worry about it. But I can't say that. Not with the taxes and the payables that I find Summer Tree as a corporation owes on it. Not with Mary Celeste, Sol, Johnson Crews, and all that crowd—even my mother, especially my mother—wanting it sold. But I can tell you this. I will do everything in my power not to sell it. And I mean everything. Then, I have to do what's best for everyone. You know that."

"Mama," Katy hollered as she jumped from the back door to the office, interrupting the conversation, Mango following close behind. Her arms were out as she ran to Genna. Genna turned where she was sitting and hugged Katy as she ran up.

"What do you have there, Katy girl? Have you been drawing pictures?"

Genna looked at her drawings—a picture of a man sitting in a boat, his hair both yellow and brown, his face and body reddened. She stayed in Genna's hug, reached out, and gave the picture to Ivey.

"It's for Ivey. It's a picture of him with sunburn on his face."

Ivey smiled as he saw it. "Thank you, Katy. I'll honor my drawing and hang it somewhere where I can always see it."

Genna looked at Ivey, a question in her mind producing furrows across her brow. She looked at her mother standing and shifting as though wondering whether to sit or stand, whether to holler with joy, or whether to file another question coming from her mind.

"Can we go out to that place we watch the sunsets tonight, Mama?" Katy cried. "I heard you say you were going to take Ivey, and he's here now. Please Mama, let's go out and watch the sunset?"

"We went today, Katy, and Ivey and I are going to go sailing later on."

"And you don't want to be around me and a swinging boom," Ivey said.

"We can plan on that for tomorrow, if you like, Ivey. It's getting late, and we can all go out to watch the sunset." She turned to Katy. "You, Miss Emily, everyone. But right now, you and Mango go back into the office and let us talk."

"You watch," Miss Emily said. "That sounds like fun to me. If those clouds come and go and it's not raining that is. You watch the clock beside the ship-to-shore, Katy, and tell us when it gets to five o'clock."

Ivey looked at the two of them as Katy left, looking as though he was searching for something to say. Nothing was said, though —just a continuation of stares -- a waiting to settle into whatever they were going to do.

Genna looked with a wide-eyed expression on her face, searching as though mathematics were running through her mind, or maybe just searching for some plan that had not been said before. She thought to herself, what do we have to do to get it all in our name? Then aloud, she asked, "Is Mary Celeste involved with this Blum character?"

"That's a good question," Ivey answered. "If she were involved in doing both the buying and the selling, it wouldn't surprise me. At any rate, no matter who it is, it looks to be a bona fide offer, and you need to make an intelligent response." He looked up—toward the sun, at Genna, then at Emily. He slid a few feet to get his sightline to the two of them out of the direct rays of the afternoon sun that was shining under a dark rain cloud floating by.

"Let me get those lounge chairs from inside the door," Emily said as she saw what he was doing. "We can set out there beside the shade of the Tiki Hut. Believe it or not, and despite the way it looks, it's dry underneath that overhang. Being protected by the banyan tree helps. If a rain comes sideways, you're soaked, but if straight down, there's no problem. Those clouds are saying it's just going be a passing shower though."

"Tell me this," Ivey started again as she started toward the office to get folding chairs for them to use. "If the offer is from this Blum guy—it's an attractive offer, by the way. If it is from him, I think we have to assume for right now that he can get building permits, Corp. of Engineers permits, and everything else he needs to do what he wants with the property. He looks like that kind."

"I will chain myself to a Banyan tree if that's what it takes," Genna said. "And I'm not talking just for the sake of rhetoric. You talk about a tree hugger—well, you just may see one, a real one. Time shares, condos, people, and all the crap that people bring… This old girl cannot, will not, take any of that."

"Play along with me for a minute there, Joan of Arc," Ivey said. "We have a quote from Blum and, for all we know, there may be more out there. As to whether Mary Celeste is involved, what does it really matter if she is?"

He looked at the others as he opened out a chair, sat down, and then fingered the top of the cool bottle he carried. "It might be a pretentious question, but if it's true—if she's involved and is on top of the receivables and the wording of the ownership papers and all that, and if she's aware of monies technically owed, and if this offer is already known to all that Orlando crowd—well, the offer may be good, but then again the whole deal may be smelling like catfish left on the dock all day. Either way, if she's involved or not, she's going to push hard to get the property sold. After all, that's what she's been asked to do, and, by nature, wants to do. You better be thinking hard about Blum's offer for the cash and to pay off the loan. In case that's the way it goes, I mean. And me... I can give you my input even if it may have to be mainly dollars and cents. But, the decision on your end needs to be yours. That's the first thing, and you two need to agree. Oh, and before I forget, Sol told me this morning that the paper—the loan on Coquina Key—has been sold, so we stand responsible for monies owed."

"We can always turn them down," said Emily, "and see if they'll come back even higher. It won't hurt me one bit to see the price go higher and higher. That won't bother me at all."

"That may be wise... it would give me time to—"

"Wait, wait... wait!" Genna said, placing her bottle between her legs and throwing out her hands like some referee stopping the play. "Ivey, tell me again what the deed, the will, and all that says about sibling approval on a sale of property."

"I called the attorney in Key West that my dad used and had him fax it up to me when I was in Orlando last. It says, and this is pretty true to the actual wording, that the property can be sold and liquidated at any time by Summer Tree Corporation under normal business practices. Denial to sell must be gained from the majority of the sons and daughters of Ben Ivan Hayes and the majority of the sons and daughters of Wiley Trace. If no majority approval to sell is gained, the deed will remain as originally drawn; that means the property may be sold."

"That's what I've been told, too," Genna said. "If your people want to sell, they can sell. The only way that can be stopped is if there's a majority vote against it. In the Hayes household, there's your mother, you, Rip, and Mary Celeste. In the Trace household, there's only Miss Emily and I. Therefore, when it comes up, if you haven't already gathered, my vote will be not to sell. And my mother?" She took her by the hand. "I'm not through with her yet... And the Hayes family?"

Ivey answered. "I would vote not to sell, but my own mother and Mary Celeste will want it sold. And Rip will do what they tell him."

Ivey looked again at Genna who looked as though she was adding and subtracting again, using her finger on the concrete tabletop. "So percentage and approval wise, it will sell."

"That's what I'm saying," Ivey said. "It's sad, but it's true. Everyone will make money and Summer Tree will get the taxman and the new loan holder away from its door."

"Then tell me this. Is there any other way to get money to pay the Summer Tree tax woes? To sway their insistence, I mean. I cannot believe that, after all these years, it falls on our home to solve a company's tax problems."

"You don't need all those old packing houses," Emily said, offering a possible way out. "I remember Ben Ivan talking about that—about them being called co-ops, but he owns them all. At least, that's the way it was."

"I've looked at that. If we sell off packinghouses, we have to hire that work done on the outside. Besides, the houses are profitable. No, the only way out is to sell assets to pay off the government before the government just comes and takes them. Besides, if Mary Celeste wants Coquina Key sold, I don't think we can stop her unless somebody knows something else—something that maybe I don't know."

"I also know that Sutton King is over those packing houses," Emily said. "And that devil, Mary Celeste, is going to protect his contriving butt 'til all hell freezes over."

"I like to think that everything stands on its own feet, profit and loss wise. But yeah, the chances are slim to none to convince Mary Celeste to sell any of the packinghouses. Even if that was an option."

"You being made president of Summer Tree," Genna said. "Am I just naïve in assuming your new responsibility might sway what goes on?"

"It will," Ivey answered. "But I have to think about the big picture—the overall picture. If Coquina Key is sold, there won't be any need to sell the packinghouses, everyone could be paid off, you could have a windfall of dollars, the company will keep functioning, paying workers, paying many, many families, paying bills, and everything will be fine."

"Except—"

"You could move onto one of the Keys with the civilized people, Genna," Miss Emily said. "We could have a house built on the quiet Gulf side—big and new and easy without the need to do all that you and I have been doing just to get by. No more having to catch those dang crabs everyday, beds to make, rental units to clean up. We could get a new place with little or no maintenance and be in hog heaven."

Genna looked away from her and to Ivey. "We have got to stop all this, Ivey. We have to stop it now. I don't care what it takes or how you do it, but you have to put a stop to it." She stood up and brushed herself off. "Besides, the rain clouds have gone and the wind smells like it might be ready for sailing, if you still want to go."

"Okay. If you need to get all this off your mind for a while."

"Sailing will do that," Miss Emily said.

"Are you going to show me what to do so I can help bring us back alive?"

"The best I remember, you taught me how to sail, ye of the forgetting mind. But yes, between the two of us, I think we can manage."

Ivey looked as though he wanted—as though he needed—to say something else, but Genna did, too. From the looks on both their faces, there was something occupying both their minds that had yet to come out. Ivey pulled himself up and walked with Genna toward the *Doubloon*.

## Seventeen

Genna sat leeward on the *Doubloon* with her knees pulled up tight against her and her head lying against the back of her hands. Ivey busied himself behind her with the wooden rudder, cutting it to port or starboard, to left or right, to keep the course they had chosen—a course to nowhere in particular, other than one heading west and into the setting sun.

She looked at the sky darkening in the south. "It looks like the storm that went by before may be changing course and is coming back at us."

"You see," Ivey said in a tone as though proving a point, but in another way almost joking. "Sometimes things do change course for one reason or the other. I mean, they reconsider and try again."

"Even if it's something that they have been dead-set against? Is that what you're saying -- mister, mister all-knowing?"

"About storms, yeah. At least, that's what I thought I was saying."

"Could be, you know. Could be like a woman turned loose. Like hell hath no fury and all those trite expressions."

"Peace! I'm talking about rain and water and wind now."

"A storm could be brewing but still be a long way away. Then, when it comes, it'll be coming from the west this time. Sometimes, storms make for tremendous sunsets if all the rest is clear. I'm talking about sunsets now."

Clouds were stretched thin and layered. A few minutes later, the entire western sky looked on fire, like a futuristic movie showing the end of the world... or maybe the beginning. Genna and Ivey sat quietly with not a sound rising from either of them, the only noise being the light smacking of waves against the wooden side and the slow rhythm of the chirping of the bell on the top of the mast. They watched the sky and the water seeming to blend into each other and producing something that was all in one—a single snapshot of what was mixed and churned together then laid out flat across the horizon for the world to see.

They watched in quiet, their eyes ahead, but both their minds locked in what was behind them at the Key, at what was in some real estate person's mind and in some attorney's files. And at what was in Ben Ivan's mind when all this originally happened—why he put some uncalled-for clause in the ownership papers about selling or not selling Coquina Key. Why did he do that? *What did he really mean?* It wasn't like him to do something just to assure that everyone was in agreement. Then, it was not like Ben Ivan to do anything without a good reason. Especially something to do with the selling of what he, and now his son after him, loved so much.

Now it was just them and nature. The other was larger than real, and they knew that they would have to take the next step, whatever that next step might be. A week ago, they both would have done something—anything—instead of waiting to see what was offered, and having to sell regardless of their wishes. Now it was something that they knew would happen, and it was up to someone—somebody—to do something about it. It was that, but, in a way, it was different, like the sky and the tides.

The evening waves seemed to sense what was going on, transgressing to only a slow murmur, as though supporting an evening sky on a painter's canvas with a song sounding like harps and only whispering winds. With pointing eyes, Genna told Ivey to look to their left—to look toward the south as a rainbow formed as a reminder of the earlier storm and as a promise that there would never be another rain exactly like the one that just skirted by them. Genna watched until the rainbow was part of her, wiping away a tear as though it was a splash of water lofted up into Coquina Key's relaxing air, as though it was hers and was then carried somewhere else by the winds. The setting of the day—the final brightness before everything was gone—showed itself through colors that looked transparent. What was still left of the sun burnished itself in the clouds like something firm and in control, like something that was supposed to be there, a view crying its majesty and hollering its beauty. It was a view that said that, if God wanted it to, it would be right where it was and would never leave again.

Ivey moved from where he was sitting and stretched out like a used sail in the bottom of the boat. He stretched out his legs and leaned back against the transom, his arm bent and lying over his shoulder and grasping the rudder.

Ivey looked up at the rainbow disappearing ahead of them and at Genna sitting like a pawn in the colored sky. The picture did not hide the setting sun, but adding to it to make what was there, in its entire wide and untamed splendor, something that was greater than anything around. The two of them sat there under sail with their eyes fixed on the glow in front of them. For those few moments, his quiet and his embedded smile said that this was what he thought perfection might possibly be.

Genna turned and moved beside Ivey. She sat beside him and leaned back against the same transom. Ivey put his arm around her as she did.

"This was not intended to be a sunset viewing trip, but it's turned out that way," she said. She did not need to speak out loudly in the quiet around her. She laughed. "We can still fit in the bottom of the boat. That's saying something."

Ivey squeezed her shoulder as if to agree.

Genna said, "It's okay for us to be riding this way. I mean, old friends, two adults, both of us in control of ourselves, both enjoying the sunset, the water, and, as I say again, old friends." She looked up at him, making him look at her, her moving eyes staring at him as though speaking on their own. They stared until Genna spoke. "Are you going to kiss me now, Ivey? You better kiss me and get it over with."

Ivey didn't speak but dropped his head to kiss her lightly on the cheek, then closer to her lips, then kissed her and pulled her to him like they maybe had done all those years before. After a timeless moment, he pulled his head away, hugged her, and then looked again at her as though she was hiding behind her gaze and as though this was where Genna Trace really was. She wrapped her arm over his and onto his shoulder.

"You knew I wanted to do that," he said. "First time in… well, the first time in a long, long, time."

"You can do it again, if you like," she smiled. Ivey only stared at her as she said, "But then, I know Ivey Hayes enough to know that guilt is probably tearing him apart on the inside even now. You of maximum control and self-assuredness."

"I know one thing; it feels natural being here with you. Not like all those years have passed and we, by fate or whatever you want to call it, have somehow appeared here together. You and I lying in the hull of a sail boat and under a sky with a color that I have never seen." She quit looking but snuggled even tighter under his arm while holding it over her like a blanket—like a security that, all of a sudden, she had found and that somehow made everything right.

"But I know, I really ought not be here," he said.

"Listen at you," she answered back. "After all these years, and now you're the one who's become so moralistic." She squeezed his arm, making it seem like a joke, then turning her glance up and at him. "You've not done anything wrong. It's okay, Ivey. You can be around more than one person in your life. Deep down inside, Addie knows that. You can even love more than one person at a time. Some people won't admit that, but it's true. You can love for a great many reasons, I think. I have always thought that love... affection... creates more love and affection. It starts something inside that can spread like the fading sunshine up there... warm and at the same time love."

Ivey twisted his body, forcing her eyes to look into his. He lightly kissed her on the forehead, on the cheek, then lightly on her lips again. But this time, it was soft, only just brushing her lips, as he might do to a child. He knew that—if he would admit it to himself. Addie and his world, the kids, the students... they were all him—all of what he knew as love. Now, Genna and Miss Emily and Katy—they were all love as well.

"You knew when I came back here that I came back because of you. I wouldn't admit it to myself, but it's true."

Her voice deepened as she suddenly leaned back from him. "Is it so bad that you won't admit it? Am I that bad that I have to be the secret hidden in your memory, like some I-hate-to-think-what? Something from somewhere else that you cannot admit to yourself? Is that what I am, Ivey Hayes?"

Ivey waited a moment, then said, "Maybe joy. Maybe that's what you are. Maybe something that I've carried around for all these years, wondering, wanting. Asking myself, where you are? How you are? Are you still here? Are you happy? Will I ever see you again? And now... now I'm here."

"You need to know what joy is Ivey. Who knows, maybe I need to know what joy is. And this, Ivey... if this is joy, this is right. Oh, I know we will never have a love like you and Addie... there I went and said her name again. I know that will never happen. But that's okay. Like I said, there's room in this world for many loves, for a love of a family, of a marriage kind of love and all that that means. I mean the caring about another, a house, kids, paying taxes, getting Christmas cards out, and somebody's birthday. That's the main kind of love. That's what makes everything that's not all right okay. I had that for a while. I knew that. Still, there can be others. One that's hidden. Even hidden for all these years. One that's separate and different and apart from the other kind."

"I know that, Genna. But when you think about it, yeah, you're probably right. Like the Greeks and their different loves."

"Exactly. Agape, Eros, all those civilized and more human words they used. You don't have to have one love, Ivey—to be only one person. You can be—you are—many people. You can be one person in one place, under one sky, and something completely different under a different setting sun and rising stars. That's only healthy, Ivey. Be what you have to be where you have to be. The world may say it differently, but that's what you have to be."

"Two different worlds is what you're saying."

"Exactly. If you try to force too many into one world, you can be miserable."

"Is that what my Dad and Miss Emily had?" Nothing else was said until Ivey spoke again. "That was unfair for me to say. I'm sorry."

Genna turned to him again. "I love you, Ivey Hayes. I love you now, I loved you then, I will love you tomorrow. You can forget that I said that or remember it in total for the rest of your life. That's for you to decide. But what you can't decide is me. And you can't decide about Coquina Key. We are here. No matter what you paint for yourself, we will be here, Ivey. Every time you see a rainbow, see a sunset, or see those little stars, you know that we are here. Don't forget that, Ivey Hayes."

Ivey leaned over, hugging her as he did. The wind died and he cut the rudder to tack and to take them back into shore.

The rains returned that night, this time with trees of lightning cutting through the one o'clock sky. Thunder could still be heard, but now it sounded only in the distance, far away and only a descending but lingering sound of what had already passed through and over them.

Lightning remained—bright enough and clustered enough to lighten up the outside and to splash light into Ivey's window. He lay in bed in a hiding zone under the turning fan and somewhere between asleep and awake. He counted the seconds between the claps of thunder to see whether the storm was going away or would make one more pass over him. He propped his arms from around his head, extending bent arms out as though listening, not caring if his eyes stayed open or not. He watched the light as it cut through the window, the flashes lighting up the room. He looked past his legs resting on top of the single sheet and at the foot of the bed, the refrigerator, the sink, the small table with his sunglasses and whatever from his pockets, the pictures on the walls of sunsets and sunrises, and the picture decoupage of blue and white cranes, silver fish, and purple coral… all flashing with the lightning. Even inside, he could smell the freshness and cleanliness of the air as it was being washed pure by the rains. He remained entranced by the syncopation of the rain as it peppered the roof and the glass of the window.

His mind entered that place where consciousness sometimes falls when it is caught between a deep and non-remembering sleep and being awake enough to know where it is but not to really care.

He lay in that stupor with his eyes continuing to look up at the fan, feeling the air blowing from it, and with his ears hearing the singing of the twirling wooden blades. Faintly in the sounds, he heard a soft opening, then a closing, of the door.

He did not move but kept his head still and himself quiet, listening. For a minute, he seemed not even to breathe. He knew what the sound was but now had to decide what had already cried to him and would cry at him again—holler at him to see what he would do if the time ever really showed itself. Now was that time. He saw her there but faintly, the flash from the lightning showing her first bright, then not at all. Through the lightning splashes in the air, he looked at her standing barefoot on the small rug between the bed and the door. Her hair hung straight and not pulled back but falling free, long, and full. She did not speak, only stood. He wanted to speak, to say something, but it seemed wrong perhaps—something to be done but at some other time. The lightning flashed again, filling the room and pouring its luminous light against her again… and then again.

Ivey turned and buried his head in the pillow. He closed his eyes so that he could not see—so that he could only remember why he was there.

He waited until the door opened and closed once again and he could breathe out slowly. He looked, and she was gone. Not forever, but for right now, for that night, but hopefully only that night, she was gone. He somehow knew, though, that she would never be gone again. The world did not know, but that didn't matter. He knew that she would always be there, if not in front of him so that he could touch and feel her, she would, at the very least, be forever in his mind. Under control and always there.

## Eighteen

Miss Emily walked out from one of the center units—one of the ones the overnight fishermen used, the ones they had rented the night before.

"Here, let me help you," Ivey said as he saw her and fluttered to put his coffee cup somewhere and move toward her. He broke the morning silence over the boatel—silence otherwise broken only by the sound of a morning game show on a television leaking through an open window of one of the units.

"Listen at you. You're the first one to ask to do that since… oh, since the last time Tommy Ripington was down here, I suppose. No, I've been doing this for more years than I'd ever tell anybody. I can take care of it. Is yours ready for a poof-poof yet?" She sat her cleaning equipment down, opened the door wide, and looked inside, then leaned against the held-open screen door.

"No. I'm going to need to head out this afternoon. I'll try to get back soon, though. This is nice, but I can't run from the rest of the world. I need to go and do whatever it is I do. Summer Tree and all that good stuff, I mean. I've been thinking about leaving mid-afternoon. That is, in time to get past Miami before the five o'clock traffic." He could see that what he had just said wasn't sinking in. "But then, traffic is always bad around Miami, isn't it?"

"I've got to talk to you before you do much, Ivey. Besides, you've just about missed this day, I mean sleeping all the way past nine o'clock and all. Those trips you made out to Forgiving Key and wherever must have been too much for you. Genna must be worn out this morning, too. She's still in bed. It catches up on you, I guess. I never have seen her sleep this late." She looked at Ivey as though looking for a reaction from him, or maybe some news, with her head tilted as though it made it easier to hear. She didn't get one, though, so she went on.

"And home—you need to get yourself home once in a while, don't you? I mean Addie… and the children."

"The children… they're big enough now that I sometimes wonder if they even know I'm there. What do you need to talk about?"

"You've raised your children, Ivey. And you've done a good job of that. Your Daddy kept me up on you and all your goings-on. And kids… kids get independent eventually, it seems. Then, I think it's good for them, if you ask me. Being independent, I mean. I never thought I would say that, but that might be what's best for them. Having everybody thinking for themselves and all and letting them think for themselves."

Ivey emptied his almost-empty cup of coffee in the grassed area in front of them. "It's too hot for coffee," he said. "I have some cold cokes left in the refrigerator. Do you want one?" He stepped past her into the room and walked over to the little refrigerator in the kitchenette—the three-by-five-foot area where he kept a few soft drinks, six or eight beers, a few things for lunches, and the bag of oranges he had first brought down. "You haven't told me what you need to talk to me about."

"Sure," she answered. "I'll take one." He returned just far enough to hand her the cold drink, retrieved a glass from the sideboard of the little sink, then reached and grabbed his own. He sat down on the edge of his already-made bed.

"You make beds like your father," she said as she walked over to the single straight-back chair in the room. She cleaned out the chair by grabbing a legal pad with notes, which Ivey had left on the chair, and set it on the bed. "Both of you grab hold of one end of the covers, pull them up, drop them down, and then hope the hell they land somewhat presentable."

"He stayed in this same room, didn't he? In this same bed."

"Yeah, this was his'n, all right. The little refrigerator and that piece of a stove were all his doings."

"I remember, I think. It was many years ago when I was down here with him—it seems like it's been a lifetime. But then, depending upon the way you look at it, it probably has."

She walked over to the pack of cigarettes left next to the refrigerator, took one, made a silent motion to Ivey—he nodded his head okay— put it in her mouth, and lit it. She looked at the book of matches after she did. Citrus Club. She held them in her hand then walked back to the straight chair and sat down.

"And Addie?" she said.

"And Addie what?"

"And Addie you need to get home to. I don't think I've ever met her. I saw her that one time… didn't get to talk to her, though… you two have been married a long time, haven't you?"

"Yes, we have. When did you see her?"

"At the funeral. There was a blond-headed lady sitting in a pew with a couple of teenagers. A little woman—a pretty lady she was. Wore glasses. I didn't see her up close or anything… or even the front of her, but I saw her. At least, I figured it was her."

"I forgot you were there. Genna did say something about it, though. Why didn't you come over and say something to us?"

She didn't answer.

"You've met my mother, haven't you?" But before she answered, he said, "I catch myself saying things like that, like it was something besides what it was. A funeral. People weren't there for meeting people."

"I don't think so, Ivey. No, I haven't met your mother. I want to; I want to very much, but that was neither the time nor place."

"You drove all that way. That's over three hundred miles up and three hundred miles back—all that way for my dad's funeral?"

Miss Emily stood up, walked over the few steps to the sink, rinsed out her glass, dried it with a towel that was in the handle of a side drawer, and put it in a cabinet overhead as though there was only one correct place for it.

"He was special to us, Ivey—special to us all. All this was a special place for him." She turned and looked at Ivey, looking him straight in the eye as though there was something there telling her what she was looking to see. "And now you're special, Ivey."

Ivey could tell that something was on her mind—something she wanted to say or maybe something she wanted to hear. There were too many things he knew that could, or should, be said. However, they were not a part of the world or were not from any place he wanted to visit. Miss Emily, though, was not a person one could run away from or to try to get something past. Ivey knew that. He didn't hear that from his father, but, in his list of good traits and bad, he knew that Ben Ivan Hayes would never know someone, no matter how intimate or not they really were, without that someone being someone, like himself, who was not afraid to say exactly what they thought.

"I could ask you as some starch-aproned and matronly mother, which I am definitely not. Nor domesticated. You can lose your dignity real fast for saying that. I could ask about your intentions, but I won't. I know about Summer Tree, about Coquina Key, about your father and his wheeling and dealing. I even know about money that we had to borrow from Ben Ivan one time. I know about that, and I know about him talking about borrowing against Coquina Key. He told me about that. He said never to worry about it, though, and I took him at his word. But I do worry. You know that, Ivey. I've known you for a long time. Oh, I've not seen you in years and years, but, like I said, I've known about you and where you were and what you've been doing."

Ivey knew there was something she was going to say, but he wasn't sure he really wanted to hear it—whether he was strong enough to weather what was really in Miss Emily's mind.

"To coin an old, old, old phrase, your father loved you more than you will ever know, Ivey. You, Mary Celeste, and Rip, too. But you're the one he used to talk about. He talked about you all the time, as though you were some medal, some prize, or award that was put on a shelf somewhere—somewhere in Virginia where it wouldn't get scarred or worn or tinted by the world around you. Then, he talked a lot about the world around him and Summer Tree. Talked as though it was something else—something he didn't know sometimes and wanted to be completely away from us. Some place that, when he was here, when he was in one of the boats, he was completely away from all that... or a step ahead of it, anyway. Yeah, 'a step ahead of it' was the way he'd put it. And you, Ivey—you were on that pedestal that was hidden away in a box that could be opened if he ever needed to. You were on a pedestal, but one that was kept away as though you were a hole card, an ace of spades that he could play when he ever needed to."

"That's a compliment, I guess. I didn't mean to—"

"Oh, he loved you, Ivey. He loved you, and he loved you having Addie and the children. He thought a lot of Addie. An awful lot of Addie Hayes. He would say that you and Addie were husband and wife, yes, but you were also friends. True-to-each-other friends. He liked that."

"Like he and my mother weren't?"

"Now, Ben Ivan, bless his heart, had good traits and he had bad. He knew that he put on an air that he didn't have anything to do with Addie. He was like that, you know. If you love something, keep it away; keep it where you know where it is, but don't get so close that your mental picture of it pops and it's not there anymore. The only person he didn't do that to was me, and I was too dang ornery—too cantankerous and downright outspoken—for him to hide me away for long."

"He did a pretty good job of it, Miss Emily."

"But do you know one thing that he knew? A thing that he'd say a thousand times a day without a soul being able to hear? Something he would say in his look, in something else he was saying? It was his need for some one, some touch, some feel, some knowledge that someone wanted to be around him for what he was. Not Summer Tree, not a house in town with country club memberships, but him. That, and that they needed him, not his money, not his name, but him—ole big-talking, big-planning Ben Ivan Hayes. And that was something he saw in you and Addie."

"He never saw Addie that much, Miss Emily."

"I know, but when he did, he really did. Your daddy never got to be where he was without that sense—that sense to see right through and to know whatever it was that needed to be known. Whether that was orange trees, scrub brush acres, or fishing boats, he somehow knew. And Addie. He always worried that something might happen—that she or you or both of you might find yourself drifting away somewhere. He worried a lot about that. Listen, I bet you don't know that your Daddy would read from time to time, and at times even remember what he read. He'd quote all the time about—now, how did he say it?—when you are friends, stay put. Stay put, because if you don't, you'll spend the rest of your life looking to find each other in the face of strangers. Or something like that."

"Were you two the strangers?"

"No, I was with him too long for that. I was the silly old lady on an island in Florida Bay that was his anchor, his cove in a storm that, whether she wanted it that way or not, Ben Ivan would never leave."

"So, you're saying that—"

"I'm saying a lot about what you have, Ivey. I love Genna Trace and Genna loves you. She really does. But Genna can take care of herself. That's hard for a mother to say, but I can say it, because it's true. Addie needs you; you need Addie. As her mother, I'm afraid that Genna may be chasing a dream that she's been dreaming for all these years—a dream about something she really can't have. The Lord has supplied, though. She can have a dream about something that she's found right here near her own little island, if she'll ever admit that he's here."

She smiled faintly, then turned back to the door. She walked to it and stood in the doorway. Looking to the outside, she put her head down and said, "Let's get serious. What I really need to talk to you about is— that Mr. Blum called again. Clayton Blum, he says his name is. I told him we weren't interested, just to see what he'd say. He asked why, and I said, amongst other things, that we wanted to know what he planned to do with it. I probably asked the wrong thing, because he jumped on that like white on rice. Like he was starving, and I was the last meal." She turned around and looked at Ivey standing just a few feet away and taking in her every word.

"Anyway, he says he wants to show some rendering or model or whatever to everybody. He tells me he's talking about me and Genna and you and your mother and sister—everybody. He wants to have everybody come in; he's going to put them up someplace—that Phillips hotel place down on the water, I think he said. Going to wine and dine us like royalty, he says. Says we'll all be enthusiastic once we see it. Talked as though he was going to show us something new. I don't know if I trust the man at all, but that's what's happening. The man talked as though we just happened in off the boat or just fell off a turnip truck, like Ben Ivan would say. I told him that the main thing that would help sway me is money. That sounds like your daddy, doesn't it? Anyway, he said that wasn't any problem."

Ivey stood with a flat, expressionless look on his face and a look of things turning inside but showing nothing of it on the outside. At least for anyone to see.

"You know, I'm for selling this place," continued Miss Emily, "even if it did fall out from Heaven. But there's something about that man. After I talk with him more, the whole thing's not setting all that well. He says he's tried to reach you and hasn't yet… said he's left messages and all that stuff… says he wants to meet with you and get your blessing to have us all to Lauderdale. He's all as brash as he can be, but that's what he's saying. I guess if he's got the money, you know how the old song goes."

"I think he and I need to talk first. We have a lot to talk about if he and his group are serious," Ivey said. "First of all, I want to know what it is and who he is. I want to know the cast of characters and who is behind all this. Then, like you, I want to know what he has in mind. I'm not going to endorse anything that's money-hungry and off the wall, even if it does turn out to be a have-to. And like I said, a have-to is a real possibility."

"That sounds like something Ben Ivan would say. All but the haveto. You're like him a whole lot, whether you want to admit it or not." Ivey didn't say anything.

"I wonder why he wants your mother there," Miss Emily said. "Has she been involved in your land dealing? She hasn't, has she?"

"It sounds like Johnson Crews' input to me—making sure everyone knows and everyone signs and all those legal things. It's probably about that sell-agreement thing—all that mumbo -jumbo about selling with heir approval and all that malarkey. Yeah, that's it, no doubt. He wants my mother— everybody—to buy into the land being disposed of so there can be a clean title."

"Then tell me, Ivey. If it gets down to a question of whether the land can be legally sold, and considering that appendix thing Ben Ivan called it and put on the title, what do you think will happen?"

"Right now, it will sell. No question. With Mother, Mary Celeste, and Rip for it to sell, there will only be you and Genna against it. So there's not a majority to stop the sale. So you see, your voting not to sell now—if you think that way—won't stop it. Nor will my vote. I might head Summer Tree, but my vote isn't going to count one iota more that anyone else's on stopping the sale. All my vote would do is tie, so it would still sell."

"I've forgotten about your little brother, Of course, he can't be little anymore. And you think he'll vote to sell? I mean, if it comes to that?"

"I went to Tom on that. Rip has friends in Key West for what that's worth, which may cause him to want this as a tie-in, so to speak. But Rip has been somewhat involved—with Sutton King, I understand. I'm only now finding out why and how involved. But right now, and hear me good, that's only rumor."

"It's drugs, isn't it?"

"I can't answer that yet and probably wouldn't if I could. I'll find out for sure, but Rip is okay. But the answer to your question is that he'll do whatever Sutton asks, and Sutton will likewise do as Mary Celeste tells him to do. And Mary Celeste is hell-bent to sell." He gave time for Miss Emily to say something, then continued, "You've said all along you want to move, but I know better. You don't want to leave here anymore than Genna wants to. They're going to have to get the Coast Guard in to do that. That's a shame, but that's the way it's starting to look."

"Yeah, deep inside, I probably don't want to. But listen, if I have to lose, a bucket-full of money could help put some nice salve on the hurt, if you know what I mean."

"And you mean?"

"I mean, air conditioning in all the rooms. Carpet on the floor, somebody to clean and take care of the place. I mean me sitting on my rear a little bit. That's what I mean."

"I know that, Miss Emily. But I also know, if truths be known, that you couldn't just sit on your duff and watch the water all day."

"You remind me more of your father every day. I've spent my life here, Ivey."

Ivey stopped as Genna walked out of the back door of the office unit across the way. She stretched out both arms as though just waking up, looked at the sun, and then looked at her watch. She shook her head and started toward them.

"There's one thing interesting about this whole thing, Ivey."

"What's that?" he asked as he watched Genna walk toward them.

"Me and Martha Hayes at the same place. Me, after all this time, getting to meet her. That's going to be a pile of it, isn't it?"

"That it will, Miss Emily. For some reason, I don't want to miss that. Yes, ma'am, that it will."

# Nineteen

They rode together to Ft. Lauderdale, Mary Celeste driving Martha's new car. Sutton sat alone in the back seat and only listening.

Hudson Ridley ordered her a new Buick when she called him the week after Ben Ivan died. Ben Ivan always bought their cars that way, seldom asking the price, just ordering out what they needed. Hudson would then pick them up for servicing or whatever when it was time, leave them loaner cars, or did whatever was needing to be done. She worried about the old one—it going on three years old and past the time when Ben Ivan usually traded. Besides, it was time she got more involved in all the things Ben Ivan always used to take care of. She knew Ivey would, but she didn't want to look completely helpless. At least until things got going the way she knew they would.

They drove down Interstate 95 after taking a short cut that Ben Ivan always took to Highway 1 and the coast, then onto the expressway and south toward Miami. Sutton sat with one leg sideways on the tufted leather-looking seat, squirming as though he was wishing to be somewhere else. He sat faking the reading of copies of business magazines from the past six months, looking and turning pages as though he was involved in something of keen interest. But Mary Celeste knew what was going through his mind. She knew what Coquina Key would bring them when it was handled correctly. The tax problem with the company would be taken care of, but even more importantly, a major cash flow stream could be started through the selling of condo units, timeshares, and whatever else the Coquina Key Club would offer. And that would take care of Sutton and all the problems he had gotten her into. It would take care of that South American lady she knew they would see with Clayton Blum—the one watching out for what was happening and reporting to her people on when their past due would be paid.

They passed the flat cattle-grazing lands, some of them probably still owned by Summer Tree. And passed the edges of citrus groves that Summer Tree surely owned. She never could tell one grove from the other, where one ended and the next one started, where oranges quit and grapefruit would grow, or any of the types of fruit Ben Ivan had started. Back when they would take a trip somewhere together or drives with the children when they were small, Ben Ivan would point out a grove that he owned here or a grove there—grapefruit, or navels, or juice trees with rusty balls hanging on them.

They passed the multitude of towns that had grown until one town ran into another—warehouses, office buildings, and discount stores on both sides of the highway. They turned off at the Sunshine Blvd. exit and into Ft. Lauderdale.

Mary Celeste found the rental office building with the "Office Space Available - $8.00 per sq. ft." sign over the entrance. She pulled into a driveway beside the building, then into a parking lot in the rear.

"This is Johnson Crew's car, isn't it?" she asked as she parked next to a window-tinted Mercedes. The other two opened their doors and stepped out. "Yeah, this is it," she answered herself. Small 'Citrus Club', '95', and 'Bay Hill' stickers were positioned on the windshield. "Looks as if he's already here." She walked around the back of the car and stuck out her arm as though to help her mother. "Ivey called again before I left and got the instructions on how to get here. He didn't say where he was, and I didn't ask. That was for him to tell me, I figure."

Martha wore her nice casual—a camel-colored-slacks-and-top combination she had bought in Orlando for the trip—it looking like something she may have worn years before. It clashed with Mary Celeste's double-knit slacks and cotton golf shirt, but was comfortable for driving, she explained. Together, they walked past the car on the other side—a white BMW with a Florida 'vanity' license tag that read BEAVA.

They walked toward the back entrance and past the first car in the parking lot—an older gray Camaro. Mary Celeste looked back at it—at the speckling of rust, at the red-and-white diver's tag—but didn't say anything. They slowed as they walked toward the building and as they heard the motor of Rip's car and the turning of tires on the pavement into a parking space in the center. He parked beside his mother, jumped out of the car, then reached in back and pulled out a canvas cover and threw it over the Miati.

When Rip joined them, they entered the conditioned air of the cigarette-smelling lobby. Sutton walked up to the tenant directory—a blackboard behind glass with white stick-on letters naming occupants and their floors. Only three of the seven floors seemed to be occupied.

They all entered the elevator, with Sutton over-politely holding the door open as they did. On the inside, Mary Celeste reached and pushed the yellow light button for the third floor. When the elevator doors opened again, they found Johnson Crews and Beava Leigh walking away from a nondescript lobby to stand in front of a pair of dark-stained doors and Clayton Blum's offices. On the sides of the doors were glass sidelights, the light beside the left door with "Clayton Blum, Realtor" etched in gold across the glass. Johnson turned back around and headed toward the open elevator door when he saw them.

"We didn't do a very good job of conserving gasoline," Martha said. "You could have ridden with us, Johnson."

"Didn't Mary Celeste tell you?" He looked at her and smiled. "I have to work here in town, so I won't be going back until tomorrow night."

"You and Rip. Rip has more business or whatever going on in places I don't even know about." She walked to Johnson, hugged him, and kissed the air as she put her cheek against his. "This isn't going to take very long is it, Johnson? I can't imagine it doing that. You're the legal person among us. I only came because of you and trying to do whatever is right. You'll tell me what's right, won't you? I mean, if his offer is like Mary Celeste says it is, and Ivey and everyone agree with it, the only thing we have to do is sign some forms, I would think—that silly thing Ben Ivan added to whatever. I still don't know why he did that. It makes no sense to me, no sense whatsoever. Anyway, I'm glad we don't have to do this every time anyone wants to buy or sell a piece of property. We'd spend all our time on that horribly hot highway and searching for smelly old office buildings."

No one answered as Johnson pushed open the door to a reception area with a large plastic-covered desk and a dark-haired and jewelryladen woman getting up from behind it.

"You must be the Hayes," she said with a Spanish accent. She walked around the corner of the desk, her hand out to shake hands. "I am Esmeralda Fuertes."

"Hi, Essie," Beava said as she stepped in front of the others. Beava hugged her, and then turned to the others. "Essie is working with Mr. Blum for a while. Essie, this is Mrs. Hayes, Sutton King and Mary Celeste King, Ripington Hayes, we call him Rip, and you of course know Johnson."

"Mr. Blum and the others are expecting you," she said as she shook hands then turned to lead them to the conference room. She stopped as though she wanted to tell them something or say something else, but she didn't.

They followed her through another set of doors and into a large room that looked to be the conference room. Thin mini blinds were pulled open to show the clear morning sky of the outside and to let light illuminate a stark white cardboard rendering sitting in the center of a long room-filling table. A short balding man with a pair of gold-framed sunglasses in his top breast pocket—Clayton Blum—stood showing a lady they didn't know (they only suspected who she must have been) the finer points of the planned condo units proposed for the Coquina Key Club.

Genna Trace sat quietly as her mother tried to pay attention to what was being shown her. She sat at the table with the open-shirted and deeply-tanned Alex Roan, her wire-rimmed and round-like-half-dollar glasses perched on her nose but attached to a silver chord that hung around her neck. She sat watching Clayton and her mother but not letting her eyes see the model at all. She looked as though they were talking about, and pointing to, something not on the table at all—or not even in the room.

The Hayes group, Martha, Rip, Mary Celeste, and Sutton fell together to walk to the other side of the table. Clayton Blum's feet fluttered like a ballerina as he stepped quickly to meet them.

Johnson, Beava Leigh, and Essie pulled out chairs then leaned across the table, groups of hands in disarray as each shook hands with the ones across the table from them. Genna stood in a bright-colored, mid-length shirt, full and past her knees and matching a pastel, longsleeved cotton top. She greeted each of them with a smile. Longhanging, gold-colored earrings darted out from the sides of her face as parentheses to pitch-black hair that was combed full and falling down to rest on the top of her shoulders.

Obligatory greetings and chatter continued until Martha Hayes stepped back and walked to the end of the table. As soon as she did, Miss Emily stepped back from the others and moved toward her. They walked toward each other and stopped as they met at the head of the table.

"I'm Emily Trace," she said as she stood in front of Martha Hayes. Martha's hands were in front of her so Emily took them both and held them in her own.

"I know," Martha answered.

At first, they did not move, but just stood and looked. The others in the room remained silent, even if they didn't understand why.

Miss Emily continued, "It didn't dawn on me until now that this would give us a chance to meet."

"It did me," Martha said. She looked at the others at the table then back at Miss Emily. Almost as though caught doing something wrong, they both turned away and returned to their chairs.

But as they did, they moved to sit across from each other with only the edges of the model in between them. They sat looking at each other, as though looking in a mirror at themselves—as though asking questions with their eyes that they somehow wanted to ask but could answer with their stares. Miss Emily sat straight, hands folded over the new black dress she had bought at the Department Store in Miami when she made the trip not that long before. She wore seldom-used lipstick with her black dress and wore her long, powdered-looking hair with thin silver barrettes on each side. They both looked at details, at hair, at the one the other always wanted to ask about—to be some fly on the wall without ever being seen. Silence remained between them, blotting out the questions each wanted to ask and the story each knew but did not want to share.

"Don't let me disturb you," Clayton said above the light niceties now falling from each side of the table and light stories and anecdotes Johnson was telling to keep everyone happy with where they were and why they were there. Rip opened up a pocket notebook and started to make notes of who was there and, by the way he was writing, notes on what was being said.

"Ivey isn't here yet, so—"

"He's on his way," Mary Celeste butted in.

"Let me start to share our excitement with you then," Clayton said.

"In front of you—" A tap on the door to the conference room caused them to look up and at Digger Riggs stepping into the room. He stood with his open-necked shirt, tanned face, and no-belt, pleated slacks. He waved a salute to each at the table. As he did, Miss Emily rose and quickly moved back to the chair beside Genna and Alex Roan.

"Everybody, this is Digger Riggs joining us," Clayton said. Genna didn't look up. "Digger is going to head our sales effort. Introduce yourself around, Digger. It'll be a short job he tells me, but that will be his responsibility. We're more than fortunate to have him with us."

"Digger knows it well," Clayton continued as Digger shook hands with Mary Celeste. "In front of you is a mock-up of our two-bedroom model units, which are found on either end of the condominium units. Each condominium unit will have three floors; all units will open to the water. One- and three-bedroom units will also be made available—we'll talk about them later—but our studies show that the two-bedroom units will presale even before we break ground. A coquina rock-and-stucco exterior finish is planned in keeping with the name, and there will be eight such units. A drawing of the interior is on the other end of the table." He stood up and walked to more drawings push-pinned to the wall. "For our quick overnight crowd and to keep within the boatel motif already established, we plan to build a twenty-four unit motel first—a place for buyers to stay until units are ready. Like all units, they will be facing the water and will open to docking right at their front door. Then, for the athletic types, we have three pools—one exclusively for the boatel, then one for families, and one reserved for adults. That one has an underground swim-in bar. Some seats in the bar will actually be in the water."

Clayton looked around the room, looking for signs of approval.

"Questions so far?" he asked.

No one answered.

"Okay. If there are no questions, I'll go on to the overnight rental units."

"No questions," Genna interrupted, breathing out pent-up air as she did. "No questions except if it will ever get off the ground. With your 'this one' and 'that one,' have you thought far enough to see that no government in its right mind is going to approve it?"

"Yes, we have, Ms. Trace. As you know, there are existing utilities. The only thing will be some pumps and those type of things that will be done on shore… I mean, on the Florida side. We've received an unofficial plan review by the Corp. of Engineers, the county concurrency people, everyone."

Johnson stared at her as Blum answered. He sat making notes of the meeting on his own legal pad but stopped to make mental notes as he listened to her speak… Such black hair, he thought. Like Beava said, the information must have been wrong about her age. Some more pretty lady. Trace's daughter. I almost forgot Wiley Trace was Indian. I wonder *why* Ivey isn't here.

"On the walls are sketches of the one- and three-bedroom condo units—the renderings of the units to go with the two-bedroom units. Note on the plan sheets in front of you that sixty percent of the units will be two-bedroom, twenty-five one-bedroom, and the rest in threebedroom units. And on this end of the table is the layout drawing showing how it's all going to fit—how it's going to be unlike anything ever even imagined for South Florida and the Keys." He continued making eye contact with each at the table, one at a time. "So, let's break, so you can walk around for a few minutes and see, think up questions for me, walk around, and ask your own questions. When Ivey gets here, we can sign forms for the land, and we can be on our way. This is a glorious day, isn't it?"

"Be on your way?" Genna's voice fluttered as she spoke. This time, she pushed her chair back and stood up. She looked down at her mother who was holding a finger to her mouth. Alex Roan sat quiet and non-committal but with a look in his eye and a quick smile telling her to go ahead. "I am not going to be 'on your way,'" she said to Clayton. And to Miss Emily, "Or shut up either. If I'm not mistaken, before you can do all these horrible things, you have to first buy the property. And unless I've been walking in my sleep, I don't believe that's been done." She looked directly at her mother as though she was speaking only to her. "In fact, I still don't know why we are here."

"You see, Genna—" Digger started.

"'You see, Genna,' hell! 'You see, Genna' going to put your pious and lying butt in jail before the sun goes down if you don't sit down, shut the hell up, and have a check for me before I leave this Godforsaken place. And I mean today. That's the only thing I see. I should have known you would get your lame-ass act into something as hairbrained as this."

Digger stopped pulling out the chair where he had chosen to sit and turned to the others. "You have to excuse my ex-wife. We sometimes don't agree." He quickly looked at her, and then just as quickly looked at Clayton Blum.

Clayton's eyes fell to Digger, then Genna and the rest of the table. "I'm always amazed as to how small this country of ours can be. Isn't this wonderful? I had no idea that Digger was once married to Miss

Trace and at one time actually lived on Coquina Key. I didn't know that until long after Digger agreed to join us."

The suspense of what was said was interrupted by another tap on the door.

"Good afternoon all," Ivey Hayes said as he walked in. He walked to the empty seat beside Genna and put a legal manila folder of notes on the table. Addie Hayes walked beside him.

Behind them, and wearing his usual Summer Tree work shirt, walked Tommy Ripington.

Ivey walked to Clayton Blum, shook hands, and said something that made them both laugh. He shook hands with Essie, walked around the table to Digger Riggs, shook his hand, went around to the other side of the table, and hugged his mother. Tommy Ripington walked first to Miss Emily, hugged her, then to Genna. He looked at Martha, then walked around and sat in the empty chair beside her. Addie waved a polite and courteous wave to the Traces and then moved to beside Tommy.

"I apologize for being late," Ivey said as Emily Trace moved away from Genna and to the other side of the table, leaving places open. Seeing the now-occupied chairs next to his mother, he went and sat next to Genna. Addie followed, sitting beside him. As he sat in the chair, he leaned forward, reached across in front of Genna, and put his hand on hers, touching her with an 'I'm here' and a 'not to worry' tap. Ivey was dressed as though he was in his college classroom—the knot of his club tie at a slight angle, a wrinkled pair of khakis, his white oxford buttondown, and wearing loafers with no socks. Addie looked like she had just come from one of his classes.

"Clayton, Essie, this is my wife, Addie." He turned to Addie then to the other side of him. "And you've heard Tommy and I speak of Emily and Genna Trace, Addie. And this is Alex Roan with the state... And Johnson Crews. You've met Johnson. And his associate, Beava Leigh." Addie acknowledged each of them with a smile.

Ivey's eyes fell again upon the model. "And Clayton, this model is indeed impressive." His eyes toured the blue-lined plans pinned on the wall, the colored layouts, and the renderings on the table. "And your layout. This is awe-inspiring. You people have gone to a lot of effort so far, haven't you?"

"Why are you so late, Ivey?" Mary Celeste asked quietly but not so quiet that the others could not hear. "I got back late last night, little sister, got a message to pick up Addie at the airport, and then we stayed out in Gotha." The children are big enough to stay by themselves, it seems, so Addie came down for a few days. It luckily coincides with this meeting." He looked around the room as he spoke as though answering to each one there. "I saw Tommy this morning and asked him if he wanted to ride down with us. He said sure, so here we are."

Essie stood up in the quiet as Ivey looked again at the model; then she looked down each side of the table as though she wanted to take an order. "Cokes? Coffee?" she said. No one answered.

"Johnson Crews," Ivey said. "I sensed that you were maybe involved with Coquina Key all along. I trust that you're here as representative of the buyer, not Summer Tree. On the other hand, maybe you are the buyer by now. Am I correct with either one or both of those assumptions?"

"Only recently, Ivey, and only partial ownership in this group. It's my interpretation that everything is legal and above board, and I mean to keep it that way. That means I will still represent Summer Tree—that is, with your approval. This is just an investment—something out in the open and something for my retirement, if it ever comes. And, it's something to help Summer Tree sell a piece of property and maybe solve some of the things we've talked about." Then, changing his tone, "I've been trying to reach you to go over everything."

Clayton Blum didn't wait for anything else to be said. "I know that some of you will want to drive back this afternoon, so let's get started with—besides seeing the model, the renderings, and our plans—why we are all here. Ivey, after we did talk briefly on the telephone—and for everyone to get on the same page, so to speak—our offer is this… We propose $5,850,000 to Summer Tree for the purchase of Coquina Key, as is. You explain the details if you will, Johnson."

Johnson looked at his notes and cleared his throat. "Yes, $5,850,000 to Summer Tree—ten percent today to hold it and the rest, plus buyer closing costs, at closing. We propose to close in thirty days." Johnson looked down the line of stares beside him, then down the line on the other side of the table. "Further, we propose a payment of $250,000 made to Summer Tree as payment of interest for monies owed to Summer Tree and money due for some time now. This will erase any clouds, past or present, on the title. The total payment of $6,100,000 will make for full ownership by—" He looked at Clayton… "The Coquina Key Corporation. So, with that, everyone gets paid what is fair and equi-

~ Coquina Key ~

table, and the ownership moves to The Coquina Key Corporation, as discussed."

Ivey looked down the row at the table until he got to Rip, who, so far, had yet to speak. "You be paying close attention, little brother. This is all stuff you're needing to know." He turned again to Johnson. "And who are the principals of The Coquina Key Corporation?"

No one answered.

"If you are a corporation, you're going to have to tell me. Or do I have to call all the way to Tallahassee to find out."

Mary Celeste answered. "Sure, I'll tell you. There's nothing to be ashamed of or to hide. Clayton is listed as President of the corporation. I am listed, as well as Sutton, Johnson Crews, and others—all listed as stockholders."

Rip butted in, "And your financing?"

Johnson and Mary Celeste exchanged questioning glances first to Rip, then to each other. "Private funding from each of us."

"Enough to purchase the land and develop the property? That must be over ten million dollars by the time it's built upon. Are you sure about the ownership names?"

"She's correct with the ownership," Johnson added. "Anything else is a loan to the corporation and will be handled like any banking transaction."

"They will receive ownership if you don't pay? Your lender, I mean," Rip said. "Is that what you're saying?"

"Yes," Johnson answered. "We, however, see no problem."

"As everyone has been made aware of the purchase price," Clayton Blum looked down the table as he spoke, then at Emily and Genna Trace, "and as we all agree that it's fair to all parties, especially the paying off of the old loan—and paying it off before it's called in with the property getting tied up in some nasty foreclosure that none of us want—Johnson has prepared the proper papers to—"

Ivey continued with his questions.

"Have you got a list of the owners of the loaning corporation? I mean Essie and her people? How many people here are parts of that corporation?"

Johnson answered, "Ownership will be made available to anyone wanting to know, Ivey. But that doesn't affect the buying of the property."

Ivey glanced over to Addie who was surveying the room and the people in it. Johnson took a group of papers stapled together from the stack in front of him and gave a set to most at the table—Genna, Miss Emily, Ivey, Rip, Mary Celeste, and Martha Hayes. Sutton King, Essie, Beava, Addie, and Tommy leaned to the papers beside them. Tommy looked at the paper, then back again to Martha.

"The Sales Agreement and a document I have prepared forgiving the loan and interest have been prepared and will be passed to you for review. Ivey, they have all been made out for your signature. And Mrs. Trace," he said, looking back down in his stack of papers. "Yes, Mrs. Trace; the forgiving of the loan and interest has been prepared for your signature."

No one moved. Then, and as though planned, Mary Celeste spoke. "I can assume that you have documentation you need to have signed on that other thing, do you not? The other little agreement my father did?"

"Yes, I do," Johnson answered. He looked at Clayton Blum. "Before I hand it out, though, are there any questions now on the use of the property or anything else that you might want to know. That question has seemed to be somehow important to some of you."

"Yes," Ivey answered. "Sutton. Mary Celeste. What is the source of funds for your participation in Coquina Key Club, or whatever you have chosen to call it?"

Mary Celeste snapped her answer. "That's not public information, Ivey. By law, we can keep it that way."

"Not if the financing comes from the misappropriation of Orange State Co-Op funds and all that's involved with the packinghouses."

"Is that what you're accusing me of?" Mary Celeste said. "I could tell something was in your craw. I've been wondering where you were going with your ownership questions."

"I'm not accusing; I'm telling," Ivey said. "But that's not the main reason for this meeting."

"Hell, I don't know what else is. You coming in here, dropping bombs out of the wild blue yonder, trying to screw up the only way Summer Tree is going to keep itself from bankruptcy."

"Don't put your hand in the hive and expect the honey without expecting to get stung, little sister."

Miss Emily buried her mouth in a folded hand and snickered as he said it.

"A-hum!" Johnson cleared his throat. "Let's get on with the reason for the meeting. The source of funding can be addressed later. The offer being made today for Coquina Key is supported by a Cashier's Check made out to Summer Tree Corporation today with the remainder to be made in thirty days. All payments to Summer Tree will be by Cashiers Checks and through Nations Bank. Now let's hope there are no more bombs to throw or misunderstandings to unravel, and we can proceed with Coquina Key. There aren't any more questions, are there?"

Miss Emily's stare caused Genna to look over at her. She winked then smiled as she did. Genna looked back at Johnson and started to speak, but Ivey interrupted her, speaking low, but not caring if he was heard. "It's okay, Genna. Wait 'til he hands it out." Genna put her hand on top of Ivey's and squeezed. The others at the table, including Addie, looked at her, at her hand, but nothing was said. Addie kept her stare at the hands as though waiting for Genna's hand to move as Mary Celeste started to say something again, but it didn't.

Johnson looked at Clayton and nodded. "So, if there are no questions, we can assume that everyone is in agreement and that I may proceed. This is the loose end about which Mary Celeste referred and it, per the attachment to the deed, needs the signature of the wife and children of Ben Ivan Hayes as well as the wife and children of Wiley Bearclaw Trace, both deceased."

Genna immediately said, "I don't remember Bearclaw being my father's middle name..."

"I think we all forgot about it," Miss Emily answered. "She looked at Martha and smiled. "I was married to the man for damn near thirty years, and I'd forgotten about it, too." Then to Johnson, "You searched wide and deep to come up with that, didn't you, son?" And to Genna, "He and Billy are third or fourth cousins or some such. Probably kept it quiet because of Billy and all his'n. You know what I mean?" She looked back at Martha. "He was good at keeping things quiet." And to Genna, "You're not the only independent one, Genna. You got it honest."

"Back to the agreement," Johnson said. "This sibling agreement, for lack of a better name, this sibling agreement you've all heard about was an agreement that Ben Ivan Hayes had added as a stipulation to the first time sale of Coquina Key. It simply states that the property may not be sold unless there is a majority agreement by the wives of the present owners, Ben Ivan Hayes and Wiley Bearclaw Trace, combined with the majority agreement of their children. The stipulation was added, as I understand, to assure that the property would not be sold after they were gone if the majority of the heirs disapproved of its sale. And with Martha Hayes, Mary-Celeste King, and Ripington Hayes, there is an approval to sell." He looked at Ivey, "With only two not to sell."

"And Ivey?" Tommy spoke for the first time.

"Ivey, in this situation, does not need to worry about it," said Johnson. "If he votes with his mother, brother, and sister, there are still only two to not sell and four to sell. For purposes of answering the question, if he were to vote with the Traces for some reason, that's still not a majority as the vote would be split three to three. Either way, there would be no majority vote to not sell the property as proposed." He looked again at each at the table. "And believe me, with the money that this proposal brings, it's the only correct thing to do for all of us. That, as I see it, is already decided."

All eyes were on Ivey to say something, but nothing came. Mary Celeste looked at him and smiled—a look down the table with an almost audible grin.

Ivey turned his eyes to Tommy Ripington but spoke to Johnson Crews as he did. "You're assuming a lot, barrister. I want to ask for a formal count. I can't believe you haven't already done that."

"There's been no need, Ivey. I mean, for God's sake, man—we've spoken to everyone and have everyone's commitment. But yes, I guess. For the record, so to speak. Let me see a show of hands from those eligible to vote—the wife and children of Ben Ivan Hayes and the wife and children of Wiley Bearclaw Trace—as wishing to accept the offer for sale of the Coquina Key property as proposed."

Martha Hayes, Mary Celeste, and Rip raised their hands.

"And a show of hands of those eligible as the wife and children of Ben Ivan Hayes and the wife and children of Wiley Bearclaw Trace wishing not to sell?"

Ivey and Genna raised their hands. "Aw, hell," said Miss Emily and raised hers. "I wouldn't know how to do anything else."

"I can't believe you're voting not to sell," Johnson said. "I mean, with the money involved. We need to talk, Ivey. Hell, we have to talk… But then, I guess it matters not. I mean, to the sale. Three to three… three to sell, three not to sell. That's a tie and not a majority."

Martha pushed herself from the table, turned, a handkerchief against her mouth, and walked quickly to the door and out of the room.

~ Coquina Key ~

Those at the table only watched.

Tommy raised his hand. Ivey pushed Genna's hand on top of her mother's, then put his hand over the top of both their hands.

"I hope she's all right," Johnson said.

Mary Celeste looked toward the open door then back at Tommy.

"Yes, do you want to add something, Tommy?" Johnson asked.

"The property don't need to be sold," Tommy said.

"And?" Johnson said.

"Packinghouse properties can be sold to pay taxes. Coquina Key don't need to be sold."

"We've been over all that, Tommy. Sutton I know for sure has looked into selling some of the packinghouses. He runs that portion, so he should know. You don't see that as a possibility, do you, Sutton?"

"No," Sutton said.

"That's been studied," Mary Celeste said. "We need to keep what we have or things will be even worse. Let's get on with it."

Johnson looked away then back at Mary Celeste. "Do you think you need to go check on your mother?"

Before she could answer, Martha reentered the room and sat back in her chair.

"I heard what he said," Martha said. She looked only at Tommy as she spoke. "That wasn't the reason he raised his hand, was it Tommy? No, that's not it at all. All this like it's in hiding. All this quiet... All these years. Tommy himself wanted to vote, and Tommy has the right to vote."

She walked around to stand beside Emily Trace and took her hand. She placed her hand to her mouth then touched her moistening eyes. "Tommy, you see... Tommy is my son."

# Twenty

Clayton Blum left the silence in the room under a transparent excuse of needing to get something from back in his own office. No one spoke, but only looked at Martha or Tommy as though wondering when something else would be said. Was what they heard right?

Johnson stated loudly, "But why? Why didn't Ben Ivan?... I mean..."

Miss Emily looked up at Martha and gave her a nod—an okay, maybe a nod of permission. Martha then walked over to Tommy as though it was an exclamation to what was just said—a sign of commitment that what was just said was true. As she stood behind him with her right hand resting on his shoulder, there was an expression on her face as though it was finally said, at long last out, a lifetime's burden snuffed out as though it was some internally burning fire. It was like something secluded for the world, for only him and his mother to ever know. And with Ben Ivan gone, only Martha to understand.

But there was more. Martha felt it being asked; she saw it in the eyes looking at her. She looked down at Emily again. She felt relief with what was opened so far but knew there was more. It was as though a command was printed in front of her to answer what was behind the questioning eyes around the table. And with Ben Ivan gone, she could do that. She could wash herself of all that was so carefully hidden—the truth that his Miss Emily had hidden inside her own self, being the only other living person to know.

"And... and Tommy was born before any of the others. Born before Ben Ivan..." Martha looked at Emily as though asking for help—asking her to say something.

Emily Trace answered, "You see, Tommy's father was Wiley Trace." She looked at Martha as she said it. Heads twisted at the table, first to Tommy, then to Martha, and then back to Emily. Despite her dreading ever having to say it—to say what would not ever go away—it was somehow all right now.

"That's why… that's why nothing could be said," Martha said. As she spoke, it was as though only to Tommy and as though no one else was in the room. "Why Tommy hasn't said anything—why no one has said or could say anything." She took a cotton handkerchief stuck inside her dress, wiped her eyes, then continued. "That was a long time ago… a long, long, time ago. Things were not as they are now. Having a baby… not being married… well… that was just not done. That wasn't even talked about, was it Emily?" Miss Emily didn't answer but sat with her eyes glued on her. "Wiley was up and working groves in the early spring that year. It was before he married Emily. I forget which year it was." She looked down at Tommy. "Forty something. Oh, it doesn't matter. I knew Ben Ivan, but we weren't even dating yet. Then the baby came and… and Tommy, you were loved and are loved more than words can ever describe. Ben Ivan wanted to marry me by that time, and Wiley knew that he, himself, could not. Ben Ivan and I agreed to marry, but I agreed, for Ben Ivan's sake, not to be raising someone else's baby. No… we agreed that no one would ever know. He was my baby brother, we agreed to say. Ben Ivan had his head in the stars, you see. There wasn't going to be anything around that could be a mark against him and his doings. No, the baby was my little brother. It was up to me to explain as to why he was with me and not my parents. That was a story I don't think I ever told the same way twice.

"I can't believe I'm standing here and telling this. However, Wiley… he and Ben Ivan agreed what they would do. Wiley was to leave and never be seen around the groves again. Wiley left, went back to his people for a while, and eventually ending up in the Keys. At first, everything was fine. No one knew, Ivey was born, then Mary Celeste… I had two children and a little brother. It stayed that way. Rip came along. No one even thought about anything different."

Emily spoke again. Not to the others, even though they could hear, but to Martha. "Except… except Ben Ivan never left Wiley alone. That's what really started him coming to Coquina Key. He wanted to beat him. Always to beat him—to somehow better him. To do something better than he could. One-upmanship, I suppose. Just like two little boys. When they would see each other, Ben Ivan was always being a little better, having three kids instead of one, catching bigger fish. Anything Wiley did, Ben Ivan wanted to take it away from him."

Martha said, "At first, he would come home after one of his trips bragging about it. Then, after a while, he never said anything."

"And Wiley never said anything," Emily said. "I knew about Tommy. Wiley, bless his heart, never could or would hide anything from me. We both knew and somehow both loved Tommy—someone I never saw until many, many years had passed. It was when Tommy was older, and he and Ben Ivan came fishing. At first, I think Ben Ivan tried purposely to keep him away from Wiley. Then he made a complete change and seemed to want to flout him in front of him. Like, he is here, but you can't have him. And the fishing boats—Ben Ivan would buy them just to show that he could. Part of Ben Ivan's little way of hurting Wiley but at the same time, helping."

"That's right," Martha said. "The *Carefrees,* he would name them… *Carefree One, Carefree Two.* Then the one that Wiley really liked—the one I understand he took as his very own besides being a fishing boat, the one Ben Ivan had to somehow do something about…"

Miss Emily snapped, "No one ever proved that, Martha. It was an accident that it burned. I'll go to my grave thinking that, Martha."

They both waited, giving the quiet and the story a few more moments to settle. Then, Miss Emily added, "Then, after that, Wiley was gone…" She looked up as though seeking permission from Martha, talking slow and almost silently. "So, after that, he took his wife. I don't like to put it that way, but yes, if there's no better way to say it, even that." She looked particularly hard at Martha—not an expectant look, but a different look, a cry-for-understanding and, at the same time, sadness for Martha Hayes. "But don't blame it all on Ben Ivan. No, don't do that. He didn't have to take as much as I had to somehow give."

Emily stood up, walked around the table, and stepped into Martha's arms. Not a sound could be heard—only the silence as the two of them shared what had been hidden, what had been stored away for no one to know for too many years. They both turned and looked at Tommy as he stared down and into folded hands. Now, like opening up a room to sunlight, it was known.

# Twenty One

Anger can linger only so long. Nevertheless, in their own ways, each of them knew that being hurt could last a lifetime.

They all sat quietly, each feeling the tears in their lives—things that happen, and one goes on with just an altered course in life, never admitting that anything is wrong. They all somehow knew that, whether spoken or not. They each sat at the long table, alone, but intermingled with the others—each a little different from when they had walked in just over an hour before. Even with all that had gone on, some things weren't spoken; they didn't have to be. Those things were not said aloud, but still hung there like signs carried around their necks.

Genna's life bore her own hidden and private chasm—a chasm that she had carried with her through every day, through every remembrance. With the help of years, she had painfully learned to accept that. The only thing that could be seen in the careful looks she and Ivey tried to hide while in that room, and the thing that could solve her hurt—every thought of what she had grown to live without—she could see now sitting across the table from her, smiling his politeness but living, she knew, a hurt of his own. Until now, Ivey would not allow himself to know what she felt, to know what she knew, but now it was all there for him to see, to know, and even touch. In its own way, the two of them looking somewhere else after accidentally catching each other's checking eye said that they both understood without needing even to say it.

Ivey looked at his mother, at Miss Emily, and at Tommy.

His look and thoughts then escaped him as he fixed his gaze on Tommy—the one who had to have known all along what had earlier surprised so many in the room. He had to have lived his life with a secret that he could never talk about from the day that he first sensed who he really was and sensed the secret he was to keep covered deep inside where only he, and maybe Tava, knew to look. Martha would say something by talking with a pat on his hand, a look in her eye, a hug when no one was around. If people had only known what they were seeing throughout the years—seeing but not understanding: a close but hidden watch over her first born. If they had only known about the caring of a mother—a caring that was maybe deeper, more hidden, and disguised by tears than anyone could have ever imagined. But deep inside, where the real decisions are made and life itself is judged and recorded, the hidden love between mother and son was strong; even though they were the only ones whoever knew, it was there.

They all stopped by Buddy's Sea Horse Inn, the old converted riverhouse on the inter-coastal waterway that Judge Leigh told Johnson about and that Johnson shared with those at the meeting. At first, Martha and Addie—who uncharacteristically made herself available for Martha to latch and hold on to—were not going to go. It seemed to be the wrong thing at the wrong time, what with the non-transferring of the title on the property, which some had worked so hard to get while others had worked so hard to retain. That and the story of Tommy Ripington and the revelations of both Martha Hayes and Miss Emily Trace. But life, albeit a new one, and smiles, and the others around them, told them to go on.

Johnson stopped long enough to pick up the tab for the drinks—pitchers of margueritas served with crushed ice in stemmed glasses with salt crusted around the rims. He carried on appropriate conversation with each one—words that were almost condolences to Martha and Miss Emily, but a squinty-eyed glare at Ivey saying get the hell away from me for screwing up and queering a deal that should have been mine. But at the same time, an apology to somehow muster up what could be found and was left of the once-proud Hayes relationship. He gave a shaking of hands and broad-grin assurance to Tommy as well as to Rip—the ones he sensed would be the Hayes management of the future. It was no more Ben Ivan with his management by the seat of his pants. It was Tommy with his knowledge of the groves, and Rip, who never talked about his dormant-but-wanting business mind that now seemed so right after things had fallen out the way they had.

Eyes seemed to stare at Rip—the one whom Ivey knew had only stayed in school and away from Florida and Summer Tree for an MBA as a convenient excuse, although he never doubted his own ability in this area if he was to ever apply himself. That was not the question. But still, he couldn't help thinking that it was just to be there—to be away from Summer Tree and all that was real to Florida, real to Johnson Crews, and real to the legal and monetary part of the family world. Or really, all that was under the all-controlling wings of Ben Ivan Hayes. He was the different-thinking kid of Ben Ivan's who went away to some Ivey league school—the strange one who nobody really knew or ever cared about. If Ben Ivan or anyone else would have just asked, what with him all but crying to be used but, until now, nobody taking the time to hear.

In quiet words to each of them, Ivey said that he would get with them back in Orlando—that the three of them... he, Tommy, and Rip... would somehow put things back in some corporate, moneymaking order. Then, almost coldly, Johnson and Essie left—Essie nervously looking at one then the other, not smiling, but holding tightly to Johnson Crews. Then, Rip and Beava Leigh left at the same time, Beava catching a ride back to Orlando with Rip and taking him by his hand as they walked to his car.

Tommy stood with Ivey, the two of them talking and, from a distance, looking to be pointing between them and explaining what they were saying with their fingers. The remainder of the crowd sat talking and enjoying the margueritas and being through with a meeting that they never wanted to attend in the first place, but that they would now never forget. Ivey and Tommy stood together, Tommy appearing to be listening while Ivey talked about crops, the need to continue with Rip in the office, and Tommy running herd in the groves.

With the others gone, Ivey, Addie, and Tommy, along with Genna, Martha, and Miss Emily had two tables pushed together in front of a large view window looking out from the restaurant. The room smelled of fish, garlic, and basil. They moved into positions at the table that looked out on the winding inter-coastal river below and beside them. They sat at the dark-stained tables and in carefully mismatched chairs. Even with darkness falling on the waterway, the view stayed on the water, with spotlights from the restaurant flowing out and lighting the sea oats, the sawgrass around them, and across the water toward the other side.

"I called and checked on the rooms," Ivey said, quieting the group as he spoke. "We've got four reserved at Pier Sixty-Six. They are there for you to take or not. You know, for some reason, I don't mind a bit letting Clayton Blum and his crowd pick up the cost. After all, he was the one who insisted when he invited us, wasn't he?" He slowed as he spoke, as though he was starting his talk again or as though to someone completely different. "And Mother, we all know how hard that was to discuss the past like you did. Somehow—" He looked around as though seeking approval from those listening. "I mean, that was a long time ago. You would think... I mean, all of a sudden being told that you have a brother," he said as he looked directly at Tommy. "But then, Tommy has always been a brother."

Tommy didn't say anything, but just remained sitting straight back in his chair looking around the table at the others. A waitress walking up caused him to divert his attention. "We have a special tonight," she said. She moved to Ivey's side, figuring he was the one who would pick up the tab. "A seafood platter, fried or broiled, the catch of the day, which is grouper, shrimp, scallops, fried oysters, crab legs, hush puppies, and cold slaw for $12.95. We also have a Crab Louis appetizer—a specialty of the house for $4.75."

Ivey looked at each one around the table, as each nodded and gave an okay to Ivey as he looked. "Six times," he said to the waitress. "Your specialties and your appetizers."

"Just so long as I don't have to catch the crabs," Miss Emily said, "or pick out the meat for the Crab Louis."

"Tea," Tommy said. "Lots of iced tea."

After the waitress checked who wanted broiled and who wanted fried and checked who wanting coffee or tea—and, in Tommy's case, it was both—the table was left quiet again.

As he had a way of doing, Ivey toured the room with his eyes—the pictures on the walls, a few stuffed fish, a lobster tank in the corner, awards from Toastmasters, a plague from Rotary. "I imagine you get enough seafood without getting it away from home," he said in the direction of Miss Emily and Genna in making conversation. He said it to break the quiet and to say something, considering the needs of those at the table. He looked at Genna, quickly away, then back, as though apologizing with his look. Thoughts raced through his mind as his quick glance left her and he looked at the others—Tommy reaching for one of the little cellophane packets of Towne House crackers and looking at Genna as he did.

Ivey said, "It's been a busy day. Before dinner arrives, let's have a word of prayer."

As heads bowed, Ivey said, "Lord, it has been so complicated that only you could bring us through the mess we got ourselves into. But you did that, and to you we give thanks.

"Now, let's each of us give a special thanks—a one-word thanks if you will—for what has happened to us, for what has occurred, for what the Lord has given us this day, and for which we are thankful."

Ivey started. He looked at each of the others and then said, "Love."
Emily said, "Remembering. Lets all remember."
Tommy said, "Friends, I guess."
Genna quietly said, "Remembering *and Love.*"
As quietly, Addie said, and stared at Ivey, "Second Chances."
Then Martha said, "Sharing. Yes, sharing. "
Rip said, "New Starts,"
Ivey ended it with, "Amen."

Genna now sat carefully not looking at Ivey, only looking to Tommy or her mother or whoever was speaking at the time. Ivey still thought of all those stories he had read throughout the years or movies or television shows with unfaithful husbands, slick masculine "wannabes" with secret and clandestine girl friends and surreptitious midafternoon get-togethers before going home to Betty Crocker wives and All-American, soccer-playing children. They were all there, the blessing had been said, but his mind still wandered. His thoughts tightened in his mind as he sat quietly now, almost afraid of what he would say, would not say, or would say that might be wrong. Or, for the first time under the new circumstances, if not said, would possibly be taken that way. He knew that secrets were long-lasting things to have to carry around. And sitting in the restaurant, he was beginning—ever so slightly, but beginning—to feel that weight.

Miss Emily answered what might have been asked. "I like seafood anywhere I can get it—at home, at a restaurant. It's all good to me. I see food, and I want it." She laughed, and the others joined her in the old joke as though it was new.

Ivey looked first to Miss Emily, then to his mother, "She's mastered the art of cooking shrimp, Mother—broils them over beer with spices I've never even heard of. She and Tava would have a lot to talk about."

"Yeah," Miss Emily said. "I've been told many times that Tava is an excellent cook."

"Sometimes what you have at home can be taken for granted," Addie said, butting into the conversation. "Cooking, I mean. I bet you only realize how good it is when you leave it and get away. Do you not find that?"

Genna just as quickly added, "Then, sometimes what you have at first, and after you have something else, you realize that what you grew up on is what you really want after all. Or so I've found."

"Well, I know one thing," Miss Emily said. "They say fresh, but grouper is a bottom-eating fish, and I know our waitress doesn't run out five miles or however close the Gulf Stream is to here and catch them for us. You just accept what there is, and enjoy the hell out of it."

Genna looked at Addie, then sideways to her mother. Miss Emily said, "No, there's too much formality nowadays on why and when and what people can do." She looked directly at Genna, then at the others. "Fish catching, I mean. It's hard for anyone just to go out and do what they want to do these days. It's a shame, but it's the truth. Go somewhere and catch a certain fish just because they like that particular fish. Sometimes, you just might love more than one fish. If they're loving people, people can love more than one. Fish, I mean. There are too many rules you have to know now on what you can love or what you can't love. Or so I've learned."

Ivey picked up one of the cracker packets, tried to tear it open, and ended up smashing the cracker into tiny bits. He put the packet down on the table beside his silverware and left it there. He looked across the table at Tommy. "Tommy, when all this settles down, you're going to be a busy man."

"What were you two talking about before?" Martha asked. "You two were hiding over there like you were telling secrets. The Lord knows there are no longer secrets to hide."

Ivey answered, "We were talking about the fact that, with Rip's business experience and education and Tommy's knowing about everything there is to know about owning groves and growing fruit, old Summer Tree is in pretty good hands."

"Does that say that you aren't going to be involved?" Addie said.

"That means that I'm not going to be day-in day-out involved, if it's okay with everyone here. Long term, I mean. Oh, I'll be for a while. Just being an extra hand, I mean. I'm talking three or four months or whatever now. I hope that everything can run without my meager daily input. We'll still need legal and accounting help; Sol Weinstein will still want to be involved, I imagine. And Johnson—we'll have to wait and see about that."

"You're forgetting something, Ivey," Martha said. "Something pretty important."

"That's up to her, I would think. That's Mary Celeste's call. I would think that if she wants to stay involved, we have responsibilities for her to handle. And Sutton—if he has problems with outside interest, he can 'fess up, call it that, and we ought to do what we can to help the man. As far as the packinghouses, those might be what Mary Celeste and Sutton both need to do —just minus one or two for tax purposes. That won't hurt all that much, according to Rip. Maybe that's the answer. Coquina Key? I can't find any real documentation on monies owed, so I—and I'm speaking for Summer Tree—I think all the talk about that needs to be quieted. Then, as far as the sale and all that, we can carry it on Summer Tree books to be sold whenever the Traces say so."

The waitress walked up with a tray of appetizers and started putting them around the table. A young Spanish waiter set his tray of iced tea and coffee down and put the drinks beside the plates. As they left, Ivey said, "I didn't mean to have a stockholders meeting. Those are just thoughts that I've had—things that I need to share. I've never been very good at keeping things quiet—I mean, business things."

"Tommy will do a slam-bang job," Miss Emily said as she reached over and put her hand on his. "No doubt about that. I figured him knowing everything in the world would ultimately get him somewhere."

"Well, Mr. Hayes," Addie said, straightening up and smoothing out the napkin in her lap. "He of not keeping any secrets. Where does that put your family in the shaking out of things?" She looked at Martha, then Miss Emily and smiled. "I mean, I would think the children are going to want to know where they will be living." She slowed her talk and looked directly at Ivey, "Or where we will be living. It sounds like you might be leaving yourself a choice."

"We need to talk about that, Addie."

"So talk about it now," she answered. "Today seems to be a bare-itall day, and I find that refreshing for a change." Now it was her time to reach and put her hand on top of Martha's.

Ivey's eyes made a quick scan of those at the table.

He fixed his eyes on Addie. "Through all that has been going on, I've had something else going through my mind. Or rather, I think I can say, Addie and I have. I've had an offer from Washington and Lee in Lexington, Virginia—to join their faculty in the English department. I plan to consider that, but don't know if I can. I want to, but I need to put Summer Tree first. Time, Rip, and Tommy should tell me that. Hopefully, through working closely with Rip and Tommy and telephones and letters and fax machines, well... maybe I can do both."

His mother said, "That's wonderful... I think."

Addie spoke while looking at Martha. "I came down this trip to look for a place to live, to see if we could all live at the house in the grove, or if we would need to find a place for all of us somewhere in town." She looked at Ivey, the others, then back to Martha. "That shows, I guess, that we haven't talked as much as we should. I hope to change that. If it works out that we're to go to W&L, or stay where we are, so be it. We can do that. If it works out that we're all meant to be in Florida, we can do that, too. Go back and to teaching English, yes, we can do that, too." She looked directly at Genna. "You take what you have, and make the best of it is what I'm saying. Or, maybe that's what today taught us." Addie looked at Ivey then back at Genna. She spoke softly to her. "Someone told me that you're separated, Genna. I'm sorry. I would imagine with all I hear about Coquina Key that there are more men around, along with all their problems, than you know what to do with." She turned toward Ivey. "Excuse us, this is girl talk."

"Genna has always been around men with their problems," Miss Emily interrupted. "The only difference between her and others is that she knows how to solve them."

"I don't know whether to thank you for a compliment or not, Mother." Genna grinned as she answered her.

"I mean men folk, Genna. You take ole Neal Roan. He's so concerned with the fish and the shrimp and the mangos, the environment and hundred-year rains that he's off most of the time in some of nature's or his own little world. But when he comes by courting, he's one more good-looking hunk of man."

"Mother!"

"You don't hush me now, Genna. Genna has her land now and that good-looking botanist fellow has always been there just for the asking."

"Mother!" Genna exclaimed again.

"That's just girl talk with Addie," she said. "You know it's true." Miss Emily looked again at Addie, this time speaking slower and more distinctly, like she sometimes did when she wanted to make sure that what she was saying was heard—a trait she must have learned from Ben Ivan. "But Genna has a way of looking right through what other people might think is there and not letting anything, and I mean anything at all, get in her way if it's something that she wants—really wants. And for that matter, anything to stop her if it does. Maybe that's something that has to be watched out for—something this white-haired lady taught her herself."

"You're to be commended, Genna," Addie said. "I feel the same way. I'm learning to be content with what I have. Then, if there's something that you want, something that you want to change or that you find you really, really want, you have to make sure that you go and get it. Like your mother says, don't let anything or anybody stand in your way. Listen to me telling you. What I'm saying is, first make sure that what you go after is there for the taking."

Genna didn't say anything else, only smiled at Addie then stared over at Ivey as he looking away from the conversation. She watched as Addie reached down and took Ivey's hand. He squeezed her hand and held onto it as the waitress started to serve.

"Looks good, doesn't it, Tommy?" Ivey said.

"Looks and smells good," he answered. "Not as good as Tava's, but it looks good."

"It'll be good to get back and tell her all that went on, won't it, Tommy?"

"Tava already knows. You don't worry about Tava. She and Ben Ivan both know people, how things happen, how things have a way of working out for the good, as she says, if things are done right. I think she knew a lot more than any of us. You don't worry none about Tava."

"She's been around us a long time," Martha said.

Genna, Miss Emily, and Martha all looked at Tommy with the same expression on their faces—a knowing tightness in their eyes as though saying to themselves the thing they all knew, things they all knew but couldn't or wouldn't say about Tommy or about the Haitian-born lady who wasn't there. "Like I've told you since you were a boy," Martha said. "Everything, and I mean everything—as long as you're right with what you do—everything has a way of working itself out okay in the end. It's taken me almost fifty years to learn that, but you know what? It's true."

"The Indians used to say," said Genna, "that no matter how muddy the backwater, there can be clear water ahead." She looked at Ivey. "That anything that has happened before can be forgiven, can even be forgotten, and there can be clear skies ahead."

Ivey smiled at her as though he knew what she meant.

## Twenty Two

After they were through with dinner, they walked out of the restaurant. In front of them, cars passed, heading back across the causeway into town, reflecting the late afternoon sun.

Ivey and Addie spoke first to Martha Hayes and Tommy as they got into her car for Tommy to drive them back to Orlando. Then, they held the door for Miss Emily and Genna to get into the old, gray Camaro with the red-and-white dive tag on the front. Ivey hugged Miss Emily tighter than he did his own mother and shut the door behind her. He walked around and opened the door for Genna, then stood as she put her arm around his neck and hugged him. He kissed her politely on the cheek, on the side of her neck, and then held her tightly in his arms. She mouthed, "I love you, Ivey Hayes," then took her eyes off Ivey as he stood watching and fighting back tears that cried out to be seen. Without speaking again, she got in the car and started the old engine. Ivey watched as she backed from the parking space, turned, and drove toward the exit and onto the highway.

Then, it was only Ivey and Addie.

It's strange, he thought as they walked to their own car, strange how bad things can come, do whatever they're going to do, then leave. Sometimes, the good things leave just as well, so that overall, the world somehow takes care of things. In the end, things seem to fall into some acceptable order whether you planned them that way or not. No, it might not be in the order I would have picked—the way I thought they were going—but things work themselves out. Ben Ivan, Martha, and their hiding behind Tommy's birth. Wiley and Emily Trace with their own problems. Miss Emily turning into what she is and where she is, admitting it, and living in a world that's hers—all hers. And Genna... Genna and her world, her students, her water, her island. And, in all probability, if she's to ever slow enough to admit it to herself, Alex Roan. No... it's him, not me. He's Florida Bay, Coquina Key, and all that's Genna Trace. But for another time, another place...

He looked at Addie and tried to get his mind on where he was going and what he was doing. Things seemed to enter his mind—uninvited things that would not leave.

Something I once read, he thought, something else I heard: when you are friends, stay that way; stay that way because if you do not, you will spend the rest of your life looking to find each other in the faces of strangers.

Ivey walked around and unlocked the door for Addie, held it, and guided her into the car as though on a first date.

Some things are just too big to change, he thought, too good to tamper with. Some things need to stay the way they are. Stay put. Me and Addie—the kids. Moving back and taking the job at Washington and Lee or wherever after all. This is best. The old established way that I somehow know and where I somehow feel at home. Everything has its place, and everything has its order. It's up to us, I suppose, to be smart enough to see what's out there and then to follow it. To do what's best for all around. Yeah, the good Lord has everything worked out.

Ivey started the car and looked over at Addie sitting beside him. He reached down and placed his hand on top of hers. He squeezed it as a mark of his acceptance of the two of them—being back together like they had been for all their years, all the years of a whole lifetime. He smiled at her that all was well.

He cut his wheels as he backed out of the parking space. Before heading forward again, he stopped and looked at the red sky in front of him, at the sun going down in the west, and at the painting of its goodbye across the water.

Ivey looked as he continued to rationalize to himself that what he was doing was right. He turned to the north and, despite the pull of the road back to the Keys and all that seemed a part of the setting sun, he turned away from a sky that he knew someday, somehow, some way, he would have to see again.

He looked at Addie, at a smile, at someone who was not just a dream that could never really come true. He looked at what he knew was love and knew that it was good. He looked again at the sunset, at the orange, and at the colors. He looked at the clouds stretched across the sky. In them, he saw the traces of where he had been, together with, maybe, just maybe, of where he was going.

Printed in the United States
25305LVS00004BA/1-24